To Mrs D, FD and SD.

"We deal in lead, friend."
Vin, 'The Magnificent Seven'

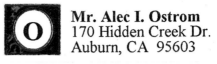

The Cleaner

A John Milton Novel

Mark Dawson

PROLOGUE

THE ROAD THROUGH THE FOREST was tranquil, the gentle quiet embroidered by the gurgling of a mountain rill and the chirruping of the birds in the canopy of trees overhead. The *route forestière de la Combe d'Ire* was potholed and narrow, often passable by just one car at a time. Evergreen pine forests clustered tightly on either side, pressing a damp gloom onto the road that was dispelled by warm sunlight wherever the trees had been chopped back. The misty slopes of the massif of the Montagne de Charbon stretched above the treeline, ribs of rock and stone running down through the vegetation. The road followed a careful route up the flank of the mountain, turning sharply to the left and right and sometimes switching back on itself as it traced the safest path upwards. The road crossed and recrossed the stream, and the humpback bridge here was constructed from ancient red bricks, held together as much by the damp lichen that clung to it as by its disintegrating putty. The bridge was next to a small enclosure signed as a car park, although that was putting it at its highest; it was little more than a lay-by hewn from the hillside, a clearing barely large enough to fit four cars side by side. Forestry reserve notices warned of "wild animals" and "hunters."

It was a quiet and isolated spot, the outside world excluded almost as if by the closing of a door.

Milton had parked his Renault there, nudged against the shoulder of the mountain. It was a nondescript hire car; he had chosen it because it was unremarkable. He had reversed into the space, leaving the engine running as he stepped out and made his way around to the boot. He unlocked and opened it and looked down at the bundle nestled in the car's small storage space. He unfolded the edges of the blanket to uncover the assault rifle that had been left at the dead drop the previous night. It was an HK53 carbine with integrated suppressor, the rifle that the SAS often used when stealth was as important as stopping power. Milton lifted the rifle from the boot and pressed a fresh twenty-five-round magazine into the breech. He opened the collapsible stock and took aim, pointing down the middle of the road. Satisfied that the weapon was functioning correctly, he made his way towards the bridge and rested it in the undergrowth, out of sight.

Milton had scouted the area and knew it well. To the north, the road eventually led to Saint-Jorioz, a medium-sized tourist resort that gathered along the shore of Lake Annecy. The descent to the south led to the small village of Chevaline. The village made its living from farming, but that was supplemented by renting the picturesque chalet farmhouses to the tourists who came for cycling and hiking. Milton had stayed in just such a chalet for the past three days. He had spent his time scouting the area, departing on his bike early in the morning and returning late at night. He had kept a low profile, staying in the chalet apart from those trips out.

Milton heard the engine of the BMW long before he saw it. He collected the rifle and slipped behind the trunk of an oak, hiding himself from the road but still able to observe it. The wine-coloured estate car was in second gear, struggling a little with the steep camber of the road. It emerged from the sharp right-hand turn, its lights illuminating a path through the gloom.

The car slowed and turned in towards the Renault. Milton held his breath, his pulse ticking up, and slipped his index finger through the trigger guard of the rifle. The driver parked alongside and switched off the engine. Milton could hear music from the interior of the car. The passenger-side door opened, and the muffled music became clearer: French pop, disposable and inoffensive. The passenger bent down and spoke sharply into the car, and the music was silenced. For a moment all Milton could hear was the crunch of the man's shoes on the gravel, the rushing of the water, and the wind in the leaves. He tightened his grip on the rifle and concentrated on keeping his breathing even and regular.

The driver's side door opened, and a tall, dark-skinned woman stepped outside.

Milton recognised both of them. The passenger was Yehya al Moussa. The driver was Sameera Najeeb.

He stepped out from behind the trunk and brought the HK53 to bear. He flicked the selector to automatic and fired off a volley of shots. The bullets struck Najeeb in the gut, perforating her liver and lungs. She put her hand to her breast, confusion spreading across her face, and then pivoted and fell back against the side of the car. Najeeb shrieked, moving quickly, ducking down beneath the line contour of the car. Milton took two smooth sidesteps to his right to open up the angle again and squeezed off another burst. The scientist was trying to get back into the car; the bullets tattooed his body in a line from throat to crotch.

The fusillade sounded around the trees for a moment. Frightened birds exploded into the air on wingbeats that sounded like claps. The echo of the reports died and faded away, and then, short moments after the brutal outburst of violence, all was quiet again: the wind rustled through the trees, the water chimed beneath the bridge, a nightingale called from high above.

Milton paused. There was another sound.

A second car approaching.

Hiding would have been pointless; the bloody tableau would give him away. The car emerged from the mouth of the forest. It was a Renault Mégane painted blue with white and red chevrons screen-printed across the bonnet. The policeman in the front of the car must have seen him immediately. The Mégane came to a sudden stop fifty feet away.

Milton ejected the magazine and slapped in a replacement.

The officer opened the door and stepped out of the car, his hand on the butt of his holstered pistol. "*Arrêt!*" he called out.

Milton did not pause to think. His reaction was hard-wired, a response that had been drilled into him across ten years so that now it was automatic, an expression of muscle memory without conscience, sudden and terribly deadly. He swung the rifle around and squeezed the trigger for a longer burst. The car was peppered with bullets, half a dozen slamming into the radiator and bonnet, another handful into the windscreen. The officer was struck in the face and chest, stumbling backwards and then dropping onto his back, where he lay for a moment, twitching horribly. Milton walked towards him, the gun cradled low, and put a final bullet into his head. Finally, the man lay still.

Peacefulness returned, ornamented now by the sound of the shards of glass that fell to shatter on the road from the breached windscreen.

Milton crossed the road to the Renault. He opened the boot and wrapped the rifle in its blanket, then stowed it away carefully beneath the spare wheel in the false floor. He pulled on a pair of latex gloves and collected the ejected shell casings from the rifle. There were forty of them, and they were still hot to the touch. He dropped them into a small evidence bag. He crouched by Najeeb's body and frisked her quickly and efficiently. He found her smartphone and a USB stick and bagged them both.

He went around to the other side of the car and lowered himself to examine al Moussa. The door was open, and as he raised his gaze from the body to peer inside, he saw a small, pale face staring back out at him. Milton did not rush. There was no need. The face belonged to a young boy, perhaps five or six years old. His skin and his hair were dark, and his features recalled those of his parents. He was cowering in the foot space, a streak of blood across his forehead as if it was paint that had been thrown over him. It was not his blood: it was blowback from his father.

Milton reached for the Sig Sauer he carried in his shoulder holster, his fingers brushing against the butt. The boy held his eyes. His face was white and quivering with fright, but he did not look away. He was brave. Milton felt a swell of vomit in his throat as his memory cast him back twenty years and a thousand miles away. He remembered another young boy, a similar age, the face peaceful despite the obscenity of his death.

He lowered his hand from the Sig and stepped back. He gently pulled the man's body onto the muddy surface of the lay-by and went back to the car.

"Stay there," he told the boy. "Help is coming."

He closed the door. He checked that he had removed the evidence of his presence and, satisfied, got into the Renault, put it into gear and drove away.

He turned to the north, upwards, and drove towards the lake.

PART ONE

The Cleaner

The man was on the bed, his hands clenched into claws over his heart and his teeth grinding over and over again. His eyelids flickered, and sometimes he moaned, strangled words that would have made no sense if anyone had been there to hear them. His body was rigid with tension, sweat drenching his body and the sheets. The dream came more often now, sometimes every night, always the same. He was lying prone, flat in the cushioned warmth of sand dunes. The sun was directly above him, a midday sun that pounded the desert with a brutal heat that made the air shimmer, the mountains in the distance swaying as if viewed through the water of a fish tank. The landscape was arid, long swathes of dead sand that stretched for as far as the eye could see. The only vegetation was close to the banks of the slow-moving river that eventually found its way into the Tigris. A single ribbon of asphalt was the only road for miles around, deep drifts of sand blown across it.

Chapter One

CONTROL SQUINTED through the windscreen of the XJS as he pulled into the empty fast lane and accelerated past a lumbering articulated lorry. The sky had been a bloody crimson last night, and when the sun returned in the morning, it had risen into a clear, untrammelled blue sky. There was heat and light in those early rays, and he angled the blind to shade his eyes. The radio was tuned to the *Today* programme and the forecaster predicted a week of searing heat. The seven o'clock news followed the weather— the lead item was the shooting of two tourists and a policeman in the French Alps. The victims had been identified, but as yet, a motive for the killing had not been found. It was "senseless," a French policeman concluded.

That, Control thought, was not true. It was far from senseless. The operation had been the result of long and meticulous planning, six months spent cultivating the targets and gaining their trust and then weeks setting up the meeting. The objective had been successfully achieved, but it had not been clean. There were two errors that would need careful handling, errors that raised doubts over the performance of the man who had carried out the operation.

The fact that it was Number One was troubling.

It had been Control's operation. He knew the targets intimately. Yehya al Moussa had been an atomic research scientist. Sameera Najeeb was an expert in microwave technology. They were married, and until recently, both had been in the employ of the Iraq Atomic Energy Agency. Following the fall of Saddam, they had been recruited by the Iranians, and with their help, the Ahmandinejad regime had made progress towards its goal of becoming a nuclear power. A decision had been made, somewhere in MI5, that the couple was too dangerous to live. That decision had been rubber-stamped in another anonymous grey office in Whitehall, and their files had been marked with red and passed to Group Fifteen to be actioned. It was important, and because of that, Control had selected Number One for the assignment.

As he turned the Jaguar off the motorway at the exit for Central London, Control reviewed his preparation. The two had come to France under the pretext of a long-deserved holiday. The real reason, however, and the reason for their diversion into the Alpine countryside, was to meet an employee of Cezus, a subsidiary of Areva, the global leader in the market for zirconium. That metal was used, among other things, for nuclear fuel cladding. Iran needed zirconium for its reactors, and al Moussa and Najeeb had been led to believe that their contact could supply as much as they needed. But there had been no employee. There was no zirconium. There was to be no meeting, at least not the rendezvous that they had been expecting.

Control tapped out a rhythm on the steering wheel as he passed into London. No, he thought, the preparation had been faultless. The problems were all of Milton's making. The dead *gendarme* would give the French police a strong personal motive to locate the killer; one of their own had been murdered. It would make them more tenacious and less likely to shelve the investigation when the trail went cold, as Control knew that it would. That was bad, but even worse was the boy. A child, orphaned by the killer, cowering in the car as he watched his parents' murders. That was dynamite, the hook upon which the press would be able to hang all of their reporting. It ensured the story would run and run.

Control slowed and turned the Jaguar into the underground car park beneath a small building huddled on the north bank of the Thames. It was a sixties build, constructed from brick and concrete without style or grace. Five floors, anonymous. The car idled as the garage door rolled up with a tired metallic creak. The sign painted onto the door read GLOBAL LOGISTICS.

He drove inside, pulled up next to the secure elevator, and got out of the car. The lift arrived, and he embarked, pressing the button for the third floor. The lift eased to a halt, the doors sighed open, and he stepped out into the bustling open-plan space beyond. Analysts stared at monitors and tapped at keyboards, printers chattered, and telephones chimed incessantly. Control passed through the chaotic space to a corridor lined with thick carpet, following it around to the right so that the clamour behind him faded to a gentle hum of activity. A number of green baize doors faced the corridor, and he picked the one at the end, pushing it open and walking through.

David Tanner, his private secretary, looked up from his computer. "Morning, sir," he said. Tanner was ex-army, infantry, like Control and all of the other operatives who worked for him. Tanner's career had been forestalled by an IED on the road outside Kabul. It had cost him his right leg below the knee and the posting to the SAS that he had craved. He was a good man, easy-going and pleasant to share a drink with, and he guarded access to his commanding officer with fierce dedication.

"Morning, Captain," he said. "What does the morning look like?"

"You're speaking to the director at midday. Wants an update on the French situation."

"I'm sure she does. And Number One?"

"Waiting for you inside, sir."

"Very good."

He went through into the office. It was a large room that offered an expansive view of the river. There was a central table with a bowl of flowers, and two comfortable club chairs on either side of the fire. There were no filing cabinets, and nothing that looked official.

Milton was standing at the wide window at the other

end of the room, smoking a cigarette and looking down on the broad sweep of the Thames. Control paused by the door and regarded him; he was dressed in a plain dark suit that looked rather cheap, a white shirt and a black tie.

"Good morning, Number One," he said.

"Morning, sir."

"Take a seat."

He watched as Milton sat down. His eyes were implacable. He looked a little shabby, a little worn around the edges. Control recalled him when he joined the service. He had sported Savile Row suits, shirts from Turnbull & Asser, and was perfectly groomed at all times. He did not seem to care for any of that any longer. Control didn't care what his agents looked like, so long as they were good at their job, and Milton was his best; that was why this latest misadventure was so troubling.

There came a knock at the door. Tanner entered bearing a tray with a pot of tea and two bone-china cups. He set the tray down on the sideboard, and after confirming that there was nothing else that Control needed, he left them alone.

Control got up and poured the tea, watching Milton as he did so. One did not apply for a job like his, one was chosen, and as was his habit with all the operatives who worked for him, Control had selected him himself and then supervised the year of rigorous training that smoothed away his rough edges and prepared him for his new role. There had been moments when Milton had doubted his own suitability for the position, and Control had not so much as assuaged the doubts as chided him for even entertaining the possibility that his judgment might have been awry. He prided himself on being an excellent judge of character, and he had known that Milton would be the perfect field agent. He had been proved right. Milton had started his career as Number Twelve, as was customary. And now, ten years later, all his predecessors were gone, and he was Number One.

Milton was tense. He gripped the armrest of the chair so tightly that his knuckles whitened. He had not shaved that morning, the strong line of his jaw darkly stubbled. "The boy?" he said.

"Traumatised but otherwise fine, from what we can gather. As you would expect. The French have him in care. We don't think they've spoken to him yet. Did he see you?"

"Yes."

"That could be awkward."

Milton ignored him "Did you know?"

"Know what?"

"That he'd be there."

"We knew he was in France. We didn't think they would bring him to the meeting."

"And you didn't think to tell me that they might?"

"Remember who you're talking to," Control said angrily. "Would it have made a difference?"

Milton's cold stare burned into him.

"There's no point in pretending otherwise—the boy is a problem. The damned policeman, too. It would've been tidy without them, but now, well, they're both loose ends. They make things more complicated. You'd better tell me what happened."

"There's not much to say. I followed the plan to the letter. The weapon was where it was supposed to be. I arrived before the targets. They were there on time. I eliminated both. As I was tidying up, the gendarme arrived. So I shot him."

"The rules of engagement were clear."

"Indeed, sir. No witnesses. I don't believe I had a choice."

"You didn't. I'm not questioning that."

"But you're questioning something?" Milton said.

Again, his tone was harsh. Control ignored it. "You said it yourself. No witnesses."

"The boy? Why I didn't shoot him?"

"It might be distasteful, but you know how clear we are about how we conduct ourselves on operations." Control was tense. The conversation was not developing as he had anticipated, and he was not in the business of being surprised. There was a whiteness around the edges of Milton's lips. The blue eyes still stared blankly, almost unseeingly.

"I've seen a lot of dead bodies since I've been working for you, sir."

Control replied with as much patience as he could manage. "Of course you have, Milton. You're an assassin. Dead bodies are your stock-in-trade."

He might not even have heard him. "I can't keep pretending to myself anymore. We make decisions about who lives and who dies, but it's not always black and white when you're in the middle of it. As you say, the rules of engagement were clear. I should have shot him. Ten years ago, when I signed up for this"—the word carried a light dusting of contempt—"I probably would have shot him. Like a good soldier."

"But you didn't."

"I couldn't."

"Why are you telling me this?"

"Ten years is a long time for this kind of work, sir. Longer than anyone else. And I haven't been happy lately. I don't think I've ever really been happy."

"I don't expect you to be happy."

Milton had become agitated and pressed on. "I've got blood on my hands. I used to tell myself the same things to justify it, but they don't work anymore. That policeman didn't deserve to die. The boy didn't deserve to lose his parents. We made a widow and an orphan because of a lie. And I'm not doing it any longer, sir. I'm finished."

Control spoke carefully. "Are you trying to resign?"

"You can call it whatever you like. My mind is made up."

Control rose. He needed a moment to tamp down his

temper. This was perilously close to insubordination, and rather than lash out, he went across to the mantelpiece and adjusted the photograph of his family. He spoke carefully: "What's the Group for, Milton?"

"Framing. Extortion. Elimination."

"Jobs that are too dirty for Her Majesty's security services to touch."

"Quite so, sir."

"And your job?"

"Cleaner."

"Which means?"

"'From time to time Her Majesty's government needs to remove people whose continued existence poses a risk to the effective conduct of public order. The government requires particularly skilled professionals who are prepared to work on a non-attributable basis to deal with these problems.' Cleaners."

He smiled without humour. That was the job description he had used when he recruited him all those years ago. All those neutral euphemisms, all designed to make the job easier to palate. "It takes a special kind of man to do that kind of work. There are so few of you— and, unfortunately, that makes you rather difficult to replace." He paused. "Do you know how many people you've eliminated for me?"

Milton replied without even thinking. "One hundred and thirty-six."

"You're my best cleaner."

"Once, perhaps. Not anymore. I can't ignore it any longer. I can't keep my mouth shut just to avoid being unprofessional. I'm lying to myself. We have to face facts, sir. Dress it up however you like—neutralisation, elimination—but those are just euphemisms for what it is I really do. I'm paid to murder people."

Control was not getting through to him. "Murder?" he exclaimed. "What are you talking about, man? Don't be so soft. You want to moralise? You know what would happen if the Iranians get the bomb. There'll be a war. A proper war that will make Iraq look like a walk in the bloody park. Thousands of people will die. Hundreds of thousands. Removing those two made that prospect a little less likely. And they knew the risk they were taking. You can call it murder if you like, but they were not innocents. They were combatants."

"And the policeman? The boy?"

"Unfortunate, but necessary."

"Collateral damage?"

Control felt he was being goaded. He took a breath and replied with a taut, "Indeed."

Milton folded his arms. "I'm sorry, sir. I'm done with you. I'm finished."

Control walked up to Milton, circled him close, noticed the tension in the shoulders and the clenched fists. "No one is ever really finished with me. You can't resign. You can't retire. You're a murderer, as you say. It's all you know. After all, what can you chaps do after you leave me? Your talents are so specialised. You use a gun. You use your fists. You use a knife. What else could you do? Work with children? In an office? No. You're unskilled labour, man. This is what you are."

"Then find yourself another labourer."

He banged a fist on the mantelpiece in frustration. "You work for me for as long as I bloody well want you to or I'll have you destroyed."

Milton rose to face him. His stature was imposing, and his eyes were chilling. They had regained their clarity and icy focus. They were the eyes of a killer, and he fixed him in a pitiless gaze. "I think we're finished, sir, aren't we? We're not going to agree with each other."

"Is that your final word?"

"It is."

Control put his desk between them and sat down. "You're making a terrible mistake. You're on suspension. Unpaid. I'll review your file, but there will be discipline.

Take the time to consider your position. It isn't too late to repair the damage this foolish stand has caused you."

"Very good, sir." Milton straightened his tie.

"You're dismissed."

"Good day, sir."

Chapter Two

MILTON FOUND A BAR. His anonymous, empty hotel room did not appeal to him. The confrontation with Control had unsettled him; his hands were shaking from anger and fear.

There was a place with a wide picture window that faced the river. He found a table that looked out onto the open water, the buildings on the opposite bank, the pleasure craft and barges churning through the surf and, above, the blazing sun in a perfectly clear sky. He wanted a large whiskey, to feel the alcohol, his head beginning to spin just a little. He knew one way to stop thinking—about everything—could be found in the bottom of his glass, but he managed to resist the urge. It was short-term relief with long-term consequences. He focussed on the number that he kept in his head—691—and ordered an orange juice instead. He sat brooding, turning the glass between his fingers, watching the boats.

There was a television above the bar. The volume was turned down with subtitles running along the bottom of the screen. The channel had been set to one of the twenty-four-hour news programmes, and an interview with a minister on Parliament Green was abruptly replaced by an overhead helicopter shot of a wooded mountain landscape. A caption flashed that it was near Lake Annecy, France. The camera jerked and zoomed until the screen was filled with a shot of a wine-coloured BMW. It was parked in a small clearing. The camera zoomed out, and a second car, blue with white-and-red chevrons, could be seen. Bloodstains were visible on the muddy ground around the cars. The captions along the bottom of the screen said "massacre," and "outrage."

The bartender shook his head. "Did you see that?"

Milton grunted.

"You know they found a boy in the car?"

Milton said nothing.

"I don't know how someone could do that—murder a family on a holiday. How cold-blooded is that? You ask me, that little boy was lucky. If whoever it was had found him, I reckon he would've been shot, too."

The news report switched to another story, but it was no good. Milton finished the juice and stood. He needed to leave.

Chapter Three

THE PLATFORM for the Underground was busy. A group of young foreign travellers who didn't know any better had congregated near the slope that led up to the surface, blocking the way with their suitcases and chattering excitedly in Portuguese. Their luggage was plastered with stickers that proclaimed their previous destinations. Brazilians, he guessed. Students. Milton picked his way through them so he could wait at the quieter, less populated end of the platform. There was a lone traveller there, standing right up at the edge. She was black, in her early thirties, and wearing the uniform of one of the fast-food chains that served the area around the station. She looked tired, and Milton saw that she was crying, her bottom lip quivering and tears rolling down her cheeks. Milton was not good with empathy, and he would not have known where to start were he to try to comfort her, but he had no interest in that. Not today. He had too much on his mind. He moved along.

He felt awful again. His mood had worsened. He felt light-headed and slumped down onto an empty bench. He started to sweat, his hands first, then his back, salty beads rolling down from his scalp into his eyes and mouth.

He recalled the overhead shot of the forest from the television helicopter. There had been three pegs on the ground, marking the spots where the bodies had been found. He knew he should stop, think of something else, but he couldn't, and soon he recalled the nightmare again, the flashes from years before: the flattened village, the blood splashed over the arid ground, the body of the boy, the peppery smell of high explosives and cloying death. He floated away from that, running onto all the other things he had done and seen in the service of Queen and country: dingy rooms and darkened streets, one hundred and thirty-six victims laid out in evidence of the terrible things he had done. A shot to the head from a sniper rifle, a knife to the heart, a garrotte around the throat pulled tight until the hacking breaths became wheezes that became silent, a body desperately jerking, then falling still. One hundred and thirty-six men and women faced him, accused him, their blood on his hands.

A loud scream yanked him around.

The students were staring down the platform at him. He took it all in, the details. Was it him they were pointing at? No. They were pointing away from him. The woman wasn't there. Another scream and one of the students pointed down onto the track. Milton stumbled to his feet and saw her deliberately laid across the rails. It was an incongruous sight. At first he thought she must have been trying to collect something that she had dropped, but then he realised that she had laid herself out in that fashion for a purpose. He spun around; the glowing digital sign said the next train was approaching, and then Milton heard it, the low rumble as the carriages rolled around the final bend in the tunnel. There wasn't any time to consider what to do. There was an emergency button on the wall fifty feet away, but he knew he wouldn't be able to reach it in time, and even if he did, he doubted the train would be able to stop.

He jumped down from the platform onto the sleepers.

He stepped over the live rail.

The train drew nearer, a blast of warm air pouring out of the mouth of the tunnel.

Milton knelt down by the woman.

"No," she said. "Leave me alone."

He slipped one hand beneath her back and the other beneath her knees. She was slight, and he lifted her easily. The train turned the final bend, its headlights shining brightly. Its horn sounded, shrill and sudden, and Milton knew it was going to be touch and go. He stepped over the live rail again and threw the woman up onto the platform. The train's brakes bit, the locked wheels sliding across the metal with a hideous shriek, as Milton planted his hands on the lip of the platform and vaulted up, rolling away just as the engine groaned by, missing him by fractions.

He rolled over, onto his back, and stared up at the curved ceiling. His breath rushed in and out.

The train had stopped halfway into the station. The driver opened the door and sprinted down the platform towards him. "Are you all right, mate?"

"Fine. Check her."

He closed his eyes and forced his breathing to return to a regular pattern. In and out, in and out.

"I thought you was a goner," the driver said. "I thought I was gonna hit you both. What happened?"

Milton didn't answer. The students had made their way down the platform, and the driver turned his attention to them. They reported what they had seen in singsong, broken English: how the woman had lowered herself from the platform and laid herself out across the rails, how Milton had gone down after her and pulled her away from danger.

"You're a bloody hero, mate," the driver said.

Milton closed his eyes again.

A hero?

He would have laughed if that wasn't so ridiculous. It was a bad joke.

Chapter Four

AN AMBULANCE arrived soon afterwards. Milton sat next to the woman on the bench as she was attended to by the paramedics. She had cried hysterically for five minutes, but she quickly stopped, and by the time the paramedics had arrived, she was silent and unmoving, staring fixedly at the large posters for exotic holidays and duty-free goods that were plastered across the curved wall on the other side of the tracks.

One of the paramedics had taken the woman's purse from her bag. "Is your name Sharon, love?" he asked. She said nothing. "Come on, love, you have to talk to us."

She remained silent.

"We're going to have to take her in," the paramedic said. "I think she's in shock."

"I'll come, too," Milton said.

"Are you a friend?"

Leaving her now would be abandoning her. He had started to help, and he wanted to finish the job. He would leave once her family had arrived

"Yes," he said.

"Come on, sweetheart. Let's get you checked out properly."

Milton followed behind the ambulance as they took the woman to the Royal Free Hospital. They wheeled her into a quiet room and made her a cup of warm tea, full of sugar. "We're just waiting for the doctor," they said to her. "Get that down you; it'll make all the difference."

"Thank you," she murmured.

The paramedic turned to Milton. "Are you all right to stay with her? He's on his way, but it might be twenty minutes."

"Yes," Milton said. "Of course."

He took the seat next to the bed and watched the girl. She had closed her eyes, and after a few minutes, Milton realised that she had drifted into a shallow sleep. Her chest rose and fell with each gentle breath. Milton regarded her. Her hair was of the deepest black, worn cut square and low on the nape of her neck, fanned out on the white hospital linen to frame a sweet almond-shaped face. Her eyes were wide under finely drawn eyebrows, slightly up tilted at the corners. Her skin was a perfect chocolate-brown and bore no trace of makeup save a light lipstick on her wide and sensual mouth. Her bare arms were slender, and her hands, folded beneath her breasts, were small and delicate. Her fingernails were chewed down, the red varnish chipped. There was no ring on her finger. The restaurant uniform was a utilitarian grey, lasciviously tight across her breasts. The trousers flowed down from a narrow, but not thin, waist. Her shoes were square-toed and of plain black leather. She was very pretty.

Milton let her rest.

Chapter Five

SHE AWOKE a full two hours later. At first her pretty face maintained the serenity of sleep, but that did not last for very long; confusion clouded across it and then, suddenly, came a terrible look of panic. She struggled upright and swung her feet off the bed and onto the floor.

"It's all right," Milton said. "You're in hospital. You've been asleep."

"What time is it?"

"Six."

"Jesus," she said. "I'm so late. My boy —I need to be home." She looked around, panicked. "Where are we?"

"Hospital."

"No," she said, pushing herself onto her feet. "I have to be home. My boy will be there. He won't know where I am; he won't have had his tea. No one's looking after him."

"The doctor's been. He wanted to speak to you. He's coming back when you're awake."

"I can't. And I'm fine, besides. I know it was a stupid thing to do. I'm not about to do it again. I don't want to die. I can't. He needs me." She looked into his face. Her expression was earnest and honest. "They can't keep me in here, can they?"

"I don't think so."

She collected her bag from the chair and started for the door.

"How are you going to get home?" Milton asked her.

"I don't know. Where is this?"

"The Royal Free."

"Hampstead? I'll get the train."

"Let me drive you."

"You don't have to do that. I live in Dalston. That

must be miles out of your way."

"No, that's fine. I live just round the corner—Islington." It was a lie. "It's not a problem."

The medical staff were uncomfortable about their patient discharging herself, but there was nothing that they could do to stop her. She was not injured, she appeared to be rational, and she was not alone. Milton answered their reflexive concern with a tone of quiet authority that was difficult to oppose. She signed her discharge papers, politely thanked the staff for their care, and followed Milton outside.

Milton had parked in the nearby NCP building. He swept the detritus from the passenger seat, opened the door, waited until she was comfortable, and then set off, cutting onto the Embankment. He glanced at her through the corner of his eye; she was staring fixedly out of the window, watching the river. It didn't look as if she wanted to talk. Fair enough. He switched on the CD player and skipped through the discs until he found the one he wanted to listen to, a Bob Dylan compilation. Dylan's reedy voice filled the car as Milton accelerated away from a set of traffic lights.

"Thanks for this," Sharon said suddenly. "I'm very grateful."

"It's not a problem."

"My boy should be home. He'll be wanting his tea."

"What's his name?"

"Elijah."

"That's a nice name."

"His father liked it. He was into his Bible."

"How old is he?"

"Fifteen. What about you? Do you have any kids?"

"No," Milton said. "It's just me."

He pulled out and overtook a slow-moving lorry, and she was silent for a moment.

"It's because of him," she said suddenly. "This morning—all that. I know it's stupid, but I didn't know what else to do. I still don't, not really. I'm at the end of my tether."

"What's happened?"

She didn't seem to hear that. "I don't have anyone else. If I lose him, there's no point in carrying on."

"Why don't you tell me about it?"

She looked out of the window, biting her lip.

"How have you lost him?"

She clenched her jaw. Milton shrugged and reached for the radio.

She spoke hurriedly. "There's a gang on the Estate where we live, these young lads. Local boys. They terrify everyone. They do what they want—cause trouble, steal things, deal their drugs. No one dares do anything against them."

"The police?"

She laughed bitterly. "No use to no one. They won't even come into the Estate unless there's half a dozen of them. It'll calm down a bit while they're around, but as soon as they go again, it's as if they were never even there."

"What do they have to do with Elijah?"

"He's got in with them. He's just a little boy, and I'm supposed to look after him, but there's nothing I can do. They've taken him away from me. He stays out late, he doesn't listen to me anymore, he won't do as he's told. I've always tried to give him a little freedom, not be one of those rowdy Jamaican mothers where the kids can't ever do anything right, but maybe now I think I ought to have been stricter. Last night was as bad as it's ever been. I know he's been sneaking out late at night to be with them. Normally he goes out of his bedroom window, so I put a lock on it. He comes into the front room, and I tell him he needs to get back to bed. He just gives me this look, and he says I can't tell him what to do anymore. I tell him I'm his mother and he has to listen to me for as long as he's under my roof. That's reasonable, isn't it?"

"Very."

"So he says that maybe he won't be under my roof for much longer, that he'll get his own money and find somewhere for himself. Where's a fifteen-year-old boy going to get the money for rent unless it's from thieving or selling drugs? He goes for the door, but he's got to come by me first, so I get up and stop him. He tells me to get out of the way, and when I won't, he says he hates me, says how it's my fault his father isn't around, and when I try to get him to calm down, he just pushes me aside, opens the door and goes. He's a big boy for his age, taller than I am already, and he's strong. If he won't do as he's told, what can I do to stop him? He didn't get back in until three in the morning, and when I woke up to go to work, he was still asleep. "

"Have you thought about moving away?"

She laughed humourlessly again. "Do you know how hard that is? We were in a hostel before. I used to live up in Manchester until my husband started knocking me about. There was this place for battered women; we ended up there when we got into London. I'm not knocking it, but it was full up. It was no place to bring up my boy. I was on at the Social for months before they gave us our flat. You have no idea the trouble it'd be to get them to move us somewhere else. No. We're stuck there."

She paused, staring out at the cars again.

"Ever since we've been in the Estate we've had problems. I worry about Elijah every single day. Every single day I worry about him. Every day I worry."

Milton had started to wonder whether there might be a way that he could help.

"I'm sorry," she said. "Here I am telling you all my troubles and I don't even know your name."

Milton almost reflexively retreated to his training and his long list of false identities, but he stopped himself. What was the point? He had no stomach for any of that any longer. A foundation of lies would not be a good place to start if he wanted to help this woman. "I'm John," he said. "John Milton."

He approached the junction for Whitechapel Road and turned off.

"I'm sorry for going on. I'm sure you've got your own problems. You don't need to hear mine."

"I'd like to help."

"That's nice of you, but I don't see how you could."

"Perhaps I could talk to him?"

"You're not police, are you?"

"No."

"Or the Social?"

"No."

"I don't want to be rude, Mr. Milton, but you don't know Elijah. He's headstrong. Why would he care what you said?"

He slowed down as they approached a queue of slower-moving traffic. "I can be persuasive."

Chapter Six

CONTROL HAD REQUESTED Milton's file from the archive, and after it had been delivered, he shut himself away in his office with a pot of tea and a cigar and spread the papers around him. It was late when he started, the sun long since set and the lights of the office blocks on the opposite side of the Thames glittering in the dark waters of the river. He lit the cigar and began his search through the documents for a clue that might explain his sudden, and uncharacteristic, decision. Their conversation had unsettled him. Milton had always been his best cleaner. His professionalism had always been complete. He maintained a vigorous regimen that meant that he was as fit as men half his age. His body was not the problem. If it was, he mused ruefully, this would have been easier to fix. The problem was with his mind, and that presented a more particular issue. Control prided himself on knowing the men and women who worked for him, and Milton's attitude had taken him by surprise. It introduced an element of doubt into his thinking, and doubt, to a man as ordered and logical as Control, was not tolerable.

He held the smoke in his mouth. Milton's dedication and professionalism had never wavered, not for a moment, and he had completed an exemplary series of assignments that could have formed the basis for an instruction manual for the successful modern operative. He was the Group's most ruthless and efficient assassin. He had always treated his vocation as something of an art form, drawing satisfaction from the knowledge of a job well done. Control knew from long and vexatious experience that such an attitude was a rarity these days. Real artisans—real *craftsmen*—were difficult to find, and when you had one, you nurtured him. The other men and women at his disposal tended towards the blunt. They were automatons that he pointed at targets, then watched and waited as they did their job. Their methods were effective but crass: a shower of bullets from a slow-moving car, a landmine detonated by mobile phone, random expressions of uncontrolled violence. It was quick and dirty, flippant and trite, a summation of all that Control despised about modern intelligence. There was no artistry left, no pride taken in the job, no assiduity, no careful deliberation. No real nerve. Milton reminded Control of the men and women he had worked with when he was a field agent himself, posted at Station M in the middle of the Cold War. They had been exact and careful, their assignments comprising long periods of planning that ended with sudden, controlled, contained violence.

Control turned through the pages and found nothing. Perhaps the answer was to be found in his history. He took another report from its storage crate and dropped it on his desk. It was as thick as a telephone directory.

In order for a new agent to be admitted to the Group, a raft of assessments were required to be carried out. The slightest impropriety—financial, personal, virtually anything—would lead to a black mark, and that would be that, the proposal would be quietly dropped and the prospective agent would never even know that they had been under consideration. Milton had been no different. MI5 were tasked with the compilation of the reports, and they had done a particularly thorough job with him. They had investigated his childhood, his education, his career in the army and his personal life.

John Milton was born in 1968. He had no brothers or sisters. His father, James Milton, had worked as a petrochemical engineer and led his family on a peripatetic existence, moving every few years as he followed work around the world. Much of Milton's early childhood was spent in the Gulf, with several years in Saudi Arabia, six months in Iran during the fall of the Shah, then Egypt,

Dubai and Oman. There had been a posting to the United States and then, finally, the directorship of a medium-sized gas exploration company in London. The young Milton picked up a smattering of Arabic and an ability to assimilate himself into different cultures; both talents had proven valuable in his later career.

His life had changed irrevocably in 1980. His mother and father were killed in a crash on a German autobahn, and John had been sent to live with his aunt and uncle in Kent. A substantial amount of money was bequeathed to him in trust, and it was put to good use. He was provided with a first-class private education, and after passing the rigorous entrance examination, he was sent up to Eton for the autumn term in 1981. His career there was not successful, and thanks to an incident that MI5 had not been able to confirm (although they suspected it involved gambling), Milton was expelled. There was a period of home tutoring before he was accepted at his father's old school. He stayed there until he was sixteen and then took a place at Cambridge to read law.

He was involved in the OTC, and it had been no surprise to anyone when he ignored the offer of a pupilage at the Bar to enlist in the army. After spending eight years with the Royal Green Jackets, he decided to attempt SAS selection. The process was renowned for being brutally difficult, but he passed, easily. While serving with Air Troop, B Squadron, 22 SAS, Milton worked on both covert and overt operations worldwide, including counterterrorism and drug operations in the Middle East and Far East, South and Central America, and Northern Ireland. Control decided that he was the perfect replacement for Number Seven, who had been killed while on operations in China. He made the pitch himself. It was a persuasive offer, and Milton had accepted immediately.

Control put the history aside and turned back to contemporary papers. Milton's recent yearly assessment had seen a significant dip in results, and as he turned back through the years, he noticed a trend that had remained hidden until then. The assessments were intense and combined a rigorous physical examination, marksmanship tests and a psychological evaluation. Milton's performance in all three elements had been in decline over the last three years. The drop was steepest this year, but it was not isolated. He chided himself for missing it. His continued success in the field had blinded him. He was so good at his job that the suggestion that he might not have been infallible was ridiculous. Now, as he examined his file with the benefit of hindsight, he saw that he had missed a series of indicators.

His physical examinations returned strong results. He was fit, with the cardiovascular profile of a man fifteen years younger. He made it his habit to run a marathon every year, and the times had been noted and added to the file, he had never finished the course in more than three and a half hours. Nevertheless, he had suffered a series of injuries in the field that had exerted a toll on his body. Since joining Group Fifteen he had been shot twice, stabbed in the leg and shoulder, and had broken more than a dozen bones. He reported the usual aches and pains, but the physician suggested that he was being stoic for the benefit of the examination and that it was likely that he was in mild to moderate pain most of the time. Blood tests detected the beginning of mild arthritis in his joints, a condition for which there was a familial history. He took a cocktail of drugs: gabapentin for his nerve damage and oxycodone for general pain relief.

Control relit his cigar and picked up his psychological assessment. He stood to stretch his legs and read the report next to the window. As he skimmed through the pages, he realised that missing the warning signs contained within had been his most egregious error. The psychiatrist noted that Milton had complained of sleeplessness and that he had been prescribed promathazine to combat it. There had been a discussion about reasons behind the problem, but Milton had become agitated and then angry, refusing to accept that it was anything other than an inability to quieten a busy mind. The psychiatrist suggested that Milton's naturally melancholic temperament indicated mild depression and that he seemed to have become introspective and doubting. The report concluded with the recommendation that he be monitored on a more regular basis. Control had ignored it.

Damn it.

Milton was a valuable asset, and he had wilfully ignored the warning signs. He did not want to admit that there might be a problem, and his inaction had allowed it to metastasise.

He put the files back into the storage crate and lit a second cigar. There came a knock at the door.

"Come in," he called.

Christopher Callan came into the office. He was Number Twelve: the most recent recruit to the Group. He had been transferred from the Special Boat Service after a career every bit as glittering as Milton's had been. He was tall and slender and impeccably dressed. His jacket was two-buttoned, cut from nine-ounce cloth. The pockets were straight, and the lining was simple and understated. There was a telltale faint bulge beneath his left armpit, where he wore his shoulder holster. He did not wear a tie. The trousers were classically cut, falling down to the back of his shoe. He was strikingly handsome although his head was round and small, supported by a muscular neck. His scalp was covered with tight blond curls that were almost white, reminding Control of the classical hair of the statues of da Vinci. His skin was a pristine white, and his grooming immaculate. There was a cruelty to his thin-lipped mouth, and the implacability that veiled those pale blue eyes seemed to infect the whole face.

"You wanted to see me, sir?" he said.

"Yes, Callan. Take a seat." He inhaled deeply, taking the smoke all the way back into his throat, then blowing it out. "We've got a bit of a problem. It's one of the other agents—do you know Number One?"

"Only by reputation."

"You've never worked with him, though?"

"No, sir. Why?"

"Afraid he's started to behave a little erratically. I want you to find out everything you can about him—where he's living, what he does with his time, who he's seeing. Everything you can."

"Yes, sir. Anything else?"

"No. Start immediately, please."

"Of course." Callan stood and straightened his jacket. "Number One was in France, sir? The Iranian scientists?"

"That's right."

Callan nodded thoughtfully. "That was unfortunate."

Control looked at him and knew that he would have followed the rules of engagement to the letter. He would not have left any witnesses. He had the same single-minded ruthlessness as Milton when he joined. He had made a reputation for it in the SBS; that was the characteristic that had appealed to Control when he had recruited him.

"Daily reports, please, Number Twelve. Get started at once. You're dismissed."

He turned to face the window again, the door closing softly behind him. He gazed through the cloud of cigar smoke, through his pensive reflection and out into the darkness beyond. Traffic streamed along Millbank on the other side of the river, tail lights leaving a red smear across the tarmac.

He thought of Milton.

Control was a craftsman, too. His agents were his tools. Sometimes, when they got old and unreliable, when their edge grew rusty and could no longer be whetted, they had to be replaced.

Perhaps it was time.

He wondered if that was what he would have to do.

Chapter Seven

ELIJAH WARRINER was frightened as he waited for the train to pull into the station. They were at Homerton, sitting on one of the metal benches, the red paint peeling away to reveal the scabrous rust beneath, the air heavy with the scent of stale urine and the sweet tang of the joint that was being passed around. Elijah stared across the track at the side of a warehouse marked with the tag that indicated that this was their territory: LFB, in ten-foot-high neon yellow and green letters, the black outline running where rain had mixed with it before it had dried.

LFB.

The London Fields Boys.

They ran things around here.

There were six of them on the platform. Pops, the oldest and the biggest, was in charge of the little crew. The other boys were arrayed around him on the platform: Little Mark was smoking a joint with his back to the wall; Pinky had his headphones pressed against his head, the low drone of the new Plan B record leaking out; Kidz and Chips were eyeing up the girls from the Gascoyne Estate, who were also waiting for the train. They were all dressed in the same way: a baseball cap, a hooded top, low-slung jeans and brand new pairs of Nikes or Reeboks. Some of them had their hoods pulled up, resting against the brim of their caps and casting their faces in dark shadow. They all wore bandanas tied around their necks.

It was just before half past five, and rush hour was just beginning.

Pops put his around Elijah's shoulders and squeezed him hard, using his other hand to scrub at his head. "JaJa, chill," he said. "Nothing to worry about."

Elijah managed to smile. Pops was wearing the same

uniform as all the others, but he had a pair of diamond earrings, a chunky ring on each hand and a heavy golden chain around his neck. They denoted his position as an Elder, and, of course, the fact that he had more money than the rest of them. Elijah watched as Pops took out his bag of weed and his packet of papers. "My grandma taught me to build zoots, get me?" Pops spread a copy of the Metro across his lap and arranged his things: the bag of weed, his papers, his lighter. "This is penging high-grade," he said, indicating the transparent bag and its green-brown contents. He unsealed it and tipped out a small pile. "You need to get yourself in the right state of mind before something like this. Can't do no better than a good zoot, know what I'm saying?"

Elijah nodded.

"You blazed before?"

"Course," Elijah said, trying to be disdainful. He had already been smoking for six months, ever since he had started hanging out with the young LFBs on the gangways and stairwells of Blissett House. That had frightened him, too, at first, and he had found that the first few drags made him retch, his eyes watering. But it was no big thing, though, and he had quickly got used to it. There was always a zoot being passed around, and he always made sure he had some.

Pops laughed at his indignant response. "Trust me, young 'un, you ain't blazed nothing like this." He opened a paper and filled it with a thick line of weed. He inserted a roach, brought the packet to his lips, licked the gummed end and sealed it. He lit the end and took a long drag, smacking his lips in appreciation. He toked again and passed the joint to Elijah. "Go on, younger, get some."

Elijah took the joint and, aware that Pops and the others were watching him, made sure that he didn't show any nerves as he put it between his lips and sucked down deep. The smoke was acrid and strong, and he spluttered helplessly. The other boys hooted at his discomfort.

"Look at the little joker," Pinky exclaimed. "He's gonna die from all that coughing."

"Hush your gums," Pops chided. "Let him enjoy himself. What you think, younger?"

"Buzzin'," Elijah managed.

"Yeah, man—buzzin'. You know what makes it so fine?"

Elijah shook his head, still dizzy.

"Piss. The growers piss on the dirt. Makes it more potent, gives the skunk a kick."

Elijah spluttered in disgust and almost retched again.

Pops grinned at him as the train rolled towards them. "Get yourself together, younger. Here it comes. This is it. You wanna be with us, you gotta do this. Everyone has to if they want to be mandem. You ready?"

"Yeah."

Elijah felt a sudden blast of light-headedness. It added to his feeling of fright, and he suddenly felt sick. He turned away from Pops, bent double, and vomited the fried chicken he had eaten ten minutes earlier, half-digested slops splashing between his legs, splattering against the new trainers he had robbed from the shop in Mare Street the previous day.

The others hollered.

"He's sicked up all over his creps!" Chips exclaimed.

"Come on," Pops said. "Get yourself together. Train's here."

The line was one of the main routes into Olympic Park, and the trains had all been cleaned up for the Games. The doors opened, and commuters working at the big new shopping centre, many still wearing their corporate uniforms, spilled out onto the platform. Pops pulled up his bandana and shrugged his hood up and over his cap until all of his face was obscured, save his eyes. The others did the same and, his hands shaking, so did Elijah. Pops was behind Elijah, and he pushed him into the crowded carriage, the others following behind.

Elijah had seen a train get steamed before, and he knew what to expect. Pushing him further into the carriage, Pops and the others started to hoot and holler, surging down the aisle between the seats. The noise was disorientating and frightening, and none of the passengers seemed able to react. Pops barged into the space between two benches that faced each other and ripped the mobile phone from the hand of a man in a suit. The others did the same, taking phones and tablets, dipping purses from handbags, removing wallets from the inside pockets of jackets and coats, yanking necklaces until they snapped and came free. Elijah followed behind Pops, and as they went from passenger to passenger, he took the items that Pops handed back to him and dropped them into his rucksack. His fright melted away as the adrenaline burned through his body at the thrill of what they were doing, robbing and stealing, and no one was doing a damned thing to stop them.

A young man in a suit stared at them as they advanced along the carriage. He had a Blackberry in his hand.

"What you looking at?" Pops said. "You wanna get slapped up?"

The man didn't reply.

"You wanna get shanked?" Chips reached into his pocket and took out a knife with a six-inch blade.

Still the man was silent. Elijah looked at him and recognised the fear in his eyes. He wasn't defying them; he was just too scared to do anything.

"Jack him, younger," Pops said to Elijah, shoving him forwards.

Elijah stepped up to him. "Give me the phone."

The man didn't resist and held it up for Elijah to take. He put it in his rucksack with all the rest. He looked down at the man, into his eyes, and made a quick, sudden movement towards him. The man flinched, expecting a blow that didn't come. Elijah had never caused that kind of reaction before. He had always been the smallest or the youngest, the butt of the joke. Just being with the LFB made all this difference. People took him seriously. He laughed, not out of malice, but out of disbelief.

Little Mark was standing in the doorway, wedging the door and preventing the train from departing. "Boi-dem!" he yelled.

It had only taken them a few seconds to work their way through the carriage although it had felt like much longer. Pops pushed Elijah ahead of him as the boys surged on, the commuters parting as they piled out of the carriage. Outside, on the platform, Elijah could hear the sound of sirens from the street below. Little Mark dropped down onto the tracks and crossed over the rails to the other side, the others following after him. Elijah clambered back onto the platform, vaulted the wooden fence, and scrambled down the loosely packed earth of the embankment, sprinting down Berger Road and turning onto Wick Road, then across that and into the Estate. They had grown up with the alleys and passageways and knew them all instinctively. The police would have no chance if they tried to follow them.

Elijah jogged in the middle of the group, his rucksack jangling and heavy with their loot. The trepidation had disappeared, its place taken by a pulsing excitement at the audacity of what they had done. They had stormed that train, and the people inside had been scared of them. They had sat there with their posh suits and expensive gadgets and no one had done anything. Elijah was used to being told what to do—his parents, teachers, the police—and this had been a complete reversal. He remembered the look on the face of the man with the BlackBerry. He was a grown man, a professional man, with expensive clothes and things, the kind of man who probably had an expensive flat in Dalston or Hackney or Bethnal Green because those places were cool, and he had been frightened of him. Scared.

Elijah had never experienced what it was like to be feared before.

Chapter Eight

MILTON DROVE THEM into Hackney. The road was lined on both sides by shops owned by Turks, Albanians and Asians—all trying to sell cheap goods to people who couldn't afford them— past fried chicken shops, garages, past a tube station, across a bridge over the A12 with cars rushing by below, past pound shops and cafés, a branch of CashConverter, a scruffy pub. The faces of the people who walked the road bore the marks of failure.

Sharon directed him to take a left turn off the main road, and they drove into an Estate. They drove slowly past a single convenience store, the windows barred and a Plexiglas screen protecting the owner from his patrons. Three huge tower blocks dominated the area, each of them named after local politicians from another time, an optimistic time when the buildings would have appeared bright, new and hopeful. That day had passed. They were monstrously big, almost too large to take in with a single glance. They drove around Carson House, the tower marked for demolition, its windows and doors sealed tight by bright orange metal covers. There was a playground in front of it, hooded kids sitting on the swings and slides, red-tipped cigarettes flaring in the hot dusky light.

Sharon directed Milton to Blissett House, and as he rolled the car into a forecourt occupied by battered wrecks and burnt-out hulks, the decay became too obvious to miss. Window frames were rotting, paint peeling like leprous scabs. Concrete had crumbled like meringue, the steel wires that lent support to the structure poking out like the ribs of a decaying carcass. Milton looked around. Blissett House looked like it had been built in the fifties. It would have seemed futuristic then, a brand-new way of living that had risen from the grotty terraces that had been cleared away, the council finishing the job that the Germans had started. It was twenty storeys high, each floor accessed by way of an external balcony that looped around a central shaft. There was a pervading sense of menace, a heavy dread that settled over everything like smog. The doors and windows were all barred. Graffitti'd tags were everywhere. One of the garages on the first-floor level had been burned out, the metal door half ripped off and hanging askance. An Audi with blacked-out windows was parked in the middle of the wide forecourt, the door open and a man lounging in the driver's seat, his legs extending out. The baleful rhythmic thump from a new dubstep track shuddered from the bass bins in the back of the car.

Milton pointed his key at his Volvo and thumbed the lock. It seemed a pointless affectation, and the car looked vulnerable as they walked away from it. He was grateful, for once, for the state of it. With the exhaust lashed to the chassis with wire and the wing folded inwards from the last time he had pranged it, it was nothing to look at. It was, he hoped, hardly worth taking, or else he was going to have a long walk home.

He followed Sharon towards the building. The man in the Audi stared at him through a blue-tinged cloud of dope smoke, his eyes lazy but menacing. Milton held his stare as he crossed his line of vision. The man's hair was arranged in long dreads, and gold necklaces were festooned around his neck. As their eyes met, the man nonchalantly flicked away the joint he had finished and tugged up his T-shirt to show the butt of the revolver shoved into the waistband of his jeans. Milton looked away. He didn't care that the man would consider that a small victory. There was nothing to be gained from causing trouble.

Sharon led the way to the lobby. "The lifts don't work," she apologised, gesturing to the signs pasted onto the closed doors. "Hope you don't mind a little climb.

We're on the sixth floor."

The stairwells were dank and dark and smelled of urine. Rubbish had been allowed to gather on the floor, and a pile of ashes marked the site of a recent fire. A youngster with his hood pulled up over his head shuffled over.

"You after something?"

Sharon stepped up to him. "Leave off, Dwayne."

"Where's JaJa?" he asked her.

"Don't you be worrying about him," she said.

"You tell him I want to see him."

"What for?"

"Just tell him, you dumb sket."

Milton stepped between them.

The boy was big for his age, only a couple of inches shorter than he was, and his shoulders were heavy with muscle. He squared up and faced him. "Yeah? What you want, big man?"

"I want you to show a little respect."

"Who are you? Her new boyfriend? She's grimey, man. Grimey. I seen half a dozen brothers going in and out of her place last week. She's easy, bro—don't think you're nothing special."

The boy was making a point; he didn't know what Milton's relationship with Sharon was, and he didn't care. He was daring Milton to do something. There didn't seem to be any point in talking to him. Milton slapped him with the back of his hand, catching him by surprise and spinning him against the wall. He followed up quickly, taking the boy's right arm and yanking it, hard, all the way up behind his back. The boy squealed in pain as Milton folded his fingers back, guiding him around so that he faced Sharon.

"Apologise," he said.

"Mr Milton," Sharon said hesitantly.

"Apologise," Milton ordered again.

The boy gritted his teeth, and Milton pulled his fingers

back another inch. "Sorry," he said. "Sorry. Please, mister—you're breaking my fingers."

Milton turned him around so that he was facing the open door and propelled him out of it. He landed on his stomach, scraping his face against the rough tarmac. The man in the tricked-out car looked over, lazy interest flickering across his face.

"You didn't need to do that," Sharon said. "It's best just to ignore them."

"Good manners don't cost anything. Come on—let's get inside. I bet you could do with a cup of tea."

They climbed the stairs to the sixth floor and followed the open walkway to the end of the block. A couple of youngsters were leaning against the balcony, looking out over the Estate below and, beyond that, the streets and houses that made up this part of Hackney. Milton recognised from experience that they had been stationed as lookouts, and that, from their perch, they would be able to see the approach of rival gang bangers or police. They would call down to the older boys selling their products on the walkways below. The dealers would vanish if it was the police or call for muscle if it was a rival crew. Milton said nothing. The boys glared at them as they approached.

Flat 609 was at the end of the block, where the walkway abutted the graffiti-marked wall. The door was protected by a metal gate and the windows were behind similar grilles. Sharon unlocked the gate and then the heavy door and went inside. Milton followed, instinctively assessing the interior. The front door opened into a tiny square hallway, one of the walls festooned with coats on a row of hooks and a dozen pairs of shoes stacked haphazardly beneath it. Post had been allowed to gather beneath the letter box, and Milton could see that most were bills, several of them showing the red ink that marked them as final demands. The hallway had three doors. Sharon opened the one to the lounge, and Milton followed her inside.

It was a large room furnished with an old sofa, a square table with four chairs and a large flat-screen television. Videogames were scattered on the floor.

"How many children do you have?" Milton asked.

"Two. My oldest, Jules, fell in with the wrong sort. He has a problem with drugs—we only ever see him when he wants money. It's just me and Elijah most of the time."

Milton was a good listener, and Sharon started to feel better. Just talking to him helped. Perhaps he was right and there was something he could do. It wasn't as if she had had any other offers of help. The Social was useless, and the last thing she wanted to do was get the police involved. They wouldn't be sympathetic, and Elijah would end up with a record or something, and that would be the end of that as far as his future was concerned.

"Why don't you sit down?" Milton suggested. "I'm guessing this is the kitchen?"

She nodded.

"So go on, sit down and relax. I'll make you a cup of tea while we wait for your son."

Chapter Nine

WHEN ELIJAH opened the door to their flat, there was a white man he had never seen before sitting in the front room. He was tall, with strong-looking shoulders and large hands, and plain to look at in a loose-fitting suit and scuffed leather shoes. The scar across his face was a little frightening. He was in the armchair Elijah used when he was on his PlayStation, drinking a cup of tea. Elijah's first thought was that he was police, a detective, and he suddenly felt horribly exposed. Pops had told him to take the gear they had tiefed from the people on the train and keep it safe while he arranged for someone to buy it from them. It swung from his shoulder, clanking and clicking.

His mother was sitting opposite the man. She got up as he came in through the door.

"Where've you been?" she said. "You're late."

"Out," he replied sullenly. The man put down his cup of tea and pulled himself out of the armchair. "Who are you?"

"This is Mr Milton."

"I was talking to him." Elijah looked up at the man. There was a flintiness in his icy blue eyes. Elijah tried to stare him out, but although the man was smiling at him, his eyes were cold and hard and unnerving. He made Elijah anxious.

He held out a hand. "You can call me John," he said.

"Yeah, whatever." The heavy rucksack slipped down his shoulder, rattling noisily. He shrugged it back into place and stepped around the man to go to his room.

Sharon got to her feet and stepped in between him and his door. "What's in the bag, Elijah?"

"Nothing. Just my stuff."

"Then you won't mind me having a look, will you?"

She took the bag from him, unzipped it and, one by one, pulled out the mobile phones, watches, wallets and two tablet computers. Silently, she lined them up on the dining table and then, when she was done, turned to face him with a frightened expression on her face. "How did you get this?"

"Looking after it for a friend."

"Did you steal it?"

"Course not," he said, but he knew he sounded unconvincing. He was aware of the big man in the room with them. "Who are you?" he asked again. "Police? Social?"

"I'm a friend of your mother. She's worried about you."

"She needn't be. I'm fine."

Sharon held up an expensive-looking watch. "This is all tiefed, isn't it?"

"I told you, I'm just looking after it."

"Then you can take it straight back to him. I don't want it in the house."

"Why don't you just mind your business?" He dropped everything back into the rucksack and slung it across his shoulder.

"Who is it?" she said as he turned for the door.

"You don't know him."

"Show your mother some respect," Milton said. "She doesn't deserve you speaking to her like that."

"Who are you to go telling me what to do?" he exploded. "I ain't never seen you before. Don't think you're anything special, neither. None of her boyfriends last long. They all get bored eventually, and we don't never see them no more. I don't know who you are, and I'm not going to bother to find out. I won't ever see you again."

"Elijah!"

Milton didn't know how to respond to that, and he stepped aside as Elijah made for the door. Sharon looked on haplessly as her son opened it, stepped out onto the landing, and slammed it behind him.

Chapter Ten

ELIJAH PASSED through the straggled group of customers that had gathered outside the entrance to Blissett House. The boys called them "cats" and took them for all they were worth. They passed out their bags of weed and heroin, their rocks of crack, snatching their money and sending them on their way. They didn't get very far. One of the empty flats had been turned into a crack house, and they scurried into it. When they shuffled out again, hours later, they were vacant and etiolated, halfway human, dead-eyed zombies, already desperately working out where they would find the money for their next fix.

Elijah made his way through the Estate to the abandoned flat that the LFB had claimed for themselves. A family had been evicted for non-payment of rent, and now the older boys had taken it over, gathering there to drink, smoke and be with their girls. Elijah had never been inside the flat before, but he didn't know where else he could take the rucksack and the things that they had stolen.

He was furious. Who was that man to tell him what to do? He didn't look like any of his mother's boyfriends— he was white, for a start—but he had no reason to come and stick his nose into his business. He told himself that he wouldn't see the man again, that he'd get bored, just like they always did, and it would be him who told his mother that it didn't matter, that he would look after her. He had been the man in the house ever since his older brother had vanished. He had been grown up about it all. He'd had to; there wasn't anyone else.

The flat was in the block opposite Blissett House. Elijah idled on the walkway, trying to muster the courage to turn the corner and approach the doorway. It was on the eleventh floor and offered a panoramic view of the area. He looked beyond the Estate, across the hotchpotch of neater housing that had replaced two other blocks that had been pulled down five years ago, past the busy ribbon of Mare Street and across East London to glittering Olympic Park beyond. He rested his elbows on the balcony and gazed down at their flat. His bedroom had a window that looked out onto the walkway. He remembered lying in bed at night and listening as the older boys gathered outside, the lookouts that were posted to watch for the police or other boys. They would talk about money, about the things they would buy, about girls. They talked for hours until the sweet smell of weed wafted in through the open window and filled the room. Elijah's mother would occasionally hustle outside, shooing them away, but they always came back, and over time, she gave up.

It was intoxicating. The boys seemed special to Elijah. They were cool. They were older, they had money, they weren't afraid of girls. They talked about dealing drugs and tiefing, the kind of things that Elijah's favourite rappers rapped about. It was a lifestyle that was glamorous beyond the day-to-day drudgery of school and then helping his mother with the flat. It didn't seem wrong to want a little bit of it for himself.

The boys knew Elijah could hear them, and eventually, they started to include him in their conversations. It wasn't long until he opened the window all the way and started talking to them. He asked how he could get his own money. They told him to stand watch for them, and he did. When they came back, they gave him a brand-new PSP. The week after that they gave him money. He had never seen a fifty-pound note before, but they pressed one into his hand. They started to talk to him more often. They offered him his first joint. He spluttered helplessly as he tried to smoke it, and they laughed at him as he desperately tried to look cool.

It wasn't long before they gave him the chance to make more money. He was small, with tiny arms that could fit through car windows that had been left open. He would open the locks from the inside, and the boys would tear out the car stereos and steal anything else that had been left behind: GPS devices, handbags. They would steal six or seven a night, and Elijah would be given fifty pounds. He put the cash in a shoebox that he hid under his bed. His mother never asked where he got the money for his new clothes. Elijah knew that she wasn't stupid. She just didn't want to hear him say it.

He watched as the door opened and the white man stepped outside. Elijah watched him make his way along the walkway and, after descending the stairs, emerge out onto the forecourt. He walked towards a beaten-up old car, pausing at the door and then crouching down at the front wheel. Elijah could tell from the way the car slumped to the side that the tyre had been slashed. He grinned as the man took off his jacket, removed a spare from the boot and started to go about changing it.

A couple of the older boys were smoking joints on the walkway.

"Alright, younger?" The boy's real name was Dylan, but they called him Fat Boy on account of how big he had been as a young teenager. He had grown out of that now; he was nineteen, six foot tall and full of muscle.

"Is Pops here?"

"He's inside. What do you want?"

"I need to see him."

"Alright, bruv. He's in the back. Knock when you get in."

The flat had been taken over by the LFB. They had sprayed their tag on every spare wall, and a huge, colourful version filled the wall in the lounge. Boys from the Estate lounged around, some playing FIFA on a stolen flat-screen television. Others were listening to the new album from Wretch, arguing that it was better or worse than the new tracks from Newham Generals or Professor Green. Trash was shoved into the corners: empty paper bags from McDonald's, chicken bones that had been sucked clean, empty cigarette packets, cigarette papers. Everyone was toking, and Elijah quickly felt dizzy from the dope smoke that rolled slowly through the room. A couple of the boys looked up, clocked him, ignored him again. No one acknowledged him. The room was hectic and confusing with noise. Elijah felt young and vulnerable but dared not show it.

"Look who it is!" whooped Little Mark.

"Baby JaJa," Pinky sneered. "It's late, younger, shouldn't you be tucked up in bed?"

"Leave him alone," Kidz chided.

Elijah reluctantly made his way across the room to them. Little Mark's real name was Edwin, and he lived in a flat on the seventh floor of Blissett House with his dad. Elijah did not know Kidz's real name, only that he lived in Regis House and had a reputation as the most prolific mugger in the crew. Pinky's real name was Shaquille, he was usually quiet and surly and had a nasty reputation. Elijah tried to keep his distance whenever he was around.

"What you doing here?" Kidz said as he came alongside them.

"Came to see Pops," he said.

Pinky nodded to the rucksack across his shoulder. "Afraid your mum finds out what you've got in there?"

"I ain't afraid," Elijah said.

"That's from earlier, right? The gear from the train?"

"Yes."

"What you bring it with you for, then? You stupid or something?"

"I ain't stupid, either."

"Look pretty stupid from where I'm sitting."

Kidz smiled at him indulgently. "How you going to explain it if you get pulled by the feds?"

Elijah felt himself blush.

"Told you he was stupid," Pinky said. "A stupid little kid. He ain't right for LFB."

"Lucky for him that's not for you to decide, then, innit? Ignore him, young 'un. Pops is in the back. Go on through."

Elijah made his way through the room. The layout of the flat was identical to his own, and he guessed that Pops was in the main bedroom. He knocked on the door. A voice called that he could come in.

The room was dark. Pops was standing next to the open window, blowing smoke into the dusky light beyond. He had removed his shirt, and his muscular torso glistened with a light film of sweat. He had a tattoo of a dragon across his shoulders and, on his bicep, the letters L, F and B. His heavy gold chain glittered against the darkness of his skin. A white woman sat on the edge of the mattress they had put in the room. She straightened her skirt as she got to her feet. She was older than Pops, looked like she was in her thirties, and dressed like the office workers from the city who had seeped into the smarter parts of the borough. Elijah had heard about her; the rumour was that she was something in the city and that she had a taste for the crack.

Pops crossed the room and kissed her gently on the cheek. "I'll see you tonight," he said. She ran her palm across his cheek, collected her jacket, and left the room.

Pops found his T-shirt and pulled it over his head. Elijah caught himself wondering how old he was. His brown skin was unmarked, his eyes bright and intense. Elijah guessed he was eighteen or nineteen, but he had a hardness about him that made him seem older. It was a forced maturity, a product of the road, of the things he had seen and done. It had flayed the innocence out of him. "What's the matter, younger?"

"My mum caught me with this," he said, shrugging the rucksack from his shoulder and letting it hang before him.

"She'll nick it off me if I have it in the house."

Pops laughed. "Don't fret about it, younger. We'll look after it here." He took the bag and tossed it onto the mattress. "Fucking day, I'm all done in." He took a bag of weed from his pocket and found a packet of rolling papers on the windowsill. "You want a smoke?"

Elijah had never been alone with Pops before. He was talking to him, taking him seriously, and it made him feel special. "Go on, then," he said, trying to sound older than he felt.

Pops busied himself with making the spliff. "You have fun this afternoon, blood?"

"Yeah."

"You nervous?"

Elijah took the joint and put it to his lips as Pops sparked it for him. "A bit."

"That's okay," he said. "S'alright to be nervous. Nerves mean adrenaline, and adrenaline is good. Keeps you sharp. You were quick when boi-dem came. Away on your toes."

"I've always been good at running," he said.

"That's the thing, younger. That's gonna be useful. You can't never let the feds get hold of you. The thing that keeps me running, even when my lungs are burning like someone's sparked up a spliff in my chest, even when the stubborn side of me wants to turn around and get ignorant, face them like a man, that's when I remember I've already spent way too many nights sitting on a blue rubber mattress in a cell, who knows how many times it's been pissed on, that's when I remember getting caught by boi-dem's a no-no. You can't come back to the manor and big up your chest about getting shift by boi-dem. Bad bwoys ain't supposed to get caught, JaJa. Especially not black boys." He grinned at him. "It's all good. You did good."

Elijah felt a blast of pride that made his heart skip. No one had said anything like that to him before. His teachers thought he was a waste of space, he didn't have a dad, and his mum was always nagging. He drew in on the joint, coughing as the smoke hit his lungs.

"We ain't really talked before, have we?"

Elijah shrugged. "Not much."

"What you going to do with your life, little man?"

The question caught him off guard. "Dunno," he said.

"You got no plans? No dreams?"

"Dunno. Maybe football. I'm not bad. Maybe that."

"'Maybe football,'" Pops repeated, smiling, taking the joint as Elijah passed it back to him.

"I'm okay at it," Elijah said defensively, wondering if he was being gently mocked. "I'm pretty fast."

"I'll say you are," Pops said, taking a long toke on the joint. "You like the Usain Bolt of Hackney."

Pops dropped down on the mattress. He patted the space next to him, and Elijah sat too. It might have been the weed, but he felt himself start to relax.

"Listen, younger, I'm going to tell you something. You won't think it's cool, but I know what I'm talking about, and you'd do yourself a favour to listen, alright?" He settled back so that he was leaning against the wall. "It's good to have dreams, but a man needs a plan, too. Maybe you are decent at football, maybe you are good enough to make it, but how many kids do you know from these ends who've done it? Maybe you can think of one, but I don't know any. Football is a dream, right, and, like I say, it's good to have dreams, but a man's got to have a plan, too. A realistic one, just in case his dreams don't pay off. You know what I'm saying?"

"What about the street?"

"Seriously, younger? The street can be a laugh, you don't get too deep into it, but the street ain't no plan."

"You're doing it."

"Only for now. It's not a long-term thing."

"I know people who do alright."

"The kids shotting drugs?"

"Nah, that's just baby steps, I mean the ones above

them."

"Listen to me, Elijah—there ain't no future on the street. Some brothers do make it through. I know some who started off as youngers, like you, younger than you, then they work their way up with shotting and tiefing until they become Elders, and then some of them keep out of trouble long enough and get made Faces. But, you look, every year, some of them get taken out. Some get lifted by the feds, others ain't so lucky, and those ones get shot and end up in the ground. Like Darwin, innit? Survival of the fittest. You want, we could have a little experiment—we could start with a hundred young boys, kids your age, and I reckon if we came back five years later to see how they be getting on, maybe one or two of them would still be making their way from the street. The others are out, one way or another. Banged up or brown bread. I don't know what you're like when it comes to numbers, but me, it's like how you are at football—I ain't too bad at all. I'm telling you, younger, one hundred to one or two ain't odds I'm that excited about."

"What about today? You were out with us."

"I know—you think I sound like a hypocrite, and that's fair enough. Maybe I am. But I ain't saying stealing stuff is bad. It ain't right that some people have everything they want and others—people like us—it ain't right that we don't have shit. That stuff we nicked today, them people was all insured. We gave them a scare, but they didn't actually lose nothing. They'll get it all back, all shiny and new. We deserve a nice phone, a camera, an iPod, whatever, and we ain't going to get it unless we take it. I reckon that's fair enough. I reckon that makes it alright to do what we did. But it ain't got a future. You do it ten times, twenty times maybe if you get lucky, eventually you're going to get nicked. Someone gets pulled and grasses you up. Your face gets on CCTV. The feds have got to do something about it in the end. See, what we did this afternoon is short-term. If you want to have those things properly, without fear that they're going to get taken away from you and you're going to get banged up, then there ain't nothing else for it—you got to play the game by their rules."

"How?"

"You got to study. You got to get your exams. You probably think I'm high saying that"—he nodded at the joint, smiled, and then handed it across—"but think about it a little, and you know I'm talking sense. I didn't pay no attention at school. I was a disaster, couldn't stand it so I hardly went at all, and I couldn't wait until I was old enough so that I didn't have to no more. I'm older now, I've got more experience, and I'm telling you that all that stuff they say about studying is true. If I'd paid attention more, did better, what I'm trying to do with myself now would've been a million times easier."

Elijah was confused. "What are you doing?"

"So I said I was okay with numbers? Always have been, just something I've got a talent for. I'm going to night school to get my A-level. Maths. You know my woman? You know what she does?"

Elijah had heard. "Something in the city?"

He nodded. "Accountant. She says if I can get my exams, she can get me a job with her firm. Nothing special, not to start with, post room or some shit like that, but it's a foot in the door. A chance to show them what I can do. After that—who knows? But I'll tell you this for nothing, younger, I ain't going to be doing what we did this afternoon for much longer."

Elijah sucked on the joint again, stifling the unavoidable cough. The conversation had taken him by surprise. He had always looked up to Pops, thought that he was cool, and he was the last person he would have expected to tell him to stay in school and work hard.

"You did good today. Like I said, you got potential. I saw it in you right away. That wasn't easy, I remember my first time, I was sick as a dog, they had to push me onto the bus, and then I was completely useless. None of that with you, was there? You got balls. That's great. But just think about what I've said, alright? There's no future there for you. For any of us."

They smoked the rest of the joint together before Pops got up. "I got to breeze. Got school. My exams are in a month, and we're revising. Equations and all that shit. Don't want to be late."

The night was warm and close, and the walkway was empty as they both stepped outside. Pops bumped fists with him and descended the stairs. Elijah rested his elbows on the balustrade, looking across to Blissett House and his mother's flat, then down into the yard as Pops emerged, walking confidently and with purpose, acknowledging the monosyllabic greetings from the strung-out cats and the boys from the gang who sold them their gear. Pops was liked. Respected. Elijah nodded to himself.

He fancied some of that himself.

PART TWO

Murder Mile

He wiped the sweat from his face and put the scope of his rifle to his eye, gazing down onto the plains below. The village was five hundred yards away, clustered around the river. Two dozen huts, the villagers making their living from the herd of goats that grazed on the scrappy pasture to the north and west. It was a small habitation gathered around a madrasa; children played in the dusty yard outside, kicking a ball, a couple of them wearing the shirts of teams he recognised. He took a breath and held it, the rifle held steady, the stock pressed into the space between his shoulder and neck. He nudged the rifle left to right, examining each hut individually. Nothing was out of place: the women were working at home while the men tended the animals in the pasture. He moved the scope right to left until the missile launcher was centred in the crosshairs. A Scud launcher, an old R-11, Russian made. He squinted down the sight, placing each member of the crew. Three men, Republican Guard. He centred each man in the crosshairs, his finger held loosely through the trigger guard, the tip trailing against the edge of the trigger. He nudged the scope away again so that he could focus on the madrasa: five children in the yard, their cheap plastic ball jerking in the wind as they kicked it against the wall of the hut. They were happy. The launcher meant nothing to them, nothing compared to their game and the fun they could have together. He heard their laughter delivered to him by a welcome breath of air.

Chapter Eleven

JOHN MILTON AWOKE at six the next morning. He had slept badly, the damned nightmare waking him in the middle of his deepest sleep and never really leaving after that, the ghostly after-effects playing across his mind. He reached out to silence his alarm and allowed himself the rare luxury of coming around slowly. His thoughts turned to the previous evening, to Sharon and Elijah. He recognised elements of his own personality in the boy: the stubbornness and the inclination to resist authority. If they lived under different circumstances, it would have done no harm for the boy to test her limits. It was natural, and he would have returned to her in time. Their circumstances did not allow him that freedom, though. Milton could see how the attraction of the gang would be difficult for him to resist. If he allowed himself to be drawn into their orbit, he risked terrible damage to his prospects: a criminal record if he was lucky, or if he wasn't, something much worse.

Milton did not own or rent a property. It was unusual for him to be in the country for long periods, and he did not see the point of it. He preferred to be unencumbered, flexible enough to be able to move quickly whenever required. His practice was to stay in hotels, so he had booked a room in an American chain, an anonymous space that could have been anywhere in the world. The hotel was on the South Bank of the Thames, next to Westminster Bridge, and when he pulled the curtains aside, he was presented with a view of the pigeons and air-conditioning units on the roof of the adjacent building and, beyond that, the tower of the Houses of Parliament. The sky above was cerulean blue, and once again, the sun was already blazing. It was going to be another hot day.

He showered and shaved, standing before the mirror with a towel around his waist. He was six foot tall and around thirteen stone, with an almost wiry solidity about him. His eyes were on the grey side of blue, his mouth had a cruel twist to it, there was a long horizontal scar from his cheek to the start of his nose, and his hair was long and a little unkempt, a frond falling over his forehead in a wandering comma. There was a large tattoo of angel wings spread across his shoulders, claws at the tips and rows of etched feathers descending down his back until they disappeared beneath the towel; it was the souvenir of a night in Guatemala, out of his mind on Quetzalteca Especial and mescaline.

Milton dressed and went down to the restaurant for breakfast. He found a table to himself and filled his plate with scrambled eggs from the buffet. He drank a glass of freshly squeezed orange juice, poured a cup of strong coffee, and flicked through the pages of the *Times*. The front page was dominated by the news of the killing in France. The *gendarmerie* were waiting to speak to the boy. It was hoped that he would be able to tell them what had happened and, perhaps, identify the man who had killed his parents.

Milton folded the paper and put it to one side.

He returned to his room and packed. He had very little in the way of possessions, but what he did own was classic and timeless: a wide, flat gun-metal cigarette case; a black oxidized Ronson lighter; a Rolex Oyster Perpetual watch. There was little else. He smoked a cigarette out of the window as he transferred his clothes from the wardrobe to his suitcase, put on a pair of Levis and a shirt, slipped his wallet and phone into his pocket, and took the lift down to reception.

"I'd like to check out, please," he told the receptionist.

She keyed his details into her computer. "Certainly, Mr. Anderson. How was your stay with us?"

"Very pleasant."

He settled the bill in cash, collected the Volvo from the underground car park, and drove back to Hackney.

He drove through the Square Mile, its clean streets, well-shod denizens, steepling towers and minarets a gleaming testament to capitalism. He continued past Liverpool Street, through trendy Shoreditch, and then passed into the hinterland beyond. Milton had noticed the arcade of shops as he had driven home last night. There was an estate agent's between a fried chicken takeaway and a minicab office. He parked and walked along the arcade, pausing to look at the properties advertised in the window. He went inside, and a man in a cheap, shiny suit asked him if he could be of help.

"I'm looking for a place to rent."

"Furnished or unfurnished?"

"Furnished."

"Anywhere in particular? We've got a nice place in a school conversion near to the station."

"Somewhere close to Blissett House."

The man looked at him as if he was mad. "That's not the best area. It's rough."

"That's all right."

"Do you work in the city?"

"No, I'm a writer," he said, using the cover story he had prepared as he had travelled across London. "I'm researching a book on police corruption. I need to be in the middle of things. I don't care if it's rough. It's better if it's authentic. Do you have anything?"

The man flicked through his folder of particulars, evidently keen not to look a gift horse in the mouth. "We just had a place come up on Grove Road. Terraced house, two bedrooms. I wouldn't say it's anything special, but it's cheap, and it's on the edge of the Estate. Best I can do, I'm afraid. Most stock in the blocks themselves are kept back for council tenants."

"Can you show me?"

"Of course."

The maisonette was close to the office, and since it was a bright, warm day, they walked. The hulk of Blissett House loomed over them as they passed beneath the railway line and into an Estate that had been cleared, the brutalist blocks replaced by neat and tidy semi-detached houses. They were painted a uniform pale orange, and each had its own little scrap of garden behind a metal fence. Some houses were occupied by their owners and marked by careful maintenance. Others were rented, distinguished by overgrown lawns that stank of dog excrement, boarded windows and wheelie bins that overflowed with trash. They continued on, picking up Grove Road.

The house that the agent led them to was the last in a terrace that was in a poor state of repair. It was a tiny sliver of a house, only as wide as a single window and the front door. Solid metal security gates had been fitted to the doors and windows, graffiti had been sprayed on the walls, and the remains of a washing machine had been dumped and left to rust in the street right next to the kerb. The agent unlocked the security door and yanked it aside. The property was spartan: a small lounge, kitchen and bathroom on the ground floor and two bedrooms above. The furniture was cheap and insubstantial. The rooms smelt of fried food and stale urine.

"It's a little basic," the agent said, not even bothering to try to pretend otherwise. "I'm sorry. We have other places, though. I've got the key for another one, much nicer, ten minutes away."

"This'll do," Milton said. "I'll take it."

Chapter Twelve

IT TOOK HALF AN HOUR back at the office for the formalities of the lease to be taken care of. Milton paid the deposit and the advance rent in cash. There were no references or credit checks required, which was just as well, since a search of Milton's details would not have returned any results. The agent asked him whether he was sure that the house was what he wanted, and, again, offered a handful of alternatives that he thought would be more appropriate. Milton politely declined the offer, thanked him for his help, took the keys, and left the office.

There was a small mini-market serving the area. It was sparsely stocked, a few bags of crisps and boxes of cereal displayed under harsh strip lights that spat and fizzed. Alcohol and cigarettes, however, were well provided for, secured behind the Perspex screen from behind which the owner surveyed his business with suspicious eyes. Milton nodded to the man as he made his way inside and received nothing but a wary tip of the head in return. He made his way through the shop, picking out cleaning products, a carton of orange juice and a bag of ice. He took his goods to the owner and arranged them on the lip of counter ahead of the screen. As the man rang his purchases up, Milton looked behind him to shelves that were loaded with alcohol: gin, vodka, whiskey.

The owner caught his glance. "You want?"

He paused and almost wavered. 692 days, he reminded himself. 692 going on 693.

He needed a meeting badly.

"No, just those, please."

Milton paid and returned to the maisonette. He unlocked the doors and scraped the security door against the concrete lintel as he yanked it aside. It didn't take long to establish himself. He unpacked in the larger of the two bedrooms, hanging the clothes in a wardrobe made of flimsy sheets of MDF. He spread his sleeping bag out across the lumpy mattress, went downstairs to the kitchen, and took out the mop and bucket he found in a small cupboard. He filled the bucket with hot water, added detergent, and started to attack the layers of grease that had stratified across the cheap linoleum floor.

It took Milton six hours to clean the house, and even then, he had only really scratched the surface. The kitchen was presentable: the floor was clean, the fridge and oven had been scoured to remove the encrusted stains; the utensils, crockery and surfaces were scrubbed until the long-neglected dirt had been ameliorated. There were mouse droppings scattered all about, but save clearing them away, there was nothing that Milton could do about that. He moved on to the bathroom, spending an hour scrubbing the toilet, the sink and the bath, and washing the floor. When he was finally finished, he undressed and stood beneath the shower, washing in its meagre stream of warm water until he felt clean. He put on a fresh T-shirt and jeans, took his leather jacket from where he had hung it over the banister, went outside and locked the door behind him. He set off for the main road.

He took out his phone and opened the bookmarked page on his internet browser. He double-tapped an icon, and his mapping application opened. His destination was a three-mile walk away. He had an hour before the meeting, and it was a hot evening. He decided that rather than take the bus, he would walk.

St Mary Magdalene church was on the left-hand side of the road, set back behind a low brick wall, well-trimmed topiary and a narrow fringe of grass studded with lichen-covered gravestones from a hundred years ago. A sign had been tied to the railings: two capital As set inside a blue triangle that was itself set within a blue circle. An arrow pointed towards the church. Milton felt a disconcerting moment of doubt and paused by the gate to adjust the lace of his shoe. He looked up and down the street, satisfying himself that he was not observed. He knew the consequences for being seen in a place like this would be draconian and swift; suspension would be immediate, the termination of his employment would follow soon after, and there was the likelihood of prosecution. He was ready to leave the service, but on his own terms and not like that.

He passed through the open gate and followed a gravel path around the side of the building, descended a flight of stairs, and entered the basement through an open door. The room inside was busy with people and full of the noise of conversation. A folding table had been set up and arranged with a vat of hot water, two rows of mismatched mugs, a plastic cup full of plastic spoons, jars of coffee and an open box of tea bags, a large two-pint container of milk, a bowl of sugar and a plate of digestive biscuits. The man behind the table was black and heavyset, with a well-trimmed salt-and-pepper beard and hair cropped close to his scalp. His arms bulged with muscle, and his shirt was tight around his chest and shoulders.

Milton approached the table.

"Can I get you a drink?" the man said.

"Coffee, please."

The man smiled, took one of the mugs, and added two spoonfuls of coffee granules. "Haven't seen you before."

"My first time."

The man poured hot water into the mug. "Your first meeting here, or your first ever?"

"First time here."

"All right then," the man said. A silence extended, but before it could become uncomfortable, the man filled it. "I'm Rutherford," he said. "Dennis Rutherford, but everyone just calls me Rutherford."

"John."

"Nice to meet you, John." He handed him the mug.

"Help yourself to biscuits. The meeting's about to get started. It's busy tonight—go in and get a seat if I were you."

Milton did. The adjacent room was larger, with a low, sloping ceiling and small windows that were cut into the thick brick walls that served as foundations for the church above. A table had been arranged at one end with two chairs behind it, and the rest of the space was filled with folding chairs. A candle had been lit on the table, and tea lights had been arranged on windowsills and against the wall. The effect was warm, intimate and atmospheric. Posters had been stuck to the walls. One was designed like a scroll, with twelve separate points set out along it. It was headed THE TWELVE STEPS TO RECOVERY.

Milton took a seat near the back and sipped the cheap coffee as the chairs around him started to fill.

A middle-aged man wearing a black polo-neck top and jeans sat at one of the chairs behind the table at the front of the room. He banged a spoon against the rim of his mug, and the quiet hush of conversation faded away. "Thank you," the man said. "Good to see so many of you—I'm glad you could come. Let's get started. My name is Alan, and I'm an alcoholic."

Milton sat quietly at the back of the room. Alan was the chairman, and he had invited another speaker to address the group. The second man said that he was a lawyer, from the city, and he told his story. It was the usual thing: a man who appeared to be successful was hiding a barrage of insecurities behind addictions to work and drink, a tactic that had worked for years but now was coming at too high a price: family, relationships, his health. The message was clichéd—Milton had heard it all before, a thousand times before—yet the passion with which the man spoke was infectious. Milton listened avidly, and when he looked at his watch at the end of the man's address, half an hour had passed.

The floor was opened after that, and the audience

contributed with observations of their own. Milton felt the urge to raise his hand and speak, but he had no idea how best to start his story. He never did. Even if had been able to tell it, he would not have known where to start. There was so much that he would not have been able to relate. He felt the usual relief to be there, the same sense of peace that he always felt, but it was something else entirely to put those thoughts into words. How would the others feel about his history? The things that he had done? It made him feel secretive, especially compared to the searing honesty of those around him. They talked openly and passionately, several of them struggling through tears of anger and sadness. Despite the sure knowledge that he belonged there with them, his inability to take part made him feel like a fraud.

Chapter Thirteen

AT THE END of the meeting a group gathered to talk and smoke cigarettes outside. They smiled at Milton as he climbed the steps from the basement. He knew that their smiles were meant as encouragement for him to stop and speak. They meant well, of course they did, but it was pointless; he couldn't possibly. He smiled back at them but didn't stop. He had no idea what he would say. Far better to make a quick exit.

"Hey, man—hey, hey, hold up."

Milton was at the gate, ready to turn onto the street to start the walk home. He paused and turned back. The man who had been serving the coffee, Rutherford, was jogging across in his direction. Milton took a moment to consider him again. He was big, over six foot tall and solid with it, several stones heavier than he was. He loped across the churchyard, moving with an easy spring that suggested plenty of strength in his legs.

"You don't hang about," he said as he reached him. "There's a café down the road. People stop for coffee or a bite to eat, have a chat. You should come."

Milton smiled. "Not for me. But thanks."

"You didn't speak in the meeting. There's no point just sitting there, man. You got to get stuck in."

"Listening's good enough."

"Not if you want to really make a difference. I had that problem myself, back when I first started coming. Thought it was crazy, no one was gonna want to listen to my shit. But I got over it in the end. Eventually, the way I saw it, coming along and not doing anything was a waste of my time. That's why I do the coffees—start small, right, and take it from there? You got to get involved." Rutherford spoke slowly and deliberately, as if measuring

74

each word. The effect was to imbue each with a persuasive weight. He was an impressive man.

"I suppose so."

"Which way you headed, man? Back to Hackney?"

"Yes."

"Me too. Come on—you don't mind, we can walk together."

"You don't want to go to the café?"

"Nah, won't make no difference if I miss it tonight. I'm up at six tomorrow; I should probably get an early night."

Milton would have preferred to walk alone, but there was something infectious in Rutherford's bearing that stalled his objections, and besides, it didn't look like he was going to take no for an answer. They set off together, making their way along Holloway Road towards Highbury Corner.

He started speaking. "What's your story, then?"

Milton took a breath. "The same as most people, I suppose. I was drinking too much, and I needed help to stop. How about you?"

"Same deal, man. I was in the Forces. Fifteen years. Saw some stuff I never want to see again. I only stopped feeling guilty about it when I was drunk." He turned to look at him. "Don't mind me being presumptuous, John, but you're a soldier too, right?"

"Is it that obvious?"

"You know what it's like—we got that look. Where did you serve? The Sandpit?"

"For a while."

"Ireland?"

"Yes."

"I been all over the place too, man. 'See the world,' that's what they told me when they were trying to get me to sign up, like it's some glamorous holiday. It was fun for a while, but then I saw what it was really all about. By the time I got wise to it, I was a raging drunk."

"What happened?"

"Look, I ain't saying I'm not grateful for what the army did for me. When I was a younger man, ten years ago, I got into all sorts of mess that I didn't want to be getting involved in. Trouble, man, all kinds of trouble. Got myself in with a bad crowd from around here. Ended up doing plenty of things I regret. Drink and drugs—you know what it's like. I got friends from around that time, plenty of them got banged up, and a couple of them are dead. Could've easily been me. The army was a way to get away from all that." He spoke fluently, settling comfortably into a story that he had clearly told many times before, probably at the meetings. "And it worked, least for a time. Took me away from here, broadened my horizons, gave me structure and discipline in my life. And those things are good things, things I needed. But they come at a price, right? The things I saw while I was out there doing my thing—" He paused. "Well, shit, it got so bad by the end that I could only live with myself with a drink inside me. You know what I mean?"

He was full of heat and passion. Milton said that he understood.

"I don't take this life lightly, John. The way I see it, the Fellowship has given me a blessing. The gift of knowledge. I can see what's wrong with how things are. I know the things that work and the things that don't. Drink and drugs—they don't. Not many people get given a chance to make a difference, but I did. And, one day at a time, I ain't going to throw it away."

They passed into the busy confluence of traffic and pedestrians circulating around the roundabout at Highbury Corner and moved onto Dalston Lane. Youngsters gathered outside the tube, ready to filter towards the pubs and bars of Islington High Street. Touts offered cheap rides, immigrants pushed burgers and hot dogs, drunken lads spilled out of the pub next to the station.

"How?" Milton asked him.

"How what, man?"

"How are you going to make a difference?"

"Boxing. I used to be a tasty heavyweight when I was a lad. I got to be big early, big and strong, and I had a right hand you didn't want to get hit by. If I'd stayed with it, who knows? I wouldn't have got into the trouble I did, that's for sure. I wouldn't have gotten into the army, and I reckon I was probably good enough to make a decent career out of it. I'm too old and out of shape for that now, but I've still got it all up in here." He tapped a finger to his temple. "So I've set up a club for youngsters, see? Amateurs, girls and boys, all ages. They ain't got nothing to do around here, nothing except run with the gangs and get into mischief, and I know better than most where that road leads. You're a younger born here, you run with one of them gangs, there are two places for you to go: prison or the crematorium. The military is one way out, but I can't recommend that no more. So I try to give them another way. Something else to do, some structure, some discipline, and you hope that's enough. It can be the difference. And the way I see it, if I help a handful of them get away from temptation, that's good enough. That's my job done."

"I used to box," Milton said, smiling for the first time. "A long time ago."

Rutherford looked him up and down: tall, lean and hard. "You've got the look for it," he said. "Cruiserweight?"

"Maybe these days." Milton smiled. "Middleweight back then. Where's the club?"

"Church hall on Grove Road, near the park. Monday, Wednesday and Friday nights and all day Saturdays. Got about twenty regulars now." His eyes flashed with passion. "Got some kids who are on the fringes of the gangs. Some of them have potential. This one girl, man, you wouldn't believe how hard she can hit. Like a piledriver, knocked this lad who was giving her lip into the middle of next week. He never gave her lip after that." He grinned at the memory of it.

They reached Milton's turning. "This is me," he said.

Rutherford cocked an eyebrow in surprise. "You living in the Estate?"

"Yes."

Rutherford sucked his teeth.

"Not good?"

"You're in the worst bit of Hackney, and Hackney's different. You talk about Waltham Forest, you talk about Camden, Southwark, Lambeth, all the rest—sure, they got bad people there. Plenty of serious players. But here? Man, Hackney's different. You understand? The boys here are more serious than anywhere else. Everyone is banging. I mean, *everyone*. You can't even compare what it's like here with them other places. You best be careful, you hear? Don't matter how big you are; they won't care about that. They got a knife or a shooter and they think you're worth rolling, I'm telling you, man, it don't matter how mean you look, they'll do it."

"Nice to meet you, Rutherford."

"You too, John. You take it easy. Maybe I'll see you at the meeting next week?"

"Maybe."

"And say something next time, all right? You look like you got plenty on your mind. You'll be surprised the difference it makes."

Milton watched as the big man walked away from him. He turned off the main road and headed into the Estate, stopping at the mini-market to buy another bag of ice. He ignored the sullen aggression of the teenagers who were gathered outside the shop, the silence as he passed through them and then the hoots of derision, the calls of "lighty!" and "batty boy" as he set off again. Most of them were young, barely in their teens. Milton didn't give them a second look.

It was half-ten by the time he returned to the

maisonette. He took the carton of orange juice and poured into one of the newly cleaned glasses. He opened the bag of ice and dropped in three chunks, putting the rest in the freezer. He took off his clothes and put his gun and holster under a pillow. He swilled the juice around to cool. He pulled a chair up to the window, then went and sat down, letting the hot air, the compound smell of baked asphalt and fried food, breathe over his body. He sipped the cool drink, feeling the tang against the back of his throat, felt it slide cold down his throat and into his stomach.

He filled up his glass again, this time with more ice, and sat back down. The bedroom overlooked the front of the house. He looked out onto the street and, beyond that, the looming mass of Blissett House. A group of young boys had gathered at the junction of the road, the glowing red tips of their cigarettes and joints flaring as they inhaled.

Milton felt restless. He went over and took his gun from beneath the pillow, slipped out the magazine, and pumped the single round onto the bed. He tested the spring of the magazine and of the breech and drew a quick bead on various objects round the room. His aim was off, just a little, but detectable nonetheless. It was the tiny tremor in his hand. He had noticed it in France, and it seemed to be getting worse. He snapped the magazine back. He pumped a round into the breech and replaced the gun under the pillow.

He watched the kids outside for another five minutes, the sound of their raucous laughter carrying all the way back to the open window. Then, tired, he closed the curtains, finished undressing, and went to bed.

Chapter Fourteen

ELIJAH WATCHED the Vietnamese hassling the shoppers as they came out of Tesco. They were in the car park, far enough away from the entrance to go unnoticed by the security guards. They stepped up to the shoppers with their trolleys full of groceries and held open the satchels that they wore around their shoulders. There were four of them, two men and two women, all of them slim and dark-haired. The satchels were full of pirated DVDs. They were given the brush-off most of the time, but occasionally, someone would stop, rifle through the bags, and hand over a ten-pound note in exchange for a couple of them.

"You ready, younger?" said Pops.

"Yeah," Elijah said. "Ready."

"Off you go, then."

He did exactly as Pops had instructed him. One of the Vietnamese women was distracted by Little Mark, who pretended to be interested in her DVDs. She kept her money in a small shoulder bag that she allowed to hang loosely across her arm. Elijah ran up to her, and her attention diverted, he yanked on the bag as hard as he could. Her arm straightened as he tugged the bag down, her fingers catching it. A second, harder tug broke her grip, and he was away. He sprinted back again, the other boys following after him in close formation. The two men started in pursuit, vaulting the wall that separated the car park from the pavement and the bus stop beyond, but it didn't take long for them to abandon the chase. They were outnumbered and being led into unfriendly territory. They knew that the money wasn't worth the risk.

The boys ran down Morning Lane, whooping and hollering, eventually taking a sharp left along the cycle path that ran underneath the East London Line. They sprinted up the shallow incline on the other side of the tunnel and slowed to a jog. Once they were in the Estate, they found a low wall and sat down along it.

Pops held up his fist, and Elijah bumped it with his. He beamed with pride. He knew he ought to keep his cool, hide away the excitement and happiness that he felt, but he couldn't help it. He didn't care how foolish it made him look.

"How much you get?"

Elijah took the notes from his pocket and fanned through them. "Two hundred," he reported.

"Not bad." Pops reached across and took the notes. He counted out fifty and gave it back to Elijah. "Go on, younger, put that towards some new Jordans. You done good."

Little Mark went into the minimart nearby and returned with a large bottle of cider and a bagful of chocolate. The cider was passed around, each boy taking a long swig of it. Elijah joined in when the plastic bottle reached him, the sickly sweet liquid tasting good as he tipped it down his throat.

"What did you get?" Kidz asked.

Little Mark opened the bag and emptied out the contents. He laid the bars out on the wall. "Twix, KitKat, Mars, Yorkie."

"Too pikey."

"Maltesers. Milky Way."

"Too gay."

"Got them for you, innit? Galaxy, Caramel—that's it. You want something else, go get it yourself."

Pops tossed the chocolate around, and they devoured it.

"I gotta jet," Pops said eventually, folding the wad of notes and sliding them into his pocket. "My woman wants to see me. I'll see you boys tomorrow, a'ight?"

"Hold up," Little Mark said. "I'm going your way."

"Me, too," Kidz said.

Elijah was left with Pinky. He wanted to go with the others, but Pinky got up and stretched. "Come on," he said. "I'll walk back with you."

They set off together, making their way through the Estate and cutting across a scrubby patch of grass. Pinky was a little older and a little taller than Elijah. His face was sharply featured, with a hook nose and prominent cheekbones. He was normally boisterous and brash, full of spiteful remarks, yet now he was quiet and brooding. Elijah quickly felt uncomfortable and wondered if there was a way he could disentangle himself without causing offence. They made their way through the Estate to a children's playground. The surface was soft and springy beneath their trainers, but the equipment had all been vandalised. The swings had been looped over the frames so that they hung high up, uselessly, and the roundabout had been pulled from its fixings. Vials of crack were crushed underfoot, shards that glittered like diamonds amid the dog mess, discarded newspaper and fast-food wrappers.

"Let's sit down here for a minute," Pinky said, pointing to a bench at the edge of the playground. "Something I want to talk to you about."

Elijah's nerves settled like a fist in his stomach. "I got to get back to my mums."

"You don't want a quick smoke?" Pinky reached into his jacket and grinned as he opened his hand; he had a small bag of weed and a packet of Rizlas. "Sit yourself down. I wanna get high. Won't take long."

Elijah did as he was told and sat.

Pinky was quiet as he held the cigarette paper open on his lap and tipped a line of marijuana along the fold. He rolled the joint with dexterous fingers, sealed it, and put it to his lips. He put flame to the end and sucked down greedily. He did not give the joint to Elijah.

"You quietened down now, little man," he said.

"Yeah?" Elijah said uncertainly.

"You don't wanna get too excited."

"What do you mean?"

"That big smile you had on your face back then. Like you'd won the fucking lottery. Robbing those nips ain't nothing. Rolling that train weren't, either. You ain't done shit yet."

Elijah was ready to fire back some lip, but he saw the look in the boy's face and decided against it. He knew banter, and this was something different; hostility sparked in his dark eyes, and he could see it would take very little for the sparks to catch and grow into something worse.

"You don't know me, do you?"

"What you mean?"

"You don't know who I am."

"Course I do."

"So?"

"You're Pinky," he said with sudden uncertainty.

"That's right. But you don't know me, do you? Not really know me."

"I guess not."

"You know my brother? Dwayne? You heard of him?"

"No."

The joint had gone out. Pinky lit it again. "Let me tell you a story. Five years ago, my brother was in the LFB, like me. They called him High Top. Your brother, Jules, he was in, too. The two of them was close, close as you can be, looked out for each other, same way that we look out for each other, innit?" He put the joint to his lips and drew down on it hard.

"There was this one time, right, there was a beef between this crew from Tottenham and the LFB. So they went over there, caused trouble, battered a couple of their boys. Tottenham came over these ends to retaliate, and they found your brother and my brother smoking in the park. Like we are right now. They got the jump on them. They was all tooled up, and our brothers didn't have nothing. Rather than stay and get stuck in, your fassy brother breezed. Straight out of the park, didn't look back, forgot all about my brother. And he wasn't so lucky. The Tottenham boys had knives and cleavers, and they wanted to make an example out of him. They cut my brother up, bruv. Sliced him—his face, across his back, his legs, all over. Ended up stabbing him in the gut. He was in hospital for two weeks while they stitched him together again. His guts—they was all fucked up. He weren't never the same again. He has to shit into a bag now, and it ain't never going to get better. Turned him into a shadow of himself."

"Fuck that," Elijah managed to say. "My brother would never have done that."

"Yeah? Really? Your brother, what's he doing now?"

"We don't see him no more."

"Don't go on like you don't know. I seen him—he's a fuckin' addict. He was a coward then, and now he's a fuckin' junkie."

Elijah got up from the bench.

"Give me that money," Pinky said.

Elijah shook his head. "No. Pops gave it to me. I earned it. It's mine."

"You wanna fall out with me, little man?"

"No—"

Pinky grabbed him by the lapels of his coat and shoved him to the ground. He fell atop him, pressing his right arm across his throat, pinning him down, and reached inside of his jacket with his left hand. He found the notes and pocketed them.

"Remember your place," he said. "You ain't nothing to me. You think you a gangster, but you ain't shit. Give me lip like that again and I'll shank you." He took out a butterfly knife, shook it open, and held the blade against Elijah's cheek. "One jerk of my hand now, bruv, and you marked for life. Know what it'll say?"

"No," Elijah said, his voice shaking.

"Pinky's bitch."

Elijah lay still as Pinky drew the cold blade slowly down his face. Pinky took a bunched handful of his jacket and pulled his head up and then, with a pivot, slammed him down again. The surface was soft but, even so, the sudden impact was dizzying. Pinky got up and backed away. He pointed at Elijah's head and laughed. Elijah felt a dampness against the back of his crown and in the nape of his neck. He reached around, gingerly, expecting to find his own blood. He did not. Pinky had pushed him back into dog mess. The shit was in his hair and against his skin, sliding down beneath the collar of his jacket.

"Later, little man." Pinky laughed at him. He left Elijah on the ground.

He bit his lip until the older boy was out of sight, and then, alone, he allowed himself to cry.

Chapter Fifteen

MILTON WAITED until the sun had sunk below the adjacent houses before he went out to scout the area. It was a humid, close evening. The stifling heat of the day had soaked into the Estate, and now it was slowly seeping out. Televisions flickered in the front rooms of the houses on his street, most of the neighbours leaving their windows uncovered. Arguments played out of open doors. The atmosphere sparked with the dull electric throb of tension, of barely suppressed aggression and incipient violence.

The area seemed to come alive at night. There were people everywhere. Youngsters gathered on street corners and on weed-strewn playgrounds. Others listlessly tossed basketballs across a pockmarked court while they were watched by girls who laced their painted nails through the wire-mesh fence. A lithe youngster faked out his doughty guard and made a stylish lay-up, the move drawing whoops from the spectators. Music played from the open windows of cars and houses. Graffiti was everywhere, one crude mural showing groups of children with guns killing one another. Milton carried on, further along the road. A railway bridge that bore the track into Liverpool Street cast the arcade of shops below into a pool of murky gloom. A man smoking Turkish cigarettes levered rolls of carpet back into his shop, drivers gathered around a minicab office, the sound of clashing metal from the open windows of a gym with a crude stencil of Charles Atlas on the glass. The arcade carried the sickly smell of kebab meat, fried chicken, and dope.

Milton took it all in, remembering the layout of the streets and the alleyways that linked them. Two streets to the east and he was in an area that bore the unmistakeable marks of gentrification: a gourmet restaurant, a chichi coffee shop that would be full of prams in the daytime, a happening pub full of hipsters in drainpipe jeans and fifties frocks, an elegant Victorian terrace in perfect repair, beautifully tended front gardens behind painted iron fences. Two streets west and he was back in the guts of the Estate, the ten-storey slabs of housing blocks with the nauseatingly bright orange balconies festooned with satellite dishes.

Milton crossed into Victoria Park, a wide-open space fringed by fume-choked fir trees. A series of paved paths cut through the park, intermittent and unreliable streetlamps providing discreet pools of light that made the darkness in between even deeper and more threatening. The area's reputation kept it quiet at night save for drunken city boys who used it as a shortcut, easy pickings for the gangs that roamed across it looking for prey.

Milton passed through the gate and walked towards the centre. A group of youngsters had congregated around one of the park benches. One of their number was showing off on his BMX, bouncing off the front wheel as the others laughed at his skill. Milton assessed them coolly. There were eight of them, mid-teens, all dressed in the uniform: caps beneath hoodies, baggy jeans and bright white trainers.

He kept walking. As he drew closer, he heard the sound of music being played through the reedy speaker of a mobile phone. It had a fast, thumping beat and aggressive lyrics. The rapper was talking about beefs and pieces and merking anyone who got in his way.

One of the group sauntered out from the pack and blocked his path.

"What you want, chichi man?" The boy showed no fear. His insolence was practiced and drew hollers of pleasure from the audience.

"I'm a journalist," he said.

"You BBC? You on the television? Can you get me on

the TV?"

"No, I'm working on a book."

Laughter rang out. "No one reads books, bro."

"It's about police corruption. You know anything about that?"

Milton watched the boy. He was a child, surely no older than fifteen. There was a disturbing aspect to his face, a lack of expression with his eyes constantly flickering to the left and right. Milton had seen that appearance before; soldiers from warzones looked that way, a pathological watchfulness to ward against the threat of sudden attack. Milton knew enough about psychology to know that kind of perpetual vigilance was unhealthy. He knew soldiers who had been constantly on the alert for danger, who equated any show of emotion with violence, and from whom all feeling had been smelted. They became machines.

"The pigs are all bent, man," the boy told him. "You might as well write about the sky being blue or water being wet. You ain't teaching no one nothing round these ends. No one's gonna read that."

"Do you know Elijah Warriner?"

"What's he got to do with the feds?"

"I want to talk to him. I heard he's around here sometimes. Is he a friend of yours?"

"That little mong ain't my friend, and there's no point talking to him. He don't know fuck all. You want, though, we could have a conversation? You and me?"

Milton noticed one of the boys in the group take his phone from his pocket and start to tap out a message. "Fine," he said. "What would you like to talk about?"

"Wanna know about violence? I shanked a guy last week. Want to know about that?"

"Not really."

"I could shank you, too. I got a knife, right here in my pocket." He sauntered forwards, towards Milton, still showing no sign of how outsized he was. He patted the bulge in his hip pocket. "Six-inch blade, lighty. I could walk up to you right now, like this, take the knife, shank you right in the guts." He made a fist and jabbed it towards Milton's stomach. "Bang, you'd be done for, blood. Finished. I could make you bleed, big man, right in the middle of the park. Ain't no one gonna come and help you out here, neither. What you think of that?"

Milton said nothing.

"Man got shook!" one of the others shouted out. "Pinky shook the big man."

Milton looked down at the boy. He was tall and thin and wiry, couldn't have been more than nine stone soaking wet. Calling his bluff would provoke the escalation he seemed to want, and there was no point in doing that. He wanted them to think he was a journalist, harmless, a little frightened and out of his depth. The hooting and hollering around them continued, but the atmosphere had become charged.

"I might shank you the moment you turn your back."

Milton noticed a group of boys cycling across to them from the edge of the park.

"Don't turn your back on me, big man. You don't mean nothing to me. I might do it just for a laugh."

The group on the bikes reached them. There were half a dozen of them. Milton recognised Elijah at the back. The biggest boy—Milton guessed he was seventeen or eighteen—propped his bike against the bench and strutted over to them.

The boy walked across to the group. "Alright, Pinky?" he said to the youngster who had threatened him. "What's the beef?"

"Nah," the boy said. "Ain't no beef."

Milton ignored him and addressed the newcomer. "Are you in charge?"

"You could say that."

Milton pointed over at Elijah. "I want to talk to him."

"You know this man, Elijah?"

A look of suspicion had fallen across his face. "Yeah," he said warily. "He was with my mums."

"And do you want to talk to him?"

Elijah shook his head.

"Sorry, bro. He don't want to talk to you."

"He say he a *writer*," one of the boys reported, loading the last word with scorn.

"That right?"

"That's right. A journalist."

"Bullshit. You ain't a journalist, mate. If you're a journalist, then I'm going to win the fucking X Factor. You must think I was born yesterday. What are you? Social?"

"He's po-po!" one of the other boys cried out. "Look at him."

"He ain't a fed. Feds don't come into the park unless they've got backup."

The atmosphere was becoming fevered. Milton could see that it had the potential to turn quickly, and dangerously. He concentrated on the older boy. "What's your name?"

"You don't need to know my name."

"I don't want any trouble."

"Then you don't wanna come walking through our ends late at night, do you, bruv?"

"I'm not police. I'm not Social. You don't have anything to worry about."

The boy laughed scornfully. "Do I look worried?"

"No, you don't," Milton said. He raised his voice so that the others could hear him. "Tell Elijah that I want to talk to him. I'm going to have my breakfast in the café on Dalston Lane every morning from now on. Nine o'clock. Tell him I'll buy him breakfast, too. Whatever he wants. And if he doesn't want to meet me, he can call me here instead." Milton reached into his pocket and took out a card with the number of his mobile printed across it. He gave it to the older boy, staring calmly into his face. A moment of doubt passed across the boy's face, Milton's sudden equanimity shaking his confidence. He took the card between thumb and forefinger.

"Thank you," Milton said.

Milton turned his back on the group and set off. He felt vulnerable, but he made a point of not looking back. He felt an itching sensation between his shoulder blades, and as he walked, an empty Coke can bounced off his shoulder and clattered to the pavement. They whooped at their insolent bravado and called out after him, but he didn't respond. He kept walking until he reached the gate next to the lido. He stopped and looked back. The boys were still gathered in the centre of the park. No one had followed.

He was satisfied that the house had not been disturbed while he was away, and allowing himself to relax, he took off his shirt and stood bare-chested at the open window. He snapped open the jaws of his lighter, put flame to a cigarette, and stared into the hot, humid night. The atmosphere was feverish, as taut as a bowstring. He took a deep lungful of smoke and expelled it between his teeth with a faint hiss. He could hear the sound of children on the street, the buzz of televisions, a siren fading in and out of London's constant metropolitan hum.

What on earth was he doing here?

Milton blew more smoke into the darkness and tossed the spent dog-end into the garden below.

He undressed and got into bed. The mattress was lumpy and uncomfortable, but he had slept on much worse. He reached one hand up beneath the pillow, his palm resting on the cold steel butt of the Sig Sauer. He calmed his thoughts and went to sleep.

Chapter Sixteen

JOHN MILTON had a strict morning regime, and he saw no reason to vary it. He pulled on a vest and a pair of shorts, slipped his feet into his running shoes, and went out for his usual run. It was just after seven, but the sun was already warm. The sky was a perfect blue, deep and dark, and Milton could see that it was going to be another blazing day.

His head had been a little foggy, but the exercise quickly woke him. He ran through the Estate and into Victoria Park, following the same route that he had taken before. The park was quiet now, and the undercurrent of incipient violence was missing. The baleful groups of boys had been replaced by people walking their dogs, and joggers and cyclists passing through the park on their way to work. Milton did two laps around the perimeter, settling into his usual loping stride, and by the time he peeled back onto the road and headed back towards the house, he was damp with sweat.

He followed a different route back through the Estate and came across an old chapel that had evidently found itself an alternative use. A sign above advertised it as Dalston Boxing Club, and posters encouraged local youngsters to join.

He ran back to the house, stripped off his sodden clothes, tentatively stepped into the grimy bath tub, and turned the taps until enough warm water dribbled out of the shower head to make for a serviceable shower. He let the water strike his broad shoulders and run down his back and chest, soothing the aches and pains that were always worse in the morning. He closed his eyes and focussed his attention on the tender spots on his body: the dull throb in his clavicle from a bullet's entry wound five years ago, the ache in the leg he had broken, the shooting pain in his shoulder from an assassin's knife. He was not as supple as he had once been, he thought ruefully. There were the undeniable signs of growing old. The toll exacted by his profession was visible, too, in the latticework of scar tissue that had been carved across his skin. The most recent damage had been caused by a kitchen knife that had scraped its point across his right bicep. It had been wielded by a bomb-maker in Helmand, a tailor who assembled suicide vests in a room at the back of his shop.

He stood beneath the water and composed his thoughts, spending ten minutes examining the details of the situation in which he had placed himself. He considered all the various circumstances that he would have to marshal in order to help Sharon and her son.

He dressed in casual clothes, left the house, and made his way back to the boxing club. The door was open, and the repeated, weighty impacts of someone working on a heavy bag were audible from inside. He went inside. The chapel's pews had been removed, and the interior was dominated by two empty boxing rings that were crammed up against each other, barely fitting in the space. They were old and tatty, the ropes sagging and the canvas torn and stained. Several heavy bags and speed bags had been suspended from the lower ceiling at the edge of the room. A large black man was facing away from him and hadn't noticed his arrival. Milton watched quietly as the man delivered powerful hooks into the sand-filled canvas bag, propelling it left and right and rattling the chain from which it had been hung. The muscles of his shoulders and back bulged from beneath the sweat-drenched fabric of a plain T-shirt, his black skin glistening, contrasting with the icy white cotton.

Milton waited for him to pause and took the opportunity to clear his throat. "Rutherford?"

He turned, and his face broke into a wide, expressive smile. "Hey! It's the quiet man."

"How are you?"

"Very good. It's John, right?"

"Yes, that's right. Sorry to disturb you. Could I have a word?"

Rutherford nodded. He reached down for a towel and a plastic water bottle and went over to a pew that had been pushed against the wall at the side of the room. He scrubbed his face with the towel and then drank deeply from the bottle.

"This is impressive," Milton said.

"Thanks. It's hard work, but we're doing good. Been here a year this weekend. Don't know how much longer we'll be around, though. Ain't got much more money. The council do us a decent price on the rent, but they're not giving it away, and I can't charge the kids much more than I'm charging at the moment. Something has to happen, or we won't be here next time this year."

"Can anyone join?"

"If they're prepared to behave and work hard. You got someone in mind?"

"I might have."

The man took another swig from his bottle. "Who is it?"

"He's the son of a friend. He's going off the rails a little. He needs some discipline."

"He wouldn't be the first boy like that I've had through those doors. We've got plenty of youngers who used to run in the gangs." The man spoke simply and inexpressively, but his words were freighted with quiet dignity and an unmistakeable authenticity. Milton couldn't help but be impressed by him. "Which gang is it?"

"I'm not sure. I met some of them in the park last night."

"That'll be the LFB, then. London Fields Boys."

"What are they like?"

"Been around for a long time—they were running around these ends before I went away, so plenty of years now. I remember we had a beef with them on more than one occasion—big fight in the park this one time, we uprooted all these fence posts and chased 'em off. The members change all the time, but they've always had a bad reputation. How deep's your boy involved?"

"Not very, I think. He's young."

"If you've caught him early, we'll have a better chance of straightening him out."

"So you take new members?"

"Always looking for them. Bring your lad along. We'll see what we can do."

"Going to the meeting on Tuesday night?"

"Perhaps," he said.

"Might see you then."

Milton made his way back to the main road.

He went into the café and took a seat.

"Scrambled eggs with cream, two rashers of bacon, and a glass of orange juice," he said when the girl came to take his order. He was hungry.

He checked his watch. It was a little after eight. The food arrived, and he set about it. When he was finished, it was a quarter past. He opened the newspaper on the table and read it. There was a short story about the killings in France, but no new details. He skipped ahead, turning the pages and reading until half past eight, and then nine. There was no sign of Elijah. Fair enough, he thought, as he went to settle his bill. He hadn't expected it to be easy. Getting through to the boy was going to take some time.

Chapter Seventeen

LITTLE MARK, Kidz and Elijah had met for lunch at the fast-food place nearest to the gates of the school. Elijah had hurried out from double science when he received the text from Pops earlier that morning. He was wearing the white shirt, green blazer and black trousers that made up his uniform, and he felt stupid as he jogged the last few yards down the road to the arcade. Little Mark was wearing his usual low-slung jeans and windcheater, and Kidz was wearing cargo pants and a hoodie.

"You look nice." They laughed at him as he drew alongside.

"I know," Elijah said ruefully. "I look stupid."

"You still going to school?"

"Yeah," Elijah said. "So?"

"Not saying nothing," Kidz said, stifling a laugh.

"I don't go all the time," he lied.

"What you doing out here anyway? Thought you'd be in the canteen with all the other little squares?"

"Got a text from Pops. He told me to be here."

Other kids from school started to arrive. The canteen was only ever half full; everyone preferred to come down here for fried chicken and pizza.

"Had an argument with my mums this morning," Little Mark said.

"Let me guess—you ate everything in the house?"

Little Mark grinned. "Nah, bro, I slept right through my alarm."

"Probably ate that, too."

"I'm in bed, right, and it's eight or something, and my mums is shouting at me to get up, says I'm gonna miss school, and this is the first time I realise, right, she still thinks I *go* to school. I ain't been for six months."

"Shows how much she pays attention to you, bro. That's child abuse, innit? That's neglect. You ought give that Childline a call."

The happy laughter paused as they heard the rumbling *thump thump thump* of the bass. It was audible long before they even saw the car, but then the black BMW turned the corner, rolled up to the side of the road, and parked.

"Shit, bruv," Little Mark said. "You know who that is?"

"What's he doing here?" Kidz said, unable to hide the quiver of nervousness in his voice.

"Who?" Elijah asked.

"You don't know shit," Kidz said sarcastically. "That's Bizness's car. You never seen him before?"

Elijah did not answer. He hadn't, but he didn't want to admit that in front of the others. He had the new BRAPPPPP! record, and their poster was on the wall of his bedroom, but that all seemed childish now.

The BMW kept its engine running. It was fitted with a powerful sound system, and heavy bass throbbed from the bass bins that had been installed where the boot had been. Elijah looked at the car with wide eyes. He knew it would have cost fifty or sixty thousand, and that was without the cost of the custom paint job, the wheel trims, the sound system and all the other accessories.

The front door of the BMW opened, and a man slid out from the driver's seat. Elijah recognised him immediately. Risky Bizness was tall and slender, a good deal over six feet, his already impressive height accentuated by an unruly afro that added another three or four inches. His face was striking rather than handsome: his nose was crooked, his forehead a little too large, his skin marked with acne scars. His eyebrows, straight and manicured, sat above cold and impenetrable black eyes. He was wearing a thin designer windcheater, black fingerless gloves, and his white Nike hi-tops were pristine. He wore two chunky gold rings on his fingers, diamond earrings through the lobes of both ears, and a heavy gold chain swung low around his neck.

"A'ight, youngers," he said.

"A'ight, Bizness?" Kidz said.

"Which one of you is JaJa?"

Elijah felt his stomach flip. "I am."

Bizness smiled at him, baring three gold teeth. "Don't worry, younger. I ain't gonna bite. I got something I want you to do for me. Get in the car. Won't take a minute."

Kidz and Little Mark gawped at that, but Elijah did as he was told. The interior of the car was finished in leather, and the bass was so loud it throbbed through his kidneys. Bizness got into the car next to him and closed the door. He leant forwards and counterclockwised the volume so he could speak more easily.

"One of my boys has clocked you, younger. Says you got a lot of fight in you. That right?"

"I don't know," he said, trying to stop his voice from trembling.

"He says you do. You hang with Pops's little crew, right?"

"Yeah," Elijah said, tripping over the word a little.

"Don't be so nervous—there ain't no need to be scared of me."

"I ain't scared."

"That's good." Bizness grinned, gold teeth glinting in his mouth. "Good to see a younger with a bit about himself. Says to me that that younger could make something of himself, get a bit of a reputation. Reminds me what I used to be like when I was green, like you, before all this." He brushed his fingers down his clothes and then extended them to encompass the car. "Get me?"

"Yes."

"So a friend of a friend says to me he's heard of a younger who's just starting running with Pops's crew, that he's got some backbone. Sound like anyone you know?"

"I guess."

Bizness snorted. "You guess." He looked him up and down. "You're big for your age."

"Big enough," he said defensively.

"That's right, bruv. Big enough. I like it. It ain't the size of the dog in the fight, it's the size of the fight in the dog, that right? You got some balls, younger. I like that. How old are you?"

"Fifteen."

"Fifteen. Just getting started in the world. Getting a name for yourself. Getting some *respect*. That's what you want, right?"

"Yeah," he said.

"Yeah. You're at what I'd call a crossroads, right—it's like *Star Wars*. You watched that, right, that last film?"

"Course," he replied indignantly.

"And it's shit, right, for the most part, except there's that one bit that makes sense, you know where Anakin has that choice where he can either go the good way or the bad way? The light or the dark? He thinks like he's got a choice, but he ain't got no choice at all, not really. It's an illusion. The dark side has him by the balls, and it ain't never going to let him go. Destiny, all that shit, you know what I mean? That's where you are, blood. Your teachers, the police, the Social, your mums—they'll all say you got a choice, you can choose to try hard at school, get your exams, get a job, except that's all bullshit. Bullshit. Brothers like us, we ain't never going to get given nothing in this world. Trouble is, a black man loves his new trainers too much. Right? And if we want to get the stuff we like, we gonna have to take it. Right?"

"Yeah." Elijah laughed nervously. Bizness was charismatic and funny, but there was a tightness about him that made it impossible to relax. Elijah got the impression that everything would be fine as long as he agreed with him. He was sure that arguing would be a bad idea.

"So we agree that getting busy on the street is the only way for you to get along in this world. It ain't easy, though, not on your own. Lots of brothers all got the same idea. You want to be successful, you want the kids you hang around with to take you seriously, you need to build up your rep. I can help you with that. You start hanging out with me, your little friends all find out you're in my crew, how quickly do you think that's going to happen?"

Elijah could hardly keep the smile from his face. "Quick."

"No, not quick, blood—instantaneously." Bizness clicked his fingers. "Just like that. So when I heard there was this new younger on the street, already making a name for himself, getting some respect, I say to myself, that's the kind of little brother I used to be like, maybe there's something I can do to help get him started in life. I'll do it for you, I guarantee it, but first I need you to prove to me that you're up to it."

"I'm up to it," Elijah insisted. "What is it? What do I have to do?"

"Nothing too bad, I just got something I need taking care of for a little while. You reckon that's the sort of thing you could do for me?"

"Course," Elijah said.

Bizness took a Tesco carrier bag and dropped it into Elijah's lap. It was heavy, solid. It felt metallic.

"Take this home and keep it safe. Somewhere your mums won't find it. You got a place like that?"

Elijah thought of his comic box. "Yeah," he said, "she don't never come into my room anyway. I can keep it safe."

"Nice."

"What is it?"

Bizness grinned at him. "You know already, right?"

"No," he said, although he thought that perhaps he did.

"There's no point me telling you not to look. I know you will as soon as I'm gone. Go on, then—open it."

Elijah opened the mouth of the bag and took out the newspaper package inside. He unfolded it carefully, gently, as if afraid that a clumsy move might cause an explosion. The gun sat in the middle of the splayed newspaper, nestling amongst the newsprint like a fat, malignant tumour. He tentatively stretched out his fingers and traced them down the barrel, the trigger guard, and then down the butt with its stippled grip. His only knowledge of guns was from his PlayStation, and this looked nothing like the sleek modern weapons you got to use in *Special Ops*. This looked older, like it might be some sort of antique, something from that *Call of Duty* where you were in the war against the Nazis. The barrel was long and thin, with a raised sight at the end. The middle part was round and bulbous, and when Elijah pushed against it, he found that it was hinged and snapped down to reveal six chambers honeycombed inside. A handful of loose bullets gathered in the creases of the newspaper.

"What is it, an antique or something?"

"Don't matter how old it is, bruv. A gun's a gun at the end of the day. You get shot, you still gonna die. Go on, it's not loaded—cock it. You know how to do that?"

The hammer was stiff, and he had to pull hard with both thumbs to bring it back. He pulled the trigger. The hammer struck down with a solid click, and the barrel rotated. The gun suddenly seemed more than just an abstract idea, it seemed real and dangerous, and Elijah was frightened.

"You keep that safe for me, bruv, and be ready— when I call you, you better be there, no hanging around, thirty minutes tops. Alright?"

"Alright," he said.

"A'ight. I was right about you—someone I can rely on. Yeah. A'ight, out you get, younger. I got to get out of here. Supposed to be seeing my manager, you know what I mean? New record out tomorrow."

He held out his closed fist for Elijah to bump. Elijah

did, everything suddenly seeming surreal. He stepped outside, holding the carrier bag tightly; it was heavy, and the solid weight within bumped up against his thigh. The bass in the BMW cranked back up, and the engine revved loudly.

Kidz and Little Mark were sitting on a wall, waiting for him. They both wore envious expressions, wide-eyed and open-mouthed.

"What did he want?" Kidz said.

Bizness sounded the horn twice, let off the handbrake, and fishtailed away from the kerb, wheelspinning until the rubber bit on the tarmac.

"Just a chat," Elijah said.

"What's that?" Little Mark said, pointing at the bag.

He clasped the bag tightly. "Nothing."

Chapter Eighteen

MILTON WAS IN THE CAFÉ AGAIN at nine o'clock. The proprietor recognised him. "Scrambled eggs with cream, two rashers of bacon and a glass of orange juice?"

Milton nodded with a smile and took the same table as before. He unfolded his copy of the *Times* and turned the pages as he waited. He turned the page to an article on a shooting in Brixton. A young boy, reported to be sixteen years old, had been shot and killed by another boy. He had passed through the territory of a rival gang to see a girl. The story was backed with a comment, the reporter recounting the deaths in what they were calling the Postcode War. Thirty young boys, almost all of them black, killed this year, and it was only halfway through August. Most of them shot or stabbed, one bludgeoned to death with a pipe.

The proprietor brought over his breakfast. "Terrible," he said, nodding at the open newspaper. He was a Greek, his face grizzled with heavy stubble. He had sad eyes. "When I was growing up, you had an argument with someone you knew and the worse thing that'd happen is you end up having a punch-up, get a black eye or a bloody nose. These days, with them all tooled up like they are, all those guns and knives, you're lucky if you just end up in hospital. And the only thing most of the victims had done wrong was going out of one area and into another."

"How many of them were from around here?"

"Three. One of them was just down the road. They shot him. Tried to get into the hardware shop, but they finished him off before he could."

"The police?"

He laughed bitterly. "They ain't got a clue half the time." He sneered at the thought of it. "Don't get me started on them; your breakfast will be cold by the time I've finished. You enjoy it, all right? There's more tea if you want it."

Milton saw Elijah Warriner standing in the doorway. He was unmistakeably nervous, and Milton thought he might be about to turn and leave. He smiled and waved at the boy, gesturing that he should come inside. Elijah took a look up and down the street and, satisfied, came inside. He was wearing brand-new trainers. Despite the heat he was wearing a bright orange puffa jacket that was obviously expensive. He had a Dallas Cowboys shirt beneath the jacket, and beneath that, Milton could see a thick gold chain.

"Sit down," Milton told him, and after another reluctant pause, he did. "I'm glad you came."

"Yeah," Elijah grunted.

"What do you fancy?"

The boy said nothing. His eyes darted around the café. A diamond stud shone against the dark skin of his ear. The jewellery looked obscene on such a young child. Milton noticed that he had chosen a chair that faced away from the window. He did not want to be seen.

"Breakfast?"

"Ain't hungry."

"Well, I am. I'll get some extra chips in case you change your mind."

Elijah slouched back in the chair, trying hard to appear nonchalant. Milton loaded his fork with eggs and put it into his mouth, watching the boy. He made sure he appeared relaxed and said nothing, leaving it for Elijah to speak first. The boy turned the newspaper around and read the short article on the murdered boy. He finished it and shook his head derisively. "Them boys in Brixton ain't shit. They come up these ends and we'd send 'em back to their mammas."

"What's your gang?"

"LFB," Elijah replied proudly.

"London Fields Boys?"

"S'right."

"I've seen the graffiti on the walls."

"Yeah, all this round here, this is our ends."

"Don't think I've seen you in the papers."

"We are—I mean, we have been."

"Perhaps you're not bad enough."

"What you mean?"

"You need a reputation, don't you?"

"We're plenty bad enough."

"But it looks like you have to kill someone to get into the papers."

"You don't think we've merked anyone?"

"I don't know. Some of the boys you've been hanging out with—maybe they have. But I know you haven't."

"Fuck you know?"

Milton put his knife and fork down and carefully wiped his mouth. He pressed his finger against the photograph of the dead boy. "Do you really think you could do that? You think you could go up to another boy, take out a gun, and pull the trigger?"

Elijah tried to hold his gaze but could not. He looked down at the table.

Milton shook his head. "You don't have it in you. You don't have it in you for your own conscience to haunt you for the rest of your whole life, telling you you've robbed a wife of her husband, children of their father, brothers, friends, everyone. Look at me—I know if a man has it in him. Do you have it in you?"

Elijah stood up. "I didn't come here to get lectured."

"I'm trying to put things into perspective."

"Don't need that," he said, making a dismissive gesture with the back of his hand.

"It's not a bad thing. Why would anyone choose to be like that?"

"You ain't got any idea what you're on about."

"Sit down, Elijah."

His words had no effect. "'Sit down, Elijah?' Who'd you think you are? You don't know shit about me. You don't know shit about anything—about these ends, what it's like to be here, what we do. You obviously think you do, but you don't."

"I'm sorry. Sit down. Let's talk."

He was angry now, and Milton could see he wouldn't be able to calm him down. "I don't know what I was thinking, coming here to see you. You can't help me. You got no idea. I must have been out of my mind."

He turned and left, the door clattering behind him. Milton rose and followed him into the street. Elijah was heading back towards the Estate, his hood pulled up and his shoulders hunched forwards. Milton was about to set off after him before he thought better of it. He went back inside and sat down again before what was left of his breakfast. He cursed himself. What had he been thinking? He had let his temper get the better of him, and now he had lost his opportunity to get through to the boy. He was stubborn and headstrong, and the direct approach was not going to be successful. He would have to try another way.

Chapter Nineteen

POPS AND LAURA had gone to the Nandos on Bethnal Green Road for dinner and then had taken the bus down towards the cinema in Shoreditch. It had been a good evening. Pops was off the Estate, and there was no need for him to impress anyone, or uphold his rep, or put anyone else down. He had an act, and he played it well: hard, impassive, sarcastic. To reveal otherwise would be dangerous, a sign of weakness. He remembered, with vivid clarity, the documentaries his biology teacher had shown them in middle school when she wanted to go off and smoke a fag in the playground. There had been one about the lions in Africa, the Serengeti or whatever the fuck place it was, and it had stuck in his head ever since. Leadership was all about image. The top lion needed to show the others in the pride that he wasn't to be messed with. If he showed weakness, they'd be on him. They'd fuck him up. Pops knew that there were other Elders in the LFB who would fuck him up, too, if he gave them reason.

It was different with Laura. He could relax and be himself. It was always like that with her. She loved her crack, but Pops knew she was into him for much more than just getting lickey. She was older than him, ten years older, and she had that sense of confidence that older women had. She wasn't like the skanky goonettes on the Estate, always mouthing off, screeching and pouting and giving attitude. They were just girls where Laura was a woman. She was cool. And, man, was she fine.

The film had been running for thirty minutes when the call came. Pops felt his phone vibrating in his pocket, and he took it out to check the caller ID: it was Bizness. His stomach plummeted, and his chest felt tight. He did not want to answer it, but he knew that there was no choice, not where Bizness was concerned. He had stabbed a boy before who had ignored his calls. He said it was a mark of disrespect. Respect was the most important thing in Bizness's life, or at least that was what he said.

He took the call, pressing the phone against his ear. "Bizness," he said quietly.

He could hear the sound of loud music in the background. "Where are you, man?"

"Watching a movie."

"Nah, bruv, don't be chatting breeze—what, you forgot the party tonight?"

Pops gritted his teeth. He hadn't forgotten, far from it. He knew about the new record, and the party to celebrate its launch, and he had decided to ignore it. He had been to the party that launched the collective's first record, eighteen months ago, and he had not enjoyed himself. The atmosphere was aggressive, feral, and there had been several beefs that had the potential to turn even more unpleasant than they already were. The relationships within the group were built on uncertain foundations. All the talk of being brothers was fine, but talk was just talk, and there was a swirl of jealousy beneath the surface that was always ready to erupt. Pops knew all of the crew, some better than others, and juggling loyalties between them was more effort than it was worth.

Bizness was currently at the top of the tree, and it had been that way for the last six months. He had replaced Lambie once he had been done for possession of a firearm and sent down for four years. There were always pretenders to his crown, and his treatment of them was always the same: constant dissing that turned violent when the dissing didn't work. Beatings, then stabbings if the beatings didn't work, and at least two shootings that he knew about. One of those shootings he knew about from close personal experience, close enough for the poor bastard's blood to land all over his jacket.

Pops didn't need that kind of aggravation in his life tonight.

"You coming, then?" Bizness pressed.

There were a couple in the seats in front of him, and the man turned around and glared at him, trying to act big in front of his woman. Pops felt his anger flare. He jerked his head up, his eyebrows cocked, and the man turned away.

"Nah, I don't know, man."

"I ain't asking," Bizness said. "I'm telling."

Pops sighed. There was no point in resisting. "Alright," he said.

"You with your gash?"

Pops looked over at Laura. She was watching the film, the light from the screen flickering against her pale skin. "Yeah."

"Bring her with you, a'ight? And bring that younger. What's his name, JaJa? Pick him up, and tell him I need that package he's holding for me. There's gonna be hype tonight, I'm hearing things. I wanna make sure I don't get caught with my dick out. Bring your piece, too."

And with that, Bizness ended the call.

Pops stared at the screen as it slowly faded to black. The first act of the film came to a crashing conclusion, yet he didn't really notice it. He was thinking of Bizness and whether there was any way they could show their faces at the party and then leave. He was unable to think of anything. Bizness would just see that as a diss, probably worse than not going at all, and he'd be in the shit.

He tried to put it into perspective. Maybe he was being ungrateful. He felt the thick wad of ten-pound notes in his pocket, the cold links of his gold chain resting against his skin, the heavy weight of the rings on his fingers. None of that came for free. You had to do things you would rather not do. That was how you got all the nice stuff you wanted. That was just the way it was.

"Come on," he whispered over to Laura.

"What?"

"We gotta split. There's a party; we got to go to it."

"Can't we go afterwards? This is good."

"Gotta go now, baby," he said, taking her by the arm and drawing her down into the aisle. He held his phone in his other hand, and using his thumb, he scrolled through his contacts until he found Elijah's number.

Chapter Twenty

THE PARTY was in Chimes nightclub on Lower Clapton Road. Pops parked next to the beaten-up Georgian houses on Clapton Square, and they walked the rest of the way, past the discount stores and kaleidoscopic ethnic restaurants, past the police posters pasted onto the lamp posts exhorting locals to "Nail the Killers in Hackney." The club was on the edge of the major roundabout that funnelled traffic between the City and the East End, and marked the beginning of Murder Mile, the long stretch of road that had become inextricably linked with gun crime over the past few years.

The club was in a large and dilapidated old building facing the minarets of an enormous mosque. It was a hot and enclosed series of rooms, and condensation dripped from the patched and sagging ceilings overhead. The largest room had been equipped with a powerful sound system, and Elijah had been able to hear the rumble of the bass from where Pops parked his car. Lights rotated and spun, lasers streaked through the damp air, strobes flickered with skittish energy. The rooms were crammed with revellers: girls in tight-fitting tops and short skirts, men gathered in surly groups at the edges of the room, drinking and smoking and aiming murderous glances at rivals. A tight wire of aggression passed through the room, thrumming with tension, ready to snap. The bass line thumped out a four-four beat, repetitive and brutal, and the noise of a hundred shouted conversations filled the spaces between as an incomprehensible buzz.

Elijah caught himself gaping. He had never been to anything like this before, and he could hardly believe he was here. All the members of BRAPPPP! were present, the whole collective, two dozen of them, each bringing their own entourage of friends and hangers-on. He recognised them from the poster in his room and the videos he had watched on YouTube. The new record had been played earlier, and now the DJ was mixing old-school Dr Dre and Snoop Dogg. Pops was alongside him, his face bleak, his hand placed possessively against the small of his girl's back.

Bizness appeared from out of the crowd, noticed them, and made his way across. He moved with exaggerated confidence, rolling his hips and shoulders, and his face was coldly impassive. He responded to the greetings from those he passed with small dips of his head or, for closer friends, a fist bump.

"A'ight," he said as he reached their group. He regarded them one at a time, his face unmoving until his gaze rested on Laura. The blank aggression lifted, and he parted his wide lips, revealing his brilliantly white teeth with the three gold caps. "Alright, darling," he said, ignoring Pops altogether. "Remember me?"

"Of course," Laura said, her eyes glittering.

"You heard the new record yet?"

"Yeah."

"You like it?"

"Course."

"That's what I like to hear. You looking *fine* tonight, darling. You totally bare choong."

She did not reply, but her helpless smile said enough. Pops noticed it, and a tremor of irritation quivered across his face.

Bizness ignored Pops and the others and turned to Elijah. "Come with me, younger," he said, and without waiting for a response, he led the way through the crowd. A tall, heavyset man wearing an earpiece was stationed at a door next to the bar, and as Bizness approached, he gave a stiff nod and stepped aside. The room beyond was small and dark, with sofas against the walls and drapes obscuring the light from the street outside. There were three others in the room, arching their backs over a long table that was festooned with two dozen lines of cocaine, arranged in parallel, each four inches long. Elijah recognised the others as members of BRAPPPP!: MC Mafia—the rapper who sounded a little like Snoop—Icarus and Bredren.

Bizness walked across to the table and took out a rolled-up twenty-pound note. He lowered his face to the nearest line, and with the note pressed tightly into his nostril, he snorted hard. Half of the line disappeared. He swapped the note into his other nostril and snorted again, finishing the line. He pressed his finger to one nostril and then the other, snorting hard again, and then rubbed a finger vigorously across his gums. With an appreciative smack of his lips, he offered the note to Elijah. "Want one?"

Elijah had never taken cocaine before, and he was scared, but he felt unable to refuse. Bizness and the others were watching them. Bizness's face was inscrutable, and he did not want him to think he was a little boy. He shrugged, doing his best to feign nonchalance, dipped his head to the table, and snorted the powder. He managed a quarter of the line, the powder tickling his nose and throat. The sneeze came before he had moved his head, and it blew the rest of the line away, a little cloud of white that bloomed across the table, the powder getting into his eyes and his mouth.

Bizness laughed at his incompetence. "You ain't done that before, have you, bruv?"

"Course I have," he said, blushing hard.

"Sure."

The word was drawn out, freighted with sarcasm, and Elijah cursed himself for being so green. They would think he was a baby, and that was no good. He would show them otherwise. He stood back from the table and shrugged his rucksack off his shoulder. He unzipped it, reached inside, and drew out the bundle wrapped with newspaper. "I brought it," he said, holding it in both hands, offering it to Bizness.

"I don't need it," he said.

"What?"

"You do."

"What?"

"Check me, younger," he said. His voice was blank, emotionless. "You like what you see here out there tonight? You were having a good look around, weren't you? I saw. You see what we got? I ain't talking about the little things. Someone like Pops, he thinks it's all about getting himself new clothes, new trainers, a good-looking gyaldem, saving up for a nice car. I ain't dissing him, each to his own and that, but he's got a severe case of what I call limited horizons. He ain't going nowhere. He's at his peak right now, that's it for him. You youngers look up to brothers like that, some of you might even get to his level, but others, the ones with ambition, that ain't never going to be good enough. The ones who are going somewhere *know* they can do better. You get me, bruv?"

Elijah nodded. Bizness's breath was heavy with the smell of booze and dope.

"I'm gonna give you a demonstration of what I mean later tonight. That bitch of his, the white girl, I know you saw the way she clocked me earlier. You see, younger— who you reckon she's going home with later? That girl's getting proper merked, and it won't have nothing to do with him."

The other men in the room laughed at that, a harsh and cruel sound. Elijah swallowed hard.

Bizness reached out a clammy hand and curled it around the back of Elijah's head. He crouched down so that they were on the same level and drew Elijah's face closer to his own. The smell of his aftershave was sickly, and as he looked into the man's face, he saw that his eyes were cold, the pupils shrunk down to pinpricks, the muscles in his cheeks and at the corners of his mouth jerking and twitching from the cocaine. "It's about power, younger. Everything else follows after it. You get me?"

"Yes."

"You want to be with us, don't you? BRAPPPP!, right, we're like brothers. We'd do anything for each other. But you wanna get in with us, be one of us like that, you got to show us you got what it takes. And I ain't talking about robbing no shop or turning over some sad mug for his iPhone. That shit's for babies. You want to get in with the real gangsters, you got to do gangster shit."

Bizness had not removed his hand from Elijah's neck. Their faces were no more than six inches apart, and his eyes bored straight into Elijah's like lasers. "Younger," he said, "I got a problem, and you're gonna help me sort it. I heard a rumour that this joker I know is coming to the party tonight. You know Wiley T?"

Elijah did. He was a young rapper who was starting to build a reputation for himself. He came from Camden, where he had shot videos of him rapping on the street. He had uploaded them to YouTube, and they had gone viral. Elijah had heard that he had been offered a record contract because of those videos. Everyone was talking about it at school, discussing it jealously, coveting his good fortune, agreeing it was proof that it could be a way out of the ghetto. A long shot, but a shot nonetheless.

"I invited him," Bizness explained. "He thinks we're gonna shake hands and make up, but we ain't. He's been dropping bars on YouTube about me. You probably heard them?"

Elijah nodded, and without thinking what he was doing, he started to intone—"'You walk around showing your body 'cause it sells / plus to avoid the fact that you ain't got skills / mad at me 'cause I kick that shit real niggaz feel…'" He realised what he was saying before the pay-off and caught himself, saying that he didn't know the rest.

"'While 99% of your fans wear high heels,'" Bizness

finished with a dry laugh with no humour in it. "Ain't a bad little diss, but bitch must've forgotten there's got to be a comeback when you drop words on me, and you better know it ain't going to be in something I put up on fucking YouTube for a laugh with my mates. He thinks he's a thug, but he ain't. He's a little joker, a little pussy, and he needs to get dooked."

Elijah's hands had started to shake. The direction the conversation was taking was frightening him, and he knew he was about to be asked to do something that he really did not want to do. Bizness unwrapped the gun from its newspaper wrapper and checked that it was loaded. "You ever shot a gun before, bruv?"

"No," Elijah managed to say.

Bizness extended his arm and pointed the gun at MC Mafia. He drew Elijah closer to him so that their heads touched. "It ain't no thing. You take the piece and aim it. That's right—look right down the sight."

"Come on, Bizness," Mafia said. "Aim that shit some other place. That ain't cool."

"Put your finger on the trigger, and give it a squeeze. It'll give you a little kick, so make sure you get in nice and close to the brother you want to shoot. You get in close, you won't miss. Easy, bruv."

He aimed away. Mafia exhaled and cracked a joke, but he could not completely hide his fear. Bizness was mental; they all knew it. Unpredictable and dangerous.

Bizness placed the gun carefully in Elijah's hands. "I want you to keep this. Keep your eyes on me tonight, a'ight? When he gets here, I'm gonna go up to him and give him a hug, like we're best friends. That's your signal. Soon as I do that, you gonna go up to him real close and put all six rounds into him. Pull the trigger until it don't fire no more. Blam, blam, blam, blam, blam, blam. You my little mash man, JaJa. We gonna make a little soldier out of you tonight, you see."

Chapter Twenty-One

RUTHERFORD PAID the barman, collected the two pints of orange juice and lemonade from the bar, and headed back outside. It was a warm evening, and he and Rutherford had found a table in the beer garden of the pub that faced onto Victoria Park. It was busy: Tuesday was quiz night, and the pub was full with teams spread out around the tables. The garden was busy, too, most of the tables occupied and with a steady stream of passers-by making their way to and from the row of chichi boutiques that had gathered along the main road. Rutherford remembered when this area had been one of the worst parts of the East End, battered and drab and the kind of place where you could get rolled just as easily as crossing the road. Now, though? The money from the city had taken over: all the old warehouses had been turned into arty studios, the terraces had been turned into apartments, and the shops were filled with butchers where you could pay a fiver for a burger made of buffalo, fancy restaurants and furniture shops. They said it was progress, and things were better now. Rutherford didn't miss the aggravation, but he did miss the soul of the place; it was as if its heart had been ripped out.

The meeting had been held in the Methodist Hall around the corner. Once again, Milton had sat quietly, keeping his own counsel. Rutherford was on the opposite side of the circle of chairs and had watched him. His face had been impassive throughout; if he had felt any response to the discussion, then he had hidden it very well. When the meeting had finished, Rutherford had suggested they go to the pub for a drink. He had not expected Milton to agree, but he had.

Rutherford set the pints down on the table and sat

down. "Cheers," he said as they touched glasses.

Milton took a long draught. "So how long were you in for?" he asked him.

"The army? Sixteen years."

He clucked his tongue. "That's a long stint. Where?"

"All the usual places: Kosovo, Iraq, Afghanistan. Lots of fun."

"I can imagine. Doing what?"

"Royal Engineers. Bomb disposal. I've always been decent enough at breaking things down and putting them back together again; it was a pretty obvious move for me once I'd got my feet wet for a couple of years. I was one of the lads they sent to defuse them for the first five years, and then when the brass thought I had enough common sense about me, they bumped me up to major and put me onto investigations—we'd get sent in when one of them went off to try to work out what it was that had caused it: pressure plate, remote detonation or something new. By the time I'd had enough, it was getting silly—the Muj started planting second and third devices in the same place to try to catch us out. A mate of mine I'd been with almost from the start lost both his legs like that. Stepped on a plate next to where they'd blown up another one fifteen minutes earlier. I was right behind him when it happened, first person there to help while they sent for the medics. I didn't need much encouragement to get out after seeing that." He looked over the rim of his pint at Milton. "What about you? What did you do? From the looks of it, I'm guessing ex-Special Forces." When Milton said nothing, Rutherford shrugged. "Well, that's your business."

He noticed that Milton's hand was shaking a little; drops fell over the lip of the glass and dribbled down the glass.

"SAS," he said eventually. "Is it that obvious?"

"Oh, I don't know—you stay in long enough and you get to know the signs."

"I was hoping it'd wash off eventually." He laughed mirthlessly. "I haven't been a soldier for years."

"Why'd you get out?"

"We've all got our own stories," he said. A jet from the city airport arced away to the south. A bloated pigeon alighted on the table opposite and was shooed off again.

Rutherford could see that Milton had no interest in talking about whatever it was that had happened to him. "What have you been doing since?"

"Some things I can't talk about," he said, with a shake of his head. They had both finished their drinks. Milton stood. "How about a coffee? We can work out how I can help you with the club."

Rutherford watched him negotiate the crowd gathered at the door. He knew that there was a lot that Milton wasn't telling him, and he guessed—well, it was pretty obvious, really—that he was still involved in soldiering in some capacity or another. The reticence was not what he would have expected of a grunt who was selling his experience as a mercenary; for his money, the discretion made it more likely that he was involved in something like intelligence. The conclusion led to more questions than it answered: what, for example, was an intelligence agent doing getting involved with a little hoodrat from Hackney? A spook? What sense did that make?

Rutherford had no idea how to even begin answering that one.

Milton returned with two cappuccinos.

"So," he said, "the boxing club. You're struggling. How can I help?"

"I can always do with more hands," Rutherford said thoughtfully. "There's a list of what's wrong with that place that's as long as my arm, man. The roof leaks, the wiring's all over the place, the walls need painting, the canvasses are torn and stained with God only knows what—there's only so much that I can do on my own, you know, with the club to run. If you're serious—?"

"I am."

"—then I'd say thank you very much. That would make a big difference."

"Fine. How about tomorrow morning? See what I can do?"

Rutherford raised his cup. "You bringing that younger you mentioned?"

"I'm working on that," Milton said.

Chapter Twenty-Two

CHRISTOPHER CALLAN, Number Twelve, drove across town to Hackney, following his satnav to Victoria Park. It was a hot, sticky night, and he drove with the windows open, the warm breeze blowing onto his face. He looked around distastefully. It was a mongrel area: million-pound houses cheek by jowl with slumlike high-rises. He reversed into a parking space in one of the better streets, locked the car, and set off the rest of the way on foot. His destination was marked on his phone's map, and he followed it across the southern end of the park, alongside a wide boating lake with a fountain throwing water into the air and Polish immigrants fishing for their dinners from the banks. Finally, he turned onto Grove Road.

Milton had used his phone earlier, and HQ had located the signal, triangulating it to the terrace that Callan was approaching. He picked his way along the untidy road until he reached the address, passing by on the other side before turning and passing back again. That side of the road was comprised of cheap terraced housing that might, once, have been pleasant. It was far from pleasant today, with the occasional property that had been well maintained standing out amidst the pitiful neglect of its neighbours.

Callan wondered what Milton was doing in a place like this. He slowed as he came up beside number eleven, taking everything in: the rotting washing machine in the gutter; the broken staves of the fencing across the road, lashed around with chicken wire; the bars on the doors and ground-floor windows. The windows of the house were open, and the curtains were drawn, the puce-coloured fabric puffing in and out of the opening, ruffled by the sweaty breeze. A lamp was on inside, the light flickering on and off as the curtains swayed. Callan couldn't tell if anyone was home.

A Volvo was parked by the side of the road. Callan recognised it from Milton's file. The car looked at home among the battered heaps that filled the parking spaces around it. He slowed as he passed the Volvo and, moving quickly and smoothly, dipped down and slapped a magnetic transmitter inside the wheel arch.

Callan did not want to tarry. He had no desire to draw attention to himself. He didn't think that he had ever met Milton before, but he could not completely discount the possibility that he might somehow have known him. No point in taking chances.

He reached the end of the road, paused for a final look back again, and set off for the main road. He took out his phone and dialled.

"Callan," said Control.

"Hello, sir. Can you talk?"

"Are you there?"

"I'm just leaving now. Awful place. Small house in a terrace. Looks like council housing. It's a sink Estate, not a good area, kids out on the street corners, pit bulls, messy, rubbish left out to rot in the gardens—you can picture the scene, I'm sure. God only knows what he's doing here."

"You've no idea?"

"None at all."

"What about the house—did you look inside?"

"Couldn't. I couldn't be sure he wasn't at home. I didn't try to get any closer than the street. I can come back for that."

As he walked back along the fringes of the Estate, he noticed that he was being followed. Two older teenagers on BMXs were lazily trailing him, kicking the bikes along on the other side of the road.

"What about his car?"

"You can tell Tech that the tracker has been fixed."

Callan took a right turn off the main road and watched

as the two boys bounced down off the kerb and crossed against the flow of the traffic. The two started to close the distance between them.

"Sorry, sir. I'll have to call you back."

He pressed the toggle on the headphones to end the call. The road turned sharply to the left, and Callan stopped to wait for the boys. They rolled up to him. They both wore baseball caps pulled down low with their hoods tugged up so that the fabric sat on the brim. The bottom half of their faces were covered with purple bandanas. Only their eyes were visible. It was impossible to guess their age, but they were both large and rangy, their bikes almost comically small for them.

"Got the time, bruv?" the first boy said with insouciant aggression, putting his foot down and stopping. If he replied to the request, no doubt the next step would have been for him to have been relieved of his watch, together with his phone and wallet.

"Time you got off home, I reckon."

The boy rolled a little closer. "You want to watch who you're giving lip to, lighty. You could end up in a lot of mess." The second boy got off his bike and walked forwards. He hawked up a ball of phlegm and spat it at Callan's feet "Give me your phone."

Callan felt his skin prickle and his muscles tightening. The sensation was familiar to him. The surge of adrenaline. Fight or flight. It was rarely flight with him. "I don't want any trouble," he said meekly.

The second boy took his hand out of the pocket of his jacket. He was holding a kitchen knife in his fist. "Give me your phone and your cash, a'ight, else you're gonna get jooked."

The boy came closer, and Callan let him. When he was within arm's reach, he lashed out suddenly with his right hand, the fingers held out straight, the thumb bracing them from beneath. The strike landed perfectly, and forcefully, Callan's hard fingertips jabbing into the boy's throat, right into the larynx. He dropped the knife and clutched his throat as he staggered back, choking, temporarily unable to draw breath. The first boy tried to hike up his jacket so that he could get to the knife he was carrying in his belt, but he was impeded by his bike and was far too slow. Callan closed the distance between them with a quick hop and, bending his arm, struck the boy in the face with the point of his right elbow. The pedals tripped the boy as he staggered away, and he fell onto his back, blood already running from his broken nose. The boy Callan had struck in the throat was still gasping for breath, and Callan almost lazily cast him to the ground, sweeping his legs out from beneath him. He crouched down and grabbed the boy by the scruff of his collar. He raised his head six inches from the pavement and then crashed it backwards, slamming his crown against the edge of the kerb, fracturing his skull and knocking him out.

Callan stood, brushed himself down, and set off again.

Chapter Twenty-Three

ELIJAH RETURNED to Pops and his woman after Bizness had finished talking to him. Pops looked surly, brooding over his JD and casting careful glances out across the room to where Bizness and MC Mafia were talking with two good-looking girls dressed in crop tops and obscenely short skirts. Elijah watched them too, unable to concentrate. He felt a dizzying mixture of emotions: fear, that he had been asked to do something that he did not want to do, but also pride. He knew it was foolish to feel that way, but he could not deny it. Where were his friends tonight? Where were Little Mark and Kidz, Pinky and the others? They weren't here. Bizness had chosen *him* for the task. Surely that must mean something. He trusted him. He could not help visualising a future in which he was a member of BRAPPPP!, too. The newest member. The youngest. The one with the reputation, the one no one would doubt. He thought of the lifestyle, the money. He would drag his family up with him, away from the Estate. His mum wouldn't need to work three jobs to make ends meet. They would buy a little house, with a little garden. Perhaps he could help Jules, too. Rehab or something. Things would be better than they were now.

He knew the price for all of this, but he tried not to think about it.

If he did, he would run.

A stir of interest rippled through the crowd as a small group of boys passed in through the entrance to the club. There were four of them, and at their head, Elijah recognised Wiley T. He knew that he was only two years older than him; he was a mixture of youth and experience. His face was fresh, and he still walked with a lazy adolescent lope, but his body language was confident. He punctuated his sentences with exaggerated gestures designed to draw attention to himself, and he smiled widely at a nearby group of girls, a confidence that Elijah could not begin to hope to emulate. Elijah knew enough about him from his YouTube profile. He was a street boy, like him, and their education was the same. He recognised the flicker of furtive watchfulness in his eyes. Boy was older than his years.

Elijah felt a nugget of ice in his gullet as Bizness approached Wiley and offered his hand. The younger man sneered and did not take it. Bizness moved forwards in an attempt to draw Wiley into an embrace, but he stepped away, a derisive expression on his face. He said something, and then, as Bizness backed away, he threw a punch that rattled against his jaw. The fight that followed flared quickly and viciously, with members of both entourages folding into one another, fists flying.

Elijah watched from the other side of the room. His rucksack was at his feet, the zip half undone, and as he looked down into it, the dull metal of the gun sparkled in the light from a glitterball overhead. Bizness separated himself from the melee and glared at Elijah, his face twisted with fury. He mouthed one word: "Now." Elijah felt his life folding down into that one small, awful point. It was over for him. He picked up his bag and lifted it to his waist, just high enough that he could reach his right hand inside for the gun. His fingers brushed the metal, encircled it so that the cold was pressed into his palm and his finger found the trigger guard and, within it, the subtle give of the trigger.

The noise of the party seemed to muffle and fade as Elijah started across the room.

Everything slowed to a crawl.

He glanced into the faces of the people around him, but nothing registered.

He felt completely alone.

He closed the distance to the brawl. He squeezed the gun into his palm and started to bring it up to the open mouth of the bag.

Pops took him by the arm and pulled him aside. "Don't be an idiot."

Elijah looked up at him dumbly.

"Be clever, younger. Do that and your life is finished. You think the feds won't find out? You think he won't rat you out to save his own skin?"

Elijah was unable to speak.

"Go home, JaJa. Go on, fuck off, fuck off now, take that bag with you, drop it in the canal, and don't ever tell no one a word about it."

On the other side of the club, the fight was getting worse. A dozen men were brawling now, and as Elijah watched, one of them fell to the ground. Bizness was onto him quickly, kicking him again and again in the head. Pops gently turned him towards the exit and pushed him on his way.

Elijah kept going. He did not look back.

Chapter Twenty-Four

POPS SAT in the front of his car, his forehead resting against the steering wheel. He had driven aimlessly for an hour, trying to arrange his thoughts into some sort of order, and had eventually found his way to Meynell Street, the sickle-shaped road that hugged the edge of Well Street Common. It was a middle-class area with big, wide houses that cost the better part of half a million pounds each. The boys rarely came up here. It wasn't worth the risk. It was a good distance from the Estate, and they knew that if they started causing trouble, the police would respond quickly, and in numbers. Far better to stay in their ends, on the streets that they knew, and where their victims were not deemed important enough to demand the same protection.

He looked out over the small park, pools of lamplight cast down at the junctions of the pathways that cut across it. He had switched off the car's engine, but the dashboard was still lit, casting queasy green light up onto his face, illuminating his reflection on the inside of the windshield. He examined himself and thought, again, that he looked older than he was. His skin looked almost grey in the artificial light, and his eyes were black and empty, denuded of life, of their sparkle. Pops was nineteen, but he felt older. He had seen things that he could not forget, no matter how hard he tried. He gave it big with the others because there was nothing else he could do. You showed weakness, you got eaten; that was the way it was. The rules of the jungle, he thought again. Just like the Serengeti.

But Pops was different. He was smart. He had a plan, and he would leave on his terms when he was ready. He was careful with his money, saving every month, and he wanted twenty grand in his account before he called it a day. He had been a decent student at school before he had been sucked down into the LFB, and he wanted to finish his education. And then, who knows, maybe he would go to college. You needed paper for that. Until then, until he had enough, there was no choice but to keep up his front. If he let down his guard, even for a minute, there were plenty of youngers who would seize their chance. There would be beef, there would be hype, and it would end up badly for all of them.

His mind flicked back to the end of the party. The fight had ended almost as quickly as it had begun, yet it had curdled the mood, like poison dripped into an open wound. Wiley and his boys had taken a terrible beating, with one young boy left unconscious on the floor, his face kicked into a mess of blood and mucus. Pops watched as his body jerked and twitched and knew that he needed a doctor, and quickly. He quietly went into the toilets and called 999, leaving an anonymous message that an ambulance was required. By the time he returned outside, the lights had been turned on, and people were starting to go. He had heard police sirens in the near distance, too. Definitely time to leave.

He looked over at the passenger seat. Laura's handbag was resting against the cushion. Pops had bought her the bag for Christmas after she mentioned that she liked the designer. It had cost plenty, but she was worth it. He had searched the club for her, but she had already gone. He didn't know where she was now, but he knew she was with Bizness. He had known that he wanted her. He made no secret of it, joking with Pops about the fact that one day he'd just take her and that there was nothing he would be able to do about it. Pops would laugh it off most of the time, making sure that he kept his seething anger to himself. As long as he kept her away from him, everything would be all right. But that had not been possible tonight. Bizness had suggested before the fight that the party would eventually relocate to his studio and that she should come. The invitation had not been extended to Pops. She had been drunk and high, and she knew that Bizness was offering her more of the same. He had lost her. He had always known it would happen, eventually, and now it had. He had gone to his car and driven away.

He looked out into the darkness, staring through his own reflection as the light of a bicycle bounced up and down, a rider passing across the park. He thought of JaJa and how close the boy had come to ruining his life. The party had made his mind up for him. Bizness was a bad man, he was out of control, and Pops knew it was insanity to think otherwise. He did not care about anyone other than himself. JaJa, young and pliable and vulnerable, the boy was just a tool to him, a means to an end. He would have used him to dook Wiley, and then, when the feds came knocking, he would give him up.

Yes, Bizness was out of control, and he had to do something.

He reached into his pocket for his wallet. Inside, hidden beneath his credit cards, was the business card that the man in the park had given him. There was something about him that stuck in his head. Pops could not put his finger on it, but there was something that said he might be able to help. He had not been able to throw the card away, and while the others had sent him off with a barrage of abuse, he had quietly slipped it into his pocket.

He took out his phone and switched it on, the display coming to life. He carefully entered the man's number. The call connected but, after ringing three times, went to voicemail. Pops listened to the bland message, then the beep, and ended the call without speaking. What was he doing? He knew nothing about this man. How could he trust him? What was he going to say?

He put the phone away, started the engine, reversed the car, and rolled slowly back towards the Estate.

Chapter Twenty-Five

MILTON WAS NOT ALONE in the waiting room. A portly middle-aged woman was slumped into one of the plastic seats, her expression bearing the marks of frustration, helplessness and anger. Her eyes followed Milton as he sat down on one of the chairs opposite her, but she didn't speak. The police station smelt the same as all the others he had visited, all around the world: the same mixture of scrubbing soap, disinfectant and body odour. It had the same weary atmosphere, the sense of a heavy relentlessness.

He gazed at the posters tacked onto a corkboard that hung from the wall; young black men staring into police cameras with expressions of dull, lazy violence. The crimes they were alleged to have committed were depressingly similar: an assault with a knife, an armed robbery at a betting shop, a shooting. There were two murders with the same police task force—Trident—dealing with them both. Black on black. A poster showed a young boy staring out from behind a lattice of bars, the message warning that this was the inevitable destination for those who got caught up with gangs. The boy in the poster was young, in his middle teens. The same age as Elijah. He looked small, vulnerable and helpless.

Milton looked at the clock on the wall for the hundredth time: it was five minutes past three in the morning.

"Who you here for?" the woman said.

"The son of a friend," Milton said.

"What've they got him in for?"

"I'm not sure."

"Won't matter," she declaimed. "Won't matter if he did it or not, neither. They need to get something cleared up, they'll say he did it, and that'll be that. Look at my boy. He ain't perfect, God knows he ain't, but he didn't do half the things they said he's done. It's because he's black, from the wrong ends, in the wrong place at the wrong time. The police are racist pigs."

Milton said nothing. He was not disposed to have a conversation with her, and after a long moment of silence, she realised that. She clucked her tongue against her teeth, shook her head, and went back to staring dully at the posters on the wall.

Sharon had called Milton just after midnight. She explained that the police had visited the flat and arrested Elijah. She had heard him coming back late. She only had vague details: the police had said something about a fight at a club, a man beaten halfway to death. Elijah was supposed to have been identified as a witness. Sharon didn't know what to do and sounded at the end of her tether. Milton had said he would deal with it.

"Is anyone here for Elijah Warriner?"

The policeman was middle-aged, a little overweight, and with wispy fronds of white hair arranged around a bald crown. He looked tired.

"I am," Milton said.

The officer opened the door and indicated inside. "Would you step in here for a moment, sir."

"What about my boy?" the woman squawked. "You've had him in there for hours."

The sergeant regarded her with a tired shrug. "They're just finishing up with him, Brenda."

"You charging him?"

"He said he did it."

"Bail?"

"I expect so. Just wait there; we'll get to you as soon as we can." He turned back to Milton. "Sir?"

Milton did as he was asked. The room beyond was small, with a table and two plastic chairs. The surface of the table had been scarified with carved graffiti, the letters

LFB repeated several times. The policeman shut the door and indicated that Milton should sit. He did, the policeman taking the other chair.

"Who are you?" the policeman asked him.

"I'm a friend of Elijah's mother. And you?"

"Detective Sergeant Shaw."

"What are you holding him for?"

"There was a serious assault at a party yesterday evening. A lad from Camden was beaten. GBH, pretty serious. Elijah was there when it happened."

"Is he a suspect?"

"I don't know yet. Probably not. But he was definitely a witness. He admitted he was there. Save that, he won't talk. Not that I'm surprised, they never do." He sighed and took a packet of cigarettes from his pocket. There were no-smoking signs on the wall, but he ignored them, taking a cigarette and lighting it. He offered one to Milton, who declined. Shaw drew deeply on the cigarette, taking the smoke into his lungs and then exhaling it in a second, longer sigh.

"Look—Mr Milton—I'm not sure what's going to happen to him, but let me make a prediction. Elijah's in a dangerous position. Chances are, he's going to get away with whatever happened this time. But that doesn't mean he's going to be all right. He's not right in the gang yet, but he's on the edge. It won't take much to tip him over, and if that happens, he'll definitely be back here again, and then he'll get nicked. He might get community service for whatever he ends up doing, but that won't straighten him out. The time after that he'll get prison. And that's if he's lucky to live that long. Plenty of them don't. I've seen it dozens of times."

"These other lads he's been messing around with—the gang? Who are they?"

"The London Fields Boys?"

"I don't know very much about them."

"Let me give you a little history, Mr Milton. I've been a

policeman around here for the best part of twenty years. That's a long time to work in one place, but it means I've got a better idea of this borough than most. I'll be honest with you—Hackney's never been a particularly nice manor. It's always been poor, there've never been enough jobs to go around, and there's never been enough for kids to do. You take a situation like that, it's normal that you're going to get a problem with crime. It's not the easiest place in the world to be a copper, but for most of those years, it's been manageable. You'd get the odd blagging, drunken lads getting into scraps after too many bevvies on a Friday night, chaps going home after the pub and slapping their women around. You'd always have a GBH on the go, and there'd be the odd murder now and again. Not the best place in the world, lots of problems, but by and large, we kept a lid on it.

"Now, you look at the last five years, and things have changed so much I hardly recognise it sometimes. We've always had gangs of young lads, and they've always gotten into scrapes. Petty stuff—fights, nicking things, just making a nuisance of themselves. But then they all started getting tooled up. They're all carrying knives. Some of them have guns. You add that to the mix, then you have a gang from another borough coming in here looking for trouble, things get serious very quickly. When I was a lad, we used to play at cops and robbers. These days, they're not playing. They're all tooled up, one way or another, and it's not all for show. The guns are real, and they don't care if they use them or not. I don't know if he'll listen to you more than he's listened to me, but you've got to get some sense into him. If you don't..." He let the words drift away before picking it up again. "If you don't, Mr Milton, then he's not going to have very much of a life."

Chapter Twenty-Six

MILTON WALKED out of the police station with Elijah behind him. He looked out into the street. It was a hot night, broiling, and even though it was coming around to four in the morning, there were still people about. The atmosphere was drunken and aggressive. Men looked at them as they passed, assuming that a white man on the steps of a police station must be a detective. There was contempt in their faces, violence behind their sleepy, hooded eyes. Milton had called a taxi while he was waiting for Elijah to be processed, and it was waiting for them by the kerb. He opened the rear door for Elijah and then slid in next to him. He gave the driver the address for Blissett House and settled back as they pulled into traffic.

He looked across at the boy. He had the downy moustache and acne of a teenager, but there was a hardness in his face. His eyes were fixed straight ahead, and his face was set, trying to appear impassive, but his hands betrayed him; they fluttered in his lap, picking at his nails and at swatches of dead skin.

"You know you're in trouble, Elijah."

He did not reply, but the fidgeting got worse.

"Let me help you."

When he finally spoke, it was quiet and quick, as if he did not want the taxi driver to overhear him. "You ain't police?"

"No."

"You swear it?"

"I'm not the police. You can trust me, and I want to help. What's the problem?"

Still he was not convinced. "Why you want to help us? What's in it for you?"

"It's a long story."

"I ain't saying nothing unless you tell me why."

Milton thought for a moment about what to say. "I've done some things in my life that I'm not proud of," he said carefully. "I'm trying to make up for them. That good enough for you?"

"What kind of things?"

"Bad things," Milton said. "That's enough for now. This is about you, not me."

Elijah looked down at his lap. Eventually, the residual fear of his situation defeated his bravado, the reluctance to admit that he needed help, and the fear of what might happen to him if the others discovered that he had spoken out of turn. "Alright," he said. "Last night. I was there. I saw what happened."

Milton told him to explain. Elijah spoke quietly and quickly.

"Who had the gun?"

"Me. Bizness gave it to me last week, told me to keep it for him until he needed it. You need heat, right, with our rep? You get a beef, like we had with Wiley and his crew, you don't have a blammer, you done for. Finished."

"Who's Wiley?"

"This rapper. He's been dissing Bizness. He had to make an example, man. Can't have that kind of nonsense going on, YouTube and everything. Bad for business. Bad for your rep."

"You gave the gun to him?"

"Nah, man. I had it. He wanted me to do it myself."

"And?"

"I didn't know what to do. I started walking over towards where this fight had started, Bizness and Wiley were going at it, I put my hand in my bag, the gun was there, and then the next thing I know Pops has come over to me, grabbed my arm, and told me to breeze. I did— went straight home."

"Did you tell the police you had the gun?"

He looked indignant. "I didn't tell them shit."

That was good, Milton thought. The boy was hanging on by his fingertips, but he still had a future. "This Bizness. Who is he?"

Elijah looked at him with a moment's incredulity before remembering that Milton was older, and naïve, and that there was no reason why he would have heard of him. "Risky Bizness. He runs things around here. He's been in the LFB for years, since he was a younger, like me. He's one of the real OGs."

"One of the what?"

"Original Gangsters, man. He's got himself involved with everything—the shotters sell the gear and pass the paper up to the Elders, and the Elders pass it up to the Faces like Bizness. He makes mad Ps. He built himself a record studio out of it, and now he's got himself a record deal. He's famous on top of everything. He's a legend, innit?"

"What's his real name?"

Elijah shrugged. "Dunno. I've never heard no one call him anything but Bizness."

The taxi turned into the road that led towards Blissett House. Milton told the driver to pull over. He guessed that Elijah would prefer not to be seen getting out of a cab with him, and he saw, from the look of relief on his face, that he had been right.

"All right, Elijah," he said. "This is what I want you to do. Go home to your mother. She's beside herself with worry. Get to bed. Don't answer your phone, particularly if it's Bizness or any of the other boys in the gang. You need a little space between you and them at the moment. Do you hear me?"

"Yes," he said. "What about the police?"

"I think that will be all right. I've given them my number. If anything comes up, they'll call me, and we can take it from there. Now then—what did you do with the gun?"

"Dropped it in the canal."

"Do you promise?"

"Yeah," he said. "I don't want nothing to do with it."

"That's good." He reached over and opened the door. "Go on, then. We'll let this blow over."

"And then?"

"I've got something for you I think you might enjoy. Meet me in the café in the morning. Nine o'clock. Bring your sports kit from school."

"Nine? That's, like, just five hours. When am I gonna get some sleep?"

"You can sleep afterwards. Nine o' clock, Elijah. I've got something for you to do that you're going to be good at."

PART THREE

Strapped

Laughter, and then something else. A low drone. His stomach knotted. No. The plane was still a dot on the horizon, but it was closing quickly. Beneath the radar. A Warthog, onion-shaped bombs hanging beneath its wings. He threw his rifle aside and scrambled down the escarpment, the loose sand sliding down with him, his boots struggling for purchase, failing, and he was tumbling down the last few metres, landing at the bottom with a heavy thump that drove the air from his lungs. He got to his knees and then to his feet, his boots skidding off the dirt and scrub as he pushed off, his arm sinking down to the wrist as he tried to keep upright.

He ran towards the village. Five hundred yards, four hundred. The sound of the Warthog's engines was louder now; it was coming in low, a thousand feet up, not rushing, the pilot taking his time. Three hundred. He ran, boots sinking up to the laces with each step, thighs pumping until they burned. He gasped in and out, his lungs so full of the scorched air that he felt like they were alight. Two hundred. He was close enough to yell out now, and he did, screaming that they had to take cover, that they had to get inside. One hundred, and he was close enough to see the faces of the children outside the madrasa. The cheap plastic ball had sailed in his direction, and he could see the confusion and fear in the face of the boy who had been sent to fetch it. Five years old? Surely no older. He yelled at him to get down, but it was too late, it had always been too late. It would not have mattered if he had been able to get to them sooner; the decision had already been taken.

The Warthog's engines boomed. The boy turned away from him to face it. The ball rolled away on the breeze. A blinding flash of white light. The deafening crack of a terrible explosion. He was picked up and thrown back twenty feet in the direction that he had come. A second and third explosion seemed to bend the world off its axis, the noise blending from a roar into a continuous, high-pitched whine. He lay staring up into the sun while the air around him seemed to vibrate as if someone had smashed a cello with a sledgehammer. He rolled over and pushed his head up, working his arm around until he could prop himself against his elbow. Above, slowly unfurling, was a dark cloud of black smoke that rose and shifted until it had obscured the sun. He smelt burning flesh and the *unmistakeable acrid tang of high explosive.*

His hearing resolved as the Warthog swooped over and away. He pushed himself up until he was on his knees. A huge crater was in the centre of the village. The launcher was gone. The madrasa was gone. The children were gone, too, or so he would have thought until his eyes tracked around to the right and he saw red splashes of colour on the ground and glistening red ribbons of flesh suspended from the bare branches of a nearby tree.

Fifty feet away, in the open desert, the plastic ball rolled with the wind.

Chapter Twenty-Seven

THE NIGHTMARE was as bad as Milton could remember it. When he awoke, the sheets were a bunched-up pile on the floor, soaked through with sweat. His brain was fogged and unclear. He rose and went for his usual run, the best way he knew to chase it away. The streets were quiet, and the park was empty. He ran two laps, following the line of trees, pushing himself harder on the second so that by the time he returned to the road, he was sweating and breathing heavily. He chose a return route that took him past the boxing club. The door was open, the slapping of a skipping rope audible from inside. He didn't stop and returned to the house, where he showered and dressed. He stood before the mirror again and checked that the outline of his pistol was not obvious against the cut of his jacket. He locked the door and went to the café for his breakfast. Elijah was already waiting for him. The boy was sitting in a booth.

"This better be good," he said, a little surly.

"Get any sleep?"

"Nah, not much. I'm knackered."

"Where's your kit?"

Elijah nodded at the black Nike sports bag resting on the chair next to him.

"Good lad. You hungry?"

"A bit," he conceded.

"All right, then. You'll need to eat. You're going to be working hard this morning."

"What are we doing?"

"You'll see," Milton said. The proprietor came over to take their order. Milton ordered two plates of scrambled eggs and bacon, a portion of chips and two glasses of orange juice.

"Is your mother all right?"

"What you mean—about me getting nicked? Yeah, she's alright."

"She worries about you, you know."

"I know," Elijah said. "I don't mean to upset her."

"I know you don't." The boy seemed more disposed to speak this morning, and Milton decided to take advantage of the boy's mood. "How are things at home?"

"How you mean?"

"How does your mum manage?"

"What you think it's like? We got no Dad, Mum works three jobs, and there's still hardly enough money coming in to feed us, buy clothes. Me and my brother—you get into a situation like that and you do what you got to do, innit? My mum knows what I've been doing—she just don't wanna ask."

"Would you have listened to her?"

The food arrived before he could answer. The proprietor handed them each a plate of eggs and bacon and left the chips in the middle of the table. "You know about Jules?" Elijah said when he had left them. "My brother?"

"Not really."

"He's five years older than me. Me and him, we grew up with nothing. You go to school and you're the one with the uniform with the holes in it. I never got no new shirts or trousers or nothing like that—all I got was his hand-me-downs; Mum would find the holes and just keep patching them up. There were patches on the patches eventually. You know how that makes you feel?"

Again, Milton shook his head.

"Makes you feel like a tramp, bruv. The other kids laugh at you like you're some kind of special case." Elijah took a chip, smeared it with ketchup, and put it into his mouth. He chewed, a little nervously, still unsure whether he was doing the right thing in talking to Milton. "Then you see the brothers with their new clothes, parking their flash cars outside their mommas' flats, you see them things, and you know what's possible. They ain't got no patched-up uniforms. Their shoes don't have holes in them. Jules saw it. He was in the LFB before me. He came back with new trainers one day, and I knew. Then he bought himself new clothes for school, more trainers, a phone, nice jewellery. He started to make a name for himself. Kids at school who used to take the piss out of him didn't do that no more. He got some respect.

"One day, he comes back, and he tells me that I have to come down to the road with him. I do like he says, and there it is, he shows me this car he's bought. It ain't nothing special, just this second-hand Nissan, beaten up to shit, but he's bought it with his own money, and it's his. The way I see it, there ain't nothing wrong with that. It don't matter where he's got it from, he's entitled."

"There are other ways to get the things you want," Milton said.

"What? School?" He laughed at that. "You think I can get out of here by getting an education? How many kids in my ends you think get through school with an education?" He spat out the word disdainfully. Just for a moment, his eyes stopped flicking back and forth and he stared straight at Milton. "I ain't gonna get the kind of education that can help me by sitting in the classroom, listening to some teacher going on about history or geography. Teachers don't give a shit about me. Let's say I did pay attention, and I get good grades so I could go to university. You have to pay thousands for that these days— so how do we afford that?" He shook his head with an expression of clear and total certainty. "Education ain't for people like me, not round here. Let me make this simple for you: my... brother... was... my... education. All I saw was guys with their cars and their clothes. His Nissan taught me more than anything I ever learned in school. Exam grades ain't gonna get me any of that. All they'll get me is a job flipping burgers in Maccy D's and that ain't never going to happen. I know what you can get if you play the game."

Milton detected a weak spot and pressed. "Where's Jules now?"

A flicker of discomfort passed across his face. "He was shotting drugs, right—the crack, selling it to the cats—then he started doing it himself. Couldn't deal with it. He got into trouble, didn't kick up the paper like he was supposed to do. He had some beef with the Elders, and he ended up getting a proper beating. Nothing he didn't deserve, mind—there are rules you got to follow, and if you don't, you get what you get. Anyway, one day he never came back home. My mums spoke to him on the phone, and he said he had to get away. I've seen him a few times since—this one time, I was in town, going to buy some new trainers from JJB, and I see him there on Oxford Street, sitting against a shop with a cap on the ground in front of him, begging for change. He's an addict now. It's disgusting. I just kept walking. Didn't say nothing to him. We don't see him no more."

"And you look up to him?"

"Not any more, man, not how he is now. But before that? Yeah—course, he's my brother, course I looked up to him. I seen how he got what he wanted, and I seen how it works better than your schools and books. I just ain't gonna make the same mistakes he did."

Milton paid after they had finished their food, and they set off. The club was a fifteen-minute walk from the main road, and Milton took the opportunity to continue the conversation. Milton sketched in the lines of a meagre, uninspiring life and quickly came to understand how the excitement and the camaraderie of the street had proven to be so attractive to the boy. He inevitably thought of his own peripatetic childhood, dragged around the embassies and consulates of Europe and the Middle East as his father followed a string of different postings. Money had never been a problem for the Miltons, but there were still comparisons to be drawn between Elijah's early years and his own. Loneliness, a lack of roots, no foundations to build on. The army had become Milton's family, and then the Group. But even that had come to an end. Now, he thought, he was on his own again. Perhaps that was for the best. For some people, people like him, perhaps that was the natural way of things.

The doors of the church hall were thrown wide, and the sound of activity was loud, spilling out into the tree-lined street. Milton led the way inside, Elijah trailing a little cautiously behind. There were two dozen boys at the club this morning, spread between the ring and the exercise equipment. Two pairs were squeezed into the ring together, sparring with one another. The heavy bag resounded with the pummelling blows of a big, muscled elder boy, and the speed bag spat out a rat-tat-tat as a wiry, sharp-elbowed girl hit it, her gloved fists rolling with the fast, repetitive rhythm. Others jumped rope or shadow-boxed, and two older boys were busy with rollers on the far side of the room, whitewashing the wall.

"Boxing?" Elijah exclaimed.

"That's right."

"I ain't into this," he said. "You're having a laugh."

Milton turned to him. "Give it a chance," he said. "Just one morning, see how you get on. If you don't like it, you don't ever have to come back. But you might surprise yourself."

Rutherford noticed them and made his way across the room. "This your boy?"

"I ain't his boy," Elijah said dismissively.

"He's not sure this is for him," Milton said, patiently ignoring his truculent attitude.

"Wouldn't be the first lad to say that the first time he comes in here. How old are you, son?"

"Fifteen."

"Big lad for your age. Reckon you might have something about you. I'm Rutherford. Who are you?"

"JaJa."

"All right then, JaJa. Have you got kit?"

Elijah gave a sullen shrug.

"I'll take that as a yes. The changing room is out the back. Get yourself sorted out and get back out here. We'll see what you can do."

Milton was surprised to see that Elijah did as he was told.

"Leave him with me for a couple of hours," Rutherford said. "I think he's going to like this more than he thinks he is."

Chapter Twenty-Eight

MILTON LOOKED at the jobs that needed doing. As Rutherford had suggested, the hall was in a bit of a state. The walls were peeling in places, large swathes of damp bubbling up beneath the paint and patches of dark fungus spreading up from the floor. Some of the floorboards were rotting, one of the toilets had been smashed, and the roof leaked in several places. Buckets had been placed to catch the falling water, and looking up to fix the position on the roof, Milton took the ladder that Rutherford offered, went outside, braced it against the wall, and climbed up to take a better look. Several of the tiles were missing. He climbed back down, went to the small hardware store that served the Estate, and bought a wide plastic sheet, a hammer and a handful of nails. He spent the next hour and a half securing the sheet so that it sheltered the missing tiles. It was only a temporary fix, but it would suffice until he could return with the materials to do the job properly.

When Milton returned to the church hall, he found Elijah sparring inside the ring. The boy was wearing a head guard, vest and shorts, his brand-new Nikes gleaming against the dirty canvas. His opponent looked to be a year or two older and was a touch taller and heavier, yet Elijah was giving him all he could handle. He was light on his feet and skipped in and out of range, absorbing his opponent's slow jabs on his gloves and retaliating with quick punches of his own. Milton had been a decent boxer in the Forces and was confident that he knew how to spot raw talent when he saw it. And Elijah had talent; he was sure about that.

Elijah allowed the bigger boy to come onto him, dropping his head so that it was shielded between his shoulders and forearms. The boy dived forward, Elijah turning at the last moment so that his jab bounced off his right shoulder, leaving his guard open and his chin exposed. Elijah fired in a straight right-hand of his own, his gloved fist crumpling into the boy's headguard with enough force to propel his mouthguard from his mouth. He was stood up by the sudden blow, dazed, and Elijah hit him with a left and another right.

The boy was staggering as Rutherford rang the bell to bring the sparring to an end.

Elijah turned to step through the ropes, but Rutherford sent him back again with a stern word. He went back to his opponent, and they touched gloves. "That's better," Rutherford said as he held the ropes open for the two of them. He sent them both to the changing rooms. He saw Milton and came across to him.

"Sorry about that," Milton said.

"Boy's keen. Needs to learn some discipline, though."

"What do you think?"

"There's potential. He's got an attitude on him, no doubt, but we can work with that."

"You'll have him back, then?"

"For sure. Bring him on Tuesday night; we'll get to setting him up a regular regime, start training him properly."

MILTON OFFERED to buy Elijah dinner wherever he liked. The boy chose the Nando's on Bethnal Green Road and led the way there. They took a bus from Dalston Junction, sitting together on the top deck, Milton with his knees pressed tight against the seat in front and Elijah alongside. The restaurant was busy, but they found a table towards the back. Milton gave Elijah a twenty-pound note and told him to get food for both of them. He returned with a tray laden with chicken, fries and soft drinks. He put the tray on the table, shrugged off his puffa jacket, and pushed a plate across the table.

"What is it?" Milton asked.

"You never eaten in Nando's before?"

"Not that I can remember."

"You got peri peri chicken and fries," he explained. "If you don't like that, there's something wrong with you, innit?"

Milton smiled at the boy's enthusiasm and took a bite out of the chicken. He looked out around the restaurant: there were tables of youngsters, some with their parents, and groups of older adolescents. There was a raucous atmosphere, loud and vibrant. He noticed a young couple with two children, probably no older than six or seven, and for a moment, his mind started to wander. He caught himself. He had moments of wistfulness now and again, but he had abandoned the thought of a family a long time ago. His line of work made that idea impossible, both practically and equitably. He was never in the same place for long enough to put down roots, and even if he did, the risks of his profession would have made it unfair to whoever might have chosen to make her life with him. The state of affairs had been settled for long enough that he had driven daydreams of domesticity from his mind. That kind of life was not for a man like him.

"So where did you learn to fight like that?" he asked him.

He shrugged. "Dunno. The street, I guess. My mums says I got a temper on me. She's probably right. I get into fights all the time."

"A temper's not going to do you any favours. You'll need to keep it under control."

Elijah dismissed the advice with a wave of his drumstick. "I know what it was. When I was younger, primary school, I was out playing football in the park when this bigger boy, Malachi, he comes onto me with his screwface on after I scored a goal against his team. He punched me right in the face, and I didn't do nothing about it. I wasn't crying or nothing, but when I got home, my mum saw that I had a cut on my head, and she was on at me about how I got it. I told her what happened, and she sent me back out again." He swallowed a mouthful and put on an exaggerated impression of his mother's voice. "'Listen good,' she said, 'I'm your mum. I protected you in my womb for nine months. I gave birth to you. I didn't do none of that so other people could just beat on you. Go outside and don't come back in until you've given that boy a good seeing to, and I'm going to be watching you from the balcony.' So I did what she said and sorted him out. I never let anyone push me around after that."

Milton couldn't help laugh, and after a moment, the boy laughed along with him.

"I don't know anything about you, do I?" he said when they had finished.

"What would you like to know?"

The boy was watching him curiously over his jumbo cup of Coke. "What do you do? For a job, I mean?"

"This and that," he said.

"Because we all knew you ain't no journalist."

"No, I'm not. We spoke about this. I'm not—"

"So what is it you do? Come on, man. I've told you plenty about me. Only fair. You want to get to know me properly, how you expect that if you got kinds of secrets and shit I don't know about?"

He said, awkwardly, "It's a little hard to explain."

"Try me."

"I'm a"—he fumbled for the right euphemism—"I'm a problem solver. Occasionally, there are situations that require solutions that are a little out of the ordinary. I'm the one who gets asked to sort them out."

"This ain't one of those situations?"

"I don't understand."

"Me, I mean. This ain't work?"

"No. I told you, it's nothing like that."

"So what, then? What kind of situations?"

"I can't really say anything else."

"So you're saying it's secret?"

"Something like that."

Elijah grinned at him. "Cool. What are you, some kind of secret agent?"

"Hardly."

"Some kind of James Bond shit, right?" He was grinning.

"Come on," Milton said. "Look at me—do I look like James Bond?"

"Nah," he said. "You way too old for that."

Milton smiled as he finished one of his chicken wings.

"So tell me what it is you do."

"Elijah, I can't tell you anything else. Give me a break, all right?"

They ate quietly for a moment. Elijah concentrated on his chicken, dipping it into the sauce, nibbling right up to the bone. He wiped his fingers on a napkin. A thoughtful look passed across his face.

"What is it?"

"Why are you helping me and my mum?"

"Because she needed it. You both did."

"She manages fine," he said, waving the chicken leg dismissively. Milton realised that Sharon had not explained to her son the circumstances of how they had met. That was probably the right thing to do; there was no sense in worrying him, but at the same time, if he knew how desperate he had made her feel, then perhaps he would have corrected his course more readily, without the need for help. It didn't really matter. He was making good progress now, and it was up to Sharon what she told her son. Milton was not about to abuse her trust.

Elijah was still regarding him carefully. Milton realised that the boy was shrewder than he looked. "No other reason?"

"Such as?"

"Such as you want to be with my mum."

Milton shook his head. "No."

"She's had boyfriends," Elijah said discursively. "Not many, but some. None of them were any good. They all give it the talk until they get what they want, but when it comes down to it, when they need to back it up, they're all full of shit. It breaks her up when they leave. It's just me and her most of the time. It's better that way."

"You don't think she's lonely?"

"Not when I'm there."

"She'll find someone eventually."

Elijah wrinkled his nose. "Nah," he said. "She don't need no one else. She's got me."

Milton felt a flicker of encouragement. The boy's attitude was changing, the hardened carapace slowly falling away. He watched him enthusiastically finishing the chicken, the sauce smearing around the corners of his mouth, and for that moment he looked exactly what he was: a fifteen-year-old boy, bravado masking a deep well of insecurity, anxiously trying to find his place in the world. Milton realised that he had started to warm towards him.

Chapter Twenty-Nine

CALLAN WALKED purposefully up the street, the row of terraced houses on his left. He passed the house that Milton had taken and slowed, glancing quickly through the single window. A net curtain obscured the view inside, but it didn't appear that the house was occupied. He continued fifty yards up the road, turned, and paused. Traffic hurried busily along the road. A few youngsters loitered aimlessly in front of the arcade of shops at the distant junction. The blocks of 1950s social housing loomed heavily behind their iron railings and scrappy lawns.

He watched carefully, assessing.

He started back towards the house, reaching into his pocket for his lock picks as he did so. A couple walked towards him, hand in hand, and Callan slowed his pace, timing his approach carefully so that the couple had passed the door to Milton's house before he reached it.

He took out his lock pick and knelt before the door. He slid the pick and a small tension wrench into the lock and lifted the pins one by one until they clicked. It had taken him less than five seconds. He turned the doorknob and passed quickly, and quietly, inside.

He took out his Sig Sauer and held it in both hands, his stance loose and easy. He held his breath and listened. The house was quiet.

He did not know how long he had before Milton returned, so he worked quickly. He pulled a pair of latex gloves onto his hands, and with his gun still held ready before him, he went from room to room.

The house was cheaply furnished and in need of repair and decoration. Milton had brought hardly anything with him. Callan found a rucksack, a handful of clothes hung carefully in a rickety cupboard, some toiletries in the bathroom, but little else. There were pints of milk and orange juice in the fridge and a half-eaten loaf of bread, but nothing else.

The investigation posed more questions than it answered. What was Milton doing here, in a place like this?

He went into the front room and shuffled through the envelopes on the table. They were old bills, addressed to a person whom Callan assumed was the previous occupier. He turned a gas bill over and saw that a note had been scribbled on the back.

SHARON WARRINER
FLAT 609, BLISSETT HOUSE

He took out his phone and took a photograph of the address. He slid the envelope back into the pile and left the room as he had found it.

He holstered the Sig Sauer, opened the door to the street, and stepped outside. The road was clear. He closed the door and stuffed the latex gloves into his pockets. He set off in the direction of the tube station.

Chapter Thirty

ELIJAH HAD BEEN working on the heavy bag and was sweating hard as he sat down on the bench. He took off his gloves and the wraps that had been wound tightly around his fists. His knuckles had cut and blistered during the session, and blood had stained the white fabric. He screwed the bandages into a tight ball and dropped them into the dustbin. The hall was busy. Two boys were sparring in the ring, and another was firing combinations into the pads that one of the men who helped Rutherford was wearing. The man moved them up and down and side to side, changing the target, barking out left and right, the boy doing his best to keep pace. Other boys skipped rope, lifted weights, or shadow-boxed in the space around the ring.

Rutherford came over to him and sat down. "How you feeling, younger?"

"I feel good."

"Looking good, too. That was a good session."

"How did I do?"

"You did good. You got to work on your guard a little. You leave your chin open like that and it don't matter how slippery and quick you are, someone'll eventually get lucky and stitch you, and that'll be that—but we can sort that for you. You got a lot of potential. You work hard at this, who knows?"

"What you mean? I could make something of it?"

"It's too early to say that, younger. But you got potential, like I said." Rutherford paused for a moment, his eyes drifting across the room. "You're running with the LFB, right?"

Elijah said that he was.

"That's right. Your friend told me. You know we don't

have none of that in here, right? No colours, no beefs, nothing. You all right with that?"

"Yeah," he said. "It's not like I'm tight with them or anything. It's a recent thing. I know some of the boys, that's it."

"Then we ain't going to have a problem, then. That's good."

"You were involved, weren't you? The streets, I mean?"

"Yeah," Rutherford said. "Long time ago. Is it obvious?"

"I see the way the other boys look at you. It's not hard to guess. Who were you with?"

"LFB."

"What did you do?"

"The usual—rolled people, shotted drugs, tiefed stuff. But my speciality was robbing dealers."

"Seriously?"

"Why not? You know they've got to be carrying plenty of Ps, and if you take it, what they going to do? I know they ain't going to the feds." He sat down on the bench next to Elijah. "Some days," he said, "we'd head down onto the Pembury or into the park and we'd rob the shotters. Same guys, every day. They'd never see us coming. You put them up against the wall, and it's 'give me your money, nigger.' They know I'm strapped; they ain't going to risk getting shot. Day in, day out, gimme the money, your jewellery, your phone—anything they had. Who they gonna tell? If we knew where there was a crack house, we'd go in there and clear the place out too. No one's packing in a crack house, see—no one wants to be caught with drugs and a gun for no reason, so you just stroll in, get your blammer out, and everyone's too wasted too argue. But you got to be strapped. Always knew that—you got to be strapped. You turn up to a place like that with a knife, man, you're gambling with your life. And you got to be strapped all the time, because when you rob another gang's crack house, the cats'll stop going, and that costs money. When the crew ask around, they'll find out who's done what they done, and they're gonna want to take action to make sure it don't happen again."

"Didn't you feel bad?"

"Sometimes, when I was lying in bed thinking about the way my life was going, course I did. But then you think about it some more, and you got money and power, so in the end you persuade yourself there was nothing in it. You tell yourself it's the law of the jungle, the strong against the weak. And I was strong, that's the way I saw it then. But I wasn't strong. I was a bully hiding behind a 2-2, and I was foolish. Young, proud, full of shit and foolish. But the way I saw it, I knew the players we was going after was doing the same shit to other people. It's kind of like—this is the road—this is how it is. If you don't like it, get off the road."

"What happened?"

"In the end?" He shook his head and sucked on his teeth. "In the end, younger, it happened like it was always gonna happen. We rolled a crack house, only this time the Tottenham boys were wise to it. They had a couple of mash men with blammers there themselves, waiting for us. Soon as we got in there, they pulled them out and started shooting the place up. I took out my strap and fired back. Didn't know who I was shooting at. Bad things happened."

"You killed someone?"

"Like I said, bad things happened. I had to get away, so I signed up for the army."

"How old were you?"

He turned the question around. "How old you say you are?"

"Fifteen."

"That's right. I had just five short years on you, younger. I'm thirty-six now. I got out six months ago. I did sixteen years in the army. Two wars. Longer than you been around in this world."

"Shit."

"Yeah, that's right—shit. You see why I do what I do now, JaJa? I know where the road is gonna take youngsters like you if you don't pay attention. There ain't no chance it can go anywhere else. I know I probably sound like it sometimes, but I ain't trying to patronise. I just *know*. You follow the road you're on for too much longer, you'll get in so deep you don't even know how to begin getting out. And then, one day, the road will take you, too. You'll get shot or shanked, or you'll do it to someone else, and the Trident will lock you up. And either way, that'll be it—the end of your life. If I can help a couple of you boys get straight, get off the road, then, the way I look at it, I'm starting to give back a little, pay back the debt I owe."

The door to the street opened, and Pinky came inside. Elijah stiffened.

"You know him?" Rutherford said.

"Yeah. Does he come here, too?"

"Used to, but I haven't seen him for a while. You two get on?"

"Not really."

"No, I bet—he's not an easy one to get along with. He's got a whole lot of troubles." Rutherford got up as Pinky approached them. "Easy, younger," he said. "How's it going? Ain't seen you for a couple of weeks."

"Been busy." The boy said it proudly, and Elijah knew exactly what he meant.

"That right? How much you made this week, playa?"

"Huh?"

"Your Ps. I know you been shotting. I saw you, up on the balcony at Blissett House. How much?"

Pinky stared at Elijah and grinned as he said, "Five-o-o."

Rutherford sucked his teeth. "Five hundred," he said. "Not bad."

"Not bad? Better than you'll make all month."

"Probably right," he conceded with an equable duck of his head. "So let me get that straight… five hundred a week, over a whole year, you keep taking that you're gonna end up with what, twenty-five thousand? What you gonna do with that much money?"

"I'm gonna buy me a big-screen TV, a new laptop, some games, some clothes and shoes, and then I'm gonna save the rest. I got plans, get me?"

"That right?"

"Yeah," he said, a little aggression laced in the reply. "What about it?"

"Where you gonna save it?"

"What you mean? In a bank—where else?"

Rutherford shook his head. "You're sixteen years old. You telling me you're going to walk into the NatWest and give them twenty grand and tell them to stick it in your account? Really? That's your plan?"

"Yeah."

"No, you ain't."

"Fuck you!" he said. "It's my money. Mine. They can't take it off me. No one can."

"You take it into a bank, and I'll tell you exactly what's gonna happen—they'll be onto the feds before you're halfway out the door. Next thing you know you're on the deck eating pavement, and then you'll do time. That's if you last that long. Because what'll most likely happen is some brother will nick it off you. And while they're at it, they'll probably merk you, too. And it's no good being rich when you're dead."

"Fuck you, man," he spat. "Fuck you know?"

Rutherford absorbed his invective and stared back at the boy with a cold hardness in his eyes that Elijah had not seen before. For a moment, it was easy to imagine the intimidating effect he must have had when he was younger. "What do you mean, what the fuck do I know? You know where I've come from. You know what I been, what I've done. I don't have to put up with your shit, either. Go on, you don't want to listen to me, fuck off. Go on. If you want to stay, then stay. I'll tell you how you can make that kind of money, but legit so you *can* put it in a bank account, so no one's gonna take it off you and drop you stone dead."

Pinky squared up, and for a moment, Elijah expected him to fire back with more lip. Rutherford stood before the boy implacably, calm certainty written across his face. He was not going to back down.

"A'ight," Pinky said, and the tension dissipated in a sudden exhale. He forced a grin across his face. "Cotch, man. I'm just creasing you."

"Get your kit on if you want to stay," Rutherford told him sternly. "You've gotten all flabby, all this time you been taking off. You got some catching up to do."

"Funny man." Pinky hiked up his Raiders T-shirt. He was thin and wiry, the muscles standing out on his abdomen in neat, compact lines. "Don't chat grease. Flabby? Look at this—I'm ripped, playa."

"Get yourself in the ring. I got someone who'll see whether you still got what it takes."

"That right? Who's that?"

Rutherford turned to Elijah. "You up, younger. Get new wraps on. The two of you can spar. Three rounds."

Pinky looked at Elijah and laughed. "Him?" he said derisively. "Seriously?"

"Talk's cheap, bruv. You think you can take him? Let's see it in the ring."

"I'm on that," he said, firing out a quick combination, right-left-right. "This little mandem gonna get himself proper sparked."

Pinky went back to the changing room, and when he returned, he had changed into a pair of baggy shorts that emphasised his thin legs. Elijah wrapped his fists again and laced up his gloves. The two boys stepped through the ropes and, at Rutherford's insistence, touched gloves.

Pinky was older than Elijah, but they were similar in

physique. He came forward aggressively, fighting behind a low guard and firing out a barrage of wild combinations. He was quick but not particularly powerful or accurate, and Elijah was able to absorb the onslaught without difficulty, taking it on his arms or dodging away. He spent the first round that way, absorbing his attacks and firing back with stiff punches that beat Pinky's absent guard, flashing into his nose or against his chin. Elijah knew that his punches were crisp rather than powerful, but that was all right. He was not trying to hurt Pinky, not yet. Each successful blow riled the older boy, and he came forward with redoubled intent. Elijah let him, dancing away or smothering the blows when he could not, letting Pinky wear himself out.

Rutherford rang the bell as the first two-minute round expired, and the two boys broke to separate corners to take a drink.

"I'm gonna dook you up, younger" Pinky called across the ring, lisping around his mouthguard.

"Didn't do nothing first round," Elijah retorted. "Look at me—I'm hardly even sweating."

The other boys had stopped to watch the action. A couple had wandered across to stand next to Rutherford, and others were idling across to join them.

Rutherford rang the bell.

They set off again. Pinky moved in aggressively, firing out another wild combination, rights and lefts that Elijah disposed of with ease. Rutherford was watching him from the side of the ring, and Elijah decided that it was time to give him his demonstration. He stepped it up a gear. Pinky moved forward again, and Elijah sidestepped his first flurry, firing in a strong right jab that stood him up, a left and a right into the kidneys and then, his guard dropped, a heavy right cross. Pinky fell back, but Elijah did not stop. He followed the boy backwards across the ring, firing hooks into the body. Pinky fell back against the ropes, and Elijah pivoted on his left foot and delivered a right cross with all of his weight behind it. Pinky took the punch square on the jaw and fell onto his back.

Rutherford rang the bell and clambered into the ring. Pinky was on his hands and knees, his mouthguard on the canvas before him, trails of spit draping down to it from his gasping mouth. Rutherford helped him to his feet and held the ropes open for him. He said nothing, barely even looking at Elijah as he slipped down to the floor and went back to the changing rooms. The watching boys were hooting and hollering, impressed with the show that Elijah had put on. One of the older boys declared that Elijah had banged Pinky out. Elijah could not prevent the grin that spread across his face.

Rutherford drew Elijah to one side and helped him to unlace his gloves. "Listen here, younger," he said. "You've got skills. You let him wear himself out there, didn't you?"

Elijah shrugged. "Didn't seem no point to get into it with him. He's bigger than me. Would've been too strong, I come onto him straight up. Seemed like a better idea to let him work himself out, let him get weak, then come in and spark him."

Rutherford smiled as he explained his tactics. "You thought all that out for yourself?"

"I used to play that way on my PlayStation. Ali and Foreman, innit? Rope-a-dope."

"You learned that from a videogame?"

"Yeah," he said.

"Why not?" Rutherford laughed. "Look, little man, I know you're only just starting out, been here just a handful of times and all, but I think you're ready to step it up. We've got a night coming up with a club in Tottenham. It's like we got here; a friend of mine runs it. He's gonna bring his boys down so we can see what's what. He'll have five of his best lads; I'll pick five of mine. I'd like to put you in the team. What you say? Sound like something you might be interested in?"

Elijah's heart filled with pride. No one had ever said he

was any good at anything. None of his teachers, none of his friends, not even his mum, not really. "Course," he said. He didn't know what else to say.

Rutherford put one of his big hands on his shoulder. "Good lad. Thought you'd be up for it. It's Thursday night. Speak to the fellow who brought you down. Mr Milton. See if he wants to come?"

Elijah thought of Milton. Would he come if he asked him? Elijah was surprised to find that he half hoped that he would. "A'ight," he said. "I'll tell him about it."

Chapter Thirty-One

MILTON LOOKED at the window of Sharon's flat. It was barred, but somehow, it had still been broken. The window faced into the sitting room, and a wide, jagged hole had been smashed in the centre. The wind had sucked the curtains out, and now they flapped uselessly, snagged on the sharp edges of the glass. Fragments had fallen out onto the walkway, and now they crunched underfoot, like ice.

He had called Sharon half an hour earlier to ask after Elijah. She had been upset, barely able to stifle the sobs, and he came straight across. A brick was lying incongruously on the cushion of the sofa, glass splinters sparkling all around it. Someone had pushed it through the glass.

"Just kids mucking about," Sharon said miserably. "They don't mean anything by it."

"Has it happened before?"

She shrugged, a little awkwardly. "Sometimes."

"You'll need to get it fixed."

"I spoke to the council. They say they can't do it until next week."

"You can't leave it like that until then. Let me take care of it."

"I can't ask you to do that."

"It's not a problem. Simple job. I just need to get some bits and pieces. It'll take me half an hour."

She smiled shyly at him. "On one condition—you let me cook you dinner."

"Deal," Milton said.

Milton sized up the job and then visited the hardware store in the centre of Hackney to collect the equipment and materials that he would need.

A handful of lazy youngsters had gathered by the time he returned, leaning against the balustrade at the end of the balcony. They stared at him with dull aggression as he set his purchases down and removed his jacket. He unscrewed the cage that contained the metal bars and stood it carefully against the wall. He spread an old sheet on the balcony outside the window and knocked out the largest fragments of glass, using a hammer and chisel to remove the smaller pieces. He chipped out the putty from the groove in the frame and plucked out the old glazing sprigs with a pair of pliers. He sanded the rough patches, applied a primer, and then filled in the holes and cracks. He kneaded putty into a thin roll and pressed it into the frame, then carefully lowered the new pane of glass into place, pressing carefully so that the putty squeezed out to form a seal. He added new sprigs to hold the glass in place and pressed more putty into the join between the panel and the frame, trimming away the excess with the edge of his chisel. He heaved the metal cage up to the window and screwed it back into place. Finally, he stepped back against the balustrade and admired his handiwork. The job was well done.

"You wasting your time," one of the kids called over to him. "No one likes her. She ain't from round these ends. She should get the hint, innit, go somewhere else?"

"She's not going anywhere," Milton said.

"It gonna get broke again, soon as you gone."

"Leave her alone. All right?"

"What you gonna do about it, old man?"

All Milton could think about was going over to teach them some manners, but he knew that that would just be for his own gratification. It wouldn't do Sharon any good. He couldn't be with her all the time, and as soon as he was gone, she would be punished. It was better to bite his tongue.

The boys stayed for another ten minutes, hooting at him to try to get a response, but when they realised he was ignoring them, they fired off another volley of abuse and slouched all the way down to the bottom of the stairs. Milton watched them go.

It was a little past seven when he had finished with the window to his satisfaction. He tidied away his tools and went inside. The television in the lounge was tuned to the BBC's news channel. A man in Tottenham had been shot dead by police. The presenter said he was a drug dealer and that the police were reporting that he had been armed. Milton watched it for a moment, not really paying attention, and then found the remote control and switched it off.

Sharon had pulled the table away from the wall and laid it for dinner. She had prepared a traditional Jamaican dish of mutton curry. Milton helped her to clear the table when they had finished. He took out his cigarettes. "Do you mind?" he asked her.

"What are they?" she said, looking at the unfamiliar black, blue and gold packet.

"Arktika. They're Russian."

"I've never seen them before. Where do you get them?"

"Internet," he said. "Every man needs at least one vice."

"Russian fags?"

"I met a man once, a long time ago. He was Russian. We found ourselves in a spot of bother, and these were all we had. Three packets. We made them last four days. I'd developed a bit of a taste for them by the end. Vodka too, but only the good stuff."

He opened the carton and offered it to Sharon. She took a cigarette and allowed Milton to light it for her. He lit his and watched as she took a deep lungful of smoke, letting it escape from between her lips in a long sigh.

"You've been so good to me," she began after a quiet moment. "I don't know why."

Milton inhaled himself, the tobacco crackling as the

flame burned higher. "You've had some bad luck," he said. "Things aren't always fair. You work hard with Elijah; you deserve some help. I'm just glad I can do that."

"But why me?"

"Why not you?" he retorted. He let the peacefulness fall between them again, his thoughts gently turning on her question. Why her? Had it just been a case of his being there at just the right time, or was there something else, something about Sharon that drew him toward her? Her vulnerability? Her helplessness? Or had he recognised in her some way to make amends for the things that he had done?

The sons that he had orphaned.

The wives that he had widowed.

He didn't know the answer to that, and he didn't think it would serve to dwell upon it.

He drew down on the cigarette again.

"Can I get you a drink? Don't have any vodka, but I think I have some gin, and some tonic, maybe."

"I don't drink anymore," he said. "A glass of water is fine."

She went through into the kitchen. Milton stood alone in the sitting room and examined it more carefully than he had before. He noticed the small details that Sharon had included in an attempt to make the blandly square box more homely: the embroidered cushions on the sofa, the box of second-hand children's toys pushed against the wall, the Ikea curtains that hid the bars on the windows outside. He went over to the sideboard. Sharon had arranged a collection of framed pictures of her children, the two boys at various stages of their lives. He picked one up and studied it; it was a professional shot, the sort that could be bought cheaply in malls, with Sharon pictured on a chair with the children arranged around her. Milton guessed it was taken four or five years ago. Sharon's hair was cut in a different shape, and her face was absent the perpetual frown of worry that must have sunk across it in the interim. Elijah was a sweet-looking ten-year-old, chubby, beaming a happy smile and without the wariness in his eyes. His older brother, Jules, looked very much like him. He had an open, honest face. He must have been the same age as Elijah was now. There was nothing to suggest a predisposition towards self-destruction, but Milton guessed that he must already have started along the path that would eventually lead him to ruin.

Sharon emerged from the kitchen with two glasses in her hands. "My boys," she said simply. "I failed with Jules. I'm not going to let the same thing happen to Elijah."

"You won't."

She smiled sadly, resting both glasses on the table. Milton watched as a single tear rolled slowly down her cheek, and he went to her, drawing her into his body and holding her there, his right hand reaching around to stroke her hair.

She gently pulled back and looked up into his face. Her eyes were wet and bright. Milton pushed her against the wall and kissed her, hard, on the mouth. She pulled away, and Milton took a step back to give her room. "I'm sorry," he said, but her hands came up, her fingers circling his wrists, and she drew him back towards her until their bodies touched. She moved his hands downwards until they were around her slender waist and angled her head to kiss him, her mouth open hungrily. Milton embraced her passionately, his tongue forcing her teeth apart, her own tongue working shyly at first and then more passionately. Milton pulled her even more tightly into his body, crushing her breasts against his chest. She gasped, disengaging her mouth and pressing her cheek against his, her mouth nuzzling his neck. They stayed like that for a moment, breathing hard, Milton feeling her hard breasts against his sternum, his hands sliding down into the small of her back.

She leant back a little so that she could look up into his face. She gently brushed aside the lock of black hair that had fallen across his damp forehead. Her hand slid into his, their fingers interlacing, and then she pulled him after her, leading the way across the sitting room to the door that led to her bedroom.

Chapter Thirty-Two

ELIJAH AWOKE AT EIGHT, just as usual, and got straight out of bed. His body felt sore from exercise, but it was a good pain, a steady ache that told him he had worked hard. He thought of his muscles, the little tears and rips that would regenerate and thicken, making him stronger. He thought of Pinky and the session in the ring. He had dreamt about that in the night, replaying the two rounds over and over again. It was one of those good dreams where it made him feel happy at the end, not the nightmares that he usually had. He thought of the boys who had been watching. "He banged Pinky out," one of them called, and there had been something different in the way that he looked at him, the way that they all looked at him. He felt a warmth in his chest as he thought about it again.

He took off his shirt, opened his cupboard door, and looked at his torso in the full-length mirror. He was lean and strong, the muscles in his stomach starting to develop, his arms thickening, his shoulders growing heavier. His puppy fat was disappearing. He knew from the few pictures he had found in his mother's room that his father had been a big man, powerfully built, and he had always hoped that he might inherit that from him. He wanted to be like Rutherford. A man that size, who was going to mess around with him?

He found a clean T-shirt and pulled on his jeans. He threw his duvet back across his bed, straightened it out, and went into the sitting room. It was empty. That was strange; his mother was normally up well before him, preparing his breakfast before she went off to work.

"Mums," he called.

There was no reply.

He went into the kitchen and poured himself an orange juice. He went and stood before the door to her bedroom. It was closed.

"Mums," he said again, "I can't find my iPod. You awake?"

He heard the sound of hasty movement from inside and, without thinking, reached for the door handle and opened it. His mother was half out of bed, fastening the belt of her dressing gown around her waist. She was not alone. Milton was sitting in her bed, the covers pulled down to reveal his hard, muscular chest.

Elijah felt his stomach drop away. He felt sick.

"Oh no," he said.

"Elijah," his mother said helplessly.

"What? What's going on?"

"*Elijah.*"

He backed out of the room.

His mother followed him, stammering something about him needing to be calm, about how he shouldn't lose his temper, how he should listen, but he hardly heard her. She came into the sitting room as he scrabbled on the floor for the trainers he had left there after he came in last night. Milton came out of the bedroom, his trousers halfway undone and hastily doing up the buttons of his shirt.

"Come on, Elijah," he said. "Let me talk to you."

"You said you weren't like the others."

"I'm not."

"I thought you wanted to help me?"

"I do."

"No, you don't. You just want her to think you do so you can get with her. What's wrong with me? You must think I'm an idiot. I can't believe I fell for it."

"You're not an idiot, and that's not how it is. I do want to help you. It's very important to me. What happens between me and your mum doesn't make any difference to that."

"You can fool her if you want, but you ain't fooling me, not anymore." He stamped his feet into his trainers and laced them hurriedly.

"Elijah…" Sharon said.

"I'll see you later, Mum."

She called after him as he slammed the door behind him. He stood on the balcony in the fresh morning air. The kids at the end of the balcony sniggered, and as he turned back, he saw why: someone had sprayed graffiti across the front door, and the paint, still wet, said SLUT.

Elijah went across to the boys. Elijah knew them by reputation; they were a year or two older than him. They occasionally passed through the Estate to sell Bizness's gear.

"You think that's funny?" he said.

"Look at the little chichi man," the oldest of the three said. "Hush your gums, younger, you know it's true."

"Wouldn't be so touchy about it if he didn't, would he? Your mum's a grimey skank, bruv, you know she is."

Elijah was blinded by a sudden, unquenchable flash of anger. He flung his arm out in a powerful right cross, catching the boy flush on the chin. He dropped to the concrete, his head bouncing back off the balustrade, and lay still. He turned to face the other two. They gaped, and then, as they saw the ire that had distorted Elijah's face, they both backed away. Elijah's fist burned from the impact, and as he opened and closed his hand, he saw that his knuckles had been painted with the boy's blood.

The door to the flat opened behind him. He turned back to see Milton emerging, barefoot. "Elijah," he called out. "Please—let me talk to you."

He leapt over the boy and made for the stairs, kicking the door open and taking them two at a time. He was crying by the time he reached the bottom; hot, gasping sobs of disappointment and disenchantment and the sure knowledge that any chance he had of striking out on a different path was gone. He could not trust Milton. He had used him, and like a callow little boy, he had given himself away cheaply and unquestioningly. He could not trust him, and there was no one else. He had always known he was alone. This had been just another false hope. He would not fall for it so easily again.

He found his phone in his pocket and swiped through his contacts until he found Bizness's number.

Chapter Thirty-Three

POPS DROVE his car into Dalston and parked next to a Turkish restaurant on Kingsland Road. He killed the engine and sat quietly, watching the pedestrians passing next to him. Bizness had called him thirty minutes earlier and told him to come to his studio. He made no mention of Laura, nor did Pops expect him to. He would feel no guilt for what he had done. The way he would see it, he was entitled to take whatever he wanted. A woman was no different to money, time, or possessions. If Bizness wanted it, then it was his.

Elijah was in the passenger seat. Bizness had told him to collect him and bring him along. Pops tried to engage him in conversation when he picked him up, but the youngster didn't respond. His face was clouded with anger, and he was completely closed off. Something had happened to him; that much was obvious.

"Here we are, younger," he said to him. "I don't know what Bizness wants with you, but be careful, alright?"

Elijah grunted, but other than that, he did not respond.

Pops tried again. "Listen to me, JaJa. You don't have to do nothing you don't want to do. Nothing's changed from before. If you'd gone through with what he wanted, you'd either be dead or in prison now. You hear me?"

Once again, Elijah said nothing. Pops hardly knew the boy, but he had never seen him like this. He looked older, more severe, his lack of emotion even a little frightening. Pops realised with a sudden flash of insight that the boy reminded him of himself, five years earlier. Anger throbbed out of him. He was frightened for him.

Elijah pulled back the handle and pushed the door open. He got out, slammed it behind him, and crossed the pavement to the door of the studio.

"Alright, then," Pops said in his wake. He got out, locked the car, and followed.

The studio was on the first floor of the building, above the restaurant. Pops held his thumb against the buzzer and spoke into the intercom. The lock popped open, and he went inside. Pops knew the history of the place. Bizness had bought the two flats that had been here before and spent fifty thousand knocking them through into one large space. He followed the dingy flight of steps upwards, frayed squares of carpet on the treads and framed posters of BRAPPPP! hung on the walls on either side of him. They were ordered chronologically, and the pictures nearer the ground floor, before the collective discovered that popularity was inextricably tied to notoriety, even seemed a little naïve. The final poster before the door at the top of the stairs was of Bizness standing alone, bare chested, holding a semi-automatic MAC-10 pistol in one hand and smoking a joint with the other. Pops remembered the first time he had seen the poster. He had been awed, then, a black man with power who was unafraid of putting a finger up at society's conventions; now, he found it all predictable and depressing. There was no message there, no purpose. The power was illusory. It was all about the money.

The sound of heavy bass thudded from the room at the top of the stairs. The interior door was open, and Pops pushed it aside. The rooms beyond comprised a small kitchen strewn with takeaway packaging and an area laid out with plush sofas and a low coffee table. At the other side of the building was the studio itself, sealed off behind a glass screen with its recording booth and mixing suite. The rest of the area was busy with people, and the noise was cacophonous; the latest BRAPPPP! record was playing through the studio's PA, the repetitive drone blending with the shouts and whoops of the people in the room, everyone struggling to make themselves heard. Pops recognised several members of the collective and the hangers-on who trailed them wherever they went. Bizness was sitting with his back against the arm of the sofa, his legs stretched out across it, his feet resting in Laura's lap. He was shirtless, exposing the litany of tattoos that stretched across his skin. The word GANGSTER had been tattooed across his stomach in gothic cursive, the letters describing a long, lazy arc above his navel. IN GUNS WE TRUST was written, two words apiece, across the backs of his hands.

Laura looked up as Pops entered, her eyes flickering to his face for a moment. There was barely a moment of recognition before her unfocussed gaze washed over him. The muscles in her face were loose, flaccid. He tried to hold her attention, but it was a waste of time. She turned her face to the low table in front of her, where several lines of cocaine had been arranged across the surface. She ignored them, languidly reaching her fingers for the crack pipe that trailed tendrils of smoke up towards the ceiling. She grasped it and put it to her lips, inhaled, and then closed her eyes. Pops's heart sank. She toked, the smoke uncurling from her nostrils and rolling up past her cheeks, obscuring her blank eyes. She ignored him completely. It was as if he wasn't there.

Bizness grinned at them both, displaying his gold teeth. He reached over for a remote control and quietened the music so he could more easily be heard. "Look who it is, my two best bredderz. Big Pops and little JaJa. A'ight, bruv?"

Pops felt his hands curling into fists. "Bizness," he said, forcing himself to smile. He could not stop himself from looking over at Laura again, just for an instant, and Bizness noticed. He said nothing—there was no need for it—but his lips curled up in a derisive grin, the light glittering off the gold caps. Everyone in the room knew what had happened, that Bizness had clicked his fingers and taken her from him, doing it without compunction, like it was no big thing. Not even acknowledging it to his face was the biggest dis of all. It said Bizness didn't care. That Pops's reaction was irrelevant, and that there was nothing he could do about any of it. Pops felt his anger flare, but he forced himself to suppress it. There was no move for him to play. Laura was gone. She was with Bizness now, for however long he wanted her. If he showed his anger, there would be hype, and there could only be one outcome after that.

Bizness turned to Elijah. "And my little soldier, how are you doing, younger?"

"I'm good," Elijah said. He went over to Bizness and held up his closed fist.

Bizness looked around the room, his mouth open in an expression of delighted surprise. "Look at the little hoodrat," he exclaimed.

Elijah ducked his head and shrugged his shoulders.

"He got some serious attitude, innit?" Bizness bumped fists with him. "So what happened to you the other night, soldier?"

"Sorry 'bout that," Elijah said. He angled his face a fraction, enough to turn his gaze onto Pops, and it was clear from his expression that he blamed him for not carrying out his instructions. "The fight—I lost my nerve. Won't happen again."

"That right? You still wanna get involved?"

"Yeah. For definite."

"Because that problem ain't gone away. We made our point, but the little fassy ain't listening. Put up another message for us last night. You see it?"

Elijah shrugged again. There was an open laptop resting on the table. Bizness stretched across and tabbed through the open windows to YouTube. The video he wanted had already been selected, and he dragged the cursor across and set it to play. Pops had seen Wiley T's uploads before, and this met the usual pattern. The boy was rapping on the streets of Camden as a friend filmed him with a handheld camera. The bars he was dropping were all about Bizness and the brawl at the party. Bizness was right: Wiley was not backing down, and if anything, the incident had made him even more brazen. It was an escalation, a direct and unambiguous dis. He questioned Bizness's heritage, his legitimacy and the size of his manhood, all in artfully rhymed couplets. He ended by calling him out for a battle, doubting that the invitation would be taken up. Wiley was good, much better than Bizness, and it was that, Pops knew, rather than the content of his bars that had upset him so badly.

Elijah watched the video, his face darkening. "He's got some front," he said when it came to an end, "don't he?"

"Fucking right he got some front. Everyone knows I'd take him down if we battled, a'ight, so what's the point? Nah, bruv. There ain't nothing else for it—he's got to get merked. Can I count on you, young 'un? You ready to stand up?"

He turned to Pops again, his eyes blazing with purpose. "Yeah," he said. "Man needs to get dooked, innit. Be my pleasure to do it for you."

Bizness laughed harshly, and following their cue, the others in the room quickly followed suit. "Little man found his balls, eh? Good for you—good for you. You still got the piece?"

"In my bedroom."

Bizness extracted himself from the sofa, stretching himself out to his full height. He took a joint from the boy next to him and inhaled deeply. He knelt down, taking Elijah by both shoulders, and breathed the smoke into his face. "We'll make a rude boy out of you, JaJa. A good little soldier."

Chapter Thirty-Four

JOHN MILTON sat in the threadbare armchair in the front room of the house, staring at the stains on the wall and thinking. He had left Blissett House soon after Elijah. Sharon had been upset at the confrontation and, apologising as she did so, told him that it was probably better if he left. She said that what had happened had been a good thing, and that she didn't regret it, but that she had to put her child first. Milton understood. He had not planned for the night to develop as it had, and he had been surprised at his reaction. There was something about her that drew him in, her endearing combination of quiet dignity and vulnerability, perhaps. She was attractive, but he wished he had shown more restraint. Elijah had been making progress, and now he didn't know how much damage had been done.

His mobile was on the table. It started to ring. Milton picked it up and checked the display. He did not recognise the number.

"Yes?" he said.

"Hello?" said the caller.

"Who's this?"

"You the man? The man in the park?"

"Who's this?"

"I met you a week ago. You were looking for Elijah."

"Which one are you?"

"You gave me your number."

Milton remembered the boy: older than the others, bigger, a strange mixture of tranquillity and threat in his expression. "I remember," he said. "What's your name?"

"Call me Pops."

"No—your real name."

There was a pause as the boy weighed up whether he

should say. "Aaron," he said eventually.

"All right, then, Aaron. I'm John. How can I help you?"

The boy's voice was tight, tense. "You were looking out for JaJa, weren't you? You wanted to help him."

There was something in the boy's tone that made him fearful. "What about him?"

"He's in trouble. He's in real trouble, man. Serious." There was a pause. "Shit, I'm in trouble too. Both of us."

"You better tell me about it. What's the matter?"

"Just so I know, you ain't a journalist, are you?"

"No."

"And you ain't no police, neither?"

"No."

"What do you do, then, you so sure you can help?"

"I can't tell you that. But all you need to know is that I have a particular set of skills and that if you're in trouble, then I can help you. Beyond that you'll have to trust me." There was a pause on the line, and Milton noticed that he was holding his breath. "Are you still there?"

"Yeah," the boy said. "I'm here."

"It sounds like we need to talk."

"Yeah. Can we meet?"

"Of course."

"Now? I'm in the park, next to the fountains. You around?"

"I can be."

"I'll be here for another thirty minutes, then."

The boy ended the call without saying anything else.

Milton walked the short distance to Victoria Park and made his way to the fountain. It had been another stifling day, and the grass was parched and flattened in squares where picnic blankets had been stretched across it. The night was darkening, the wide expanses gloomy between the amber cones from the occasional streetlamp. A jumbo jet slid across the gloaming, its lights winking red as it curled away to the west. The big Estate buildings on the southern edges of the park hunched over the fringe of trees and railings, twenty-storey blocks of concrete, depressingly stolid, oppressive. It was a changing of the guard: the last joggers, cyclists and dog walkers passed around the outer circle as groups of youngsters gathered on the benches beneath the streetlamps to smoke and joke with one another. Milton noticed all of them, a habitual caution so ingrained that he did not even realise it, but he paid them no heed. He followed the outer circle around from the pub and then took the diagonal path that cut straight to the memorial and the glassy squares of water that attended it. A homeless man sat at one of the benches, massaging the ears of the thin greyhound huddling next to him. There was no one else. Milton walked slowly around the monument, making a show of examining it, before sitting at one of the empty benches to fuss with a lace that did not need tying. The water was still and flat and perfectly reflective, a rind of moon floating in the shallow depth. He set to waiting.

Twenty minutes passed before he looked up to see someone else turn off the outer path and head towards the monument. Despite the late heat, the figure was wearing a bomber jacket over the top of a hoodie, the hood pulled over the head like a cowl. Pristine white trainers almost shone in the gloom.

Milton got up from the bench and idled towards the monument. As the boy got closer, he recognised the face beneath the hood. His skin was black and perfectly smooth, his eyes and teeth shining.

"A'ight," the boy said in a low monotone, angling his head in greeting.

"Hello, Aaron."

"We can head towards the pond, over there. Ain't no one there this time of the day."

They set off side by side. Milton studied the boy through the corner of his eye. He was large, not much shorter than Milton but heavier, and he walked with a roll to his step, his head and shoulders slouched forwards. He dressed like all the others: hooded jacket, low-slung jeans with the crotch somewhere between his knees, the brand-new trainers, pieces of expensive jewellery. It was the uniform of the gang, topped off by the purple bandana knotted around his throat. He wore it all naturally. He was quiet and composed, his eyes on the path. They continued that way for a minute, Milton happy to wait until the boy was ready to speak.

They were approaching the pond when he finally spoke. "JaJa needs help," he said. "He's got in with a bad man. I tried to keep him out of it, but he ain't listening to me anymore. Ain't nothing else I can do for him."

"Is it Bizness?"

"You know him?"

"Elijah spoke to me after he was arrested. I know a little about him. Is he dangerous?"

"What, man, are you fucking high? Is he *dangerous?* Seriously? Bizness's a psycho, innit? He was always bad, but since his ego got to be like it is now, he's turned into a monster."

"What about you?"

"What about me?"

"You said you needed help, too."

He cleared his throat awkwardly. "Bizness's the same age as I am. We were at school together. We used to be tight, but we ain't no more, and he's finished with me. I dunno, the last few weeks it's as if he's been provoking me, starting hype like he wants to get a reaction. I seen it happen before. He don't let anyone get too influential, start taking his thunder, see, and then when they do, when he thinks they might be getting to be a threat"—he clicked his fingers—"then he gets rid of them. One way or another."

"And you're a threat."

"Nah, man. I ain't like that. I want out, but he don't know that."

"So tell him."

He laughed bitterly. "Don't work that way, man. You get in, you're all the way in. You ain't done until he tells you you're done. And there ain't no talking with him."

Milton reflected that he knew what that felt like. He said nothing.

"Look, it ain't about me, not really. I *am* getting out, whether he likes it or not. It's the younger who needs help."

They reached the pond. A sign describing the nearby flora and fauna had been defaced with graffiti—Milton guessed that the 925 was a rival gang tag—and the bracket that should have held the buoyancy aid had been vandalised, snapped wood showing white through the creosote like splintered bone. Pops sat down on the bench and took a joint from his pocket. "I come down here now and again," he said, lighting the joint with his lighter. "I know it sounds pathetic, but I used to be in the Scouts when I was younger. The fucking Scouts. We used to come down here once a year and dredge the whole lot. You wouldn't believe the things people used to dump—washing machines, shopping trolleys, everything covered in sludge and weeds. We always joked we'd pull out a dead body one day. What I know now, I'm half surprised we never did. There are guns and shanks in there. I know *that* for a fact."

The boy offered the joint to Milton. He shook his head. The boy shrugged and smoked hard on it instead.

"So tell me about Elijah."

"You know about what happened at the party?"

"He told me."

"There's a man Bizness wants to have shot. JaJa mention Wiley?"

"A little."

"Bizness's got beef with him. Wants him gone. That was what the club was all about. He wants JaJa to do it. He had the gun that night. I thought I'd got through to him. I sent him home when I saw what was happening. I thought he'd listen to me. Something must've happened since." His voice trailed off. Milton said nothing. "So then I got a call from Bizness yesterday to say I had to pick JaJa up and bring him to his studio. I never seen the younger like that before—he was angry, man, he had this proper screwface on like he was ready to fucking *explode*. Bizness loves that, course, and he asks him whether he's ready to do what he wants him to do with Wiley."

A dog walker skirted the far side of the pond. His dog, a pit bull heavy with a fat collar of muscle, chased the ducks into the water.

"And Elijah said he'd do it?"

Pops nodded.

Milton felt sick in the pit of his stomach. "When?"

"I don't know the details. Bizness won't tell me. I'm not that close to him, and I don't think he trusts me no more, anyway."

"Is there anything else?"

"Can't think of nothing." He paused. "Except—"

"Go on."

The boy clenched his teeth so hard that the strong line of his jaw jutted from his face. "My girl's got involved with him, too. She's vulnerable. Got a weakness for drugs, and he won't look out for her like I did. Last time I saw her, she was smoking crack with him. It'll be skag next. She'll end up on the streets for him, I seen that before, too. Or she'll end up raped or dead."

Milton sat quietly.

"So what are you going to do?"

"I don't know," Milton said.

"You said you could help me, man."

"I will. But you have to work with me."

"How?"

"First things first: you have to speak to the police."

Pops kissed his teeth. "Go to the feds? You know what would happen to me if Bizness found out I'd been grassing? I'd end up in that fucking pond with a bullet between my eyes." Pops stood abruptly. "If that's the best you can do, we're finished. Police aren't going to do nothing until JaJa's got blood on his hands and my girl is fucking dead. I'm wasting my time with this bullshit."

"Grow up, Aaron," Milton said. His voice was emotionless, iron hard and utterly authoritative. "Sit down."

He did as he was told, adding, self-pityingly, "What's the point?"

"Because I'm going to take him out of the picture," Milton said. "Tell them what happened at the club. The boy who got beaten, you saw all that?"

Pops looked down at his feet. "Yeah, man, I saw it."

"That's good," Milton said. "They'll have to take that seriously."

"What you gonna do?"

"I'm going to have a word with Bizness."

He laughed. "A word? No offence, man, but he ain't gonna listen to you."

"He'll listen to me," Milton said. "You'll have to trust me about that."

Milton stood, and they started back towards the main road. "This is what we're going to do—you're going to go to the police and tell them about what happened at the club. Leave Elijah out of it, but tell them everything else."

"It won't do nothing. It'll be my word against theirs."

"Maybe. But it will be a useful distraction."

"And then what?"

"You'll get your friend off balance just as I give him something else to think about. I want him to take me seriously when we speak. I'm going to need some information from you about how his operation is put together—who works for him, how he makes his money, where he keeps it. Can you help me with that?"

"Yeah."

Milton asked a series of questions, and Pops provided

awkward, but reasonably comprehensive, answers. Milton memorised the information, filtering it and arranging it as he built a picture of Bizness's business. The man had numerous interests in the local underworld, his malign influence stretching from drugs to prostitution and robbery. His music was clearly lucrative, but it would be as nothing compared to the profit he was turning from his illegal businesses. It was good that he was spread among different businesses and areas. That would mean that there would be plenty of vulnerable spots that Milton would be able to exploit.

"How does he communicate with everyone?"

Pops looked at him derisively. "How'd you think, man? Smoke signals? Homing pigeons? Facebook, BBM, texts. Pay-As-You-Go phones. Nothing he could ever get nailed with by the feds if they got hold of it. If he needs to meet to talk business, he'll get someone else to make the call to set it up and then arrange the meet somewhere, in the open, where it's impossible for the boi-dem to bug him. He's careful, man. Precise. Plans everything like he's in the military or something. Police think their old ways still work, but people—the real players like him—man, they been around long enough to have seen brothers get nicked all sorts of different ways, and they remember all of them. You got to get up early to pull a fast one on him."

They reached the fringe of trees that provided a canopy of leaves over the path at the outer edge of the park. The pub at the junction was growing busier, with loud customers spilling into a beer garden decorated with fairy lights.

"All right," Milton said. "That's enough for now. Go to the police tomorrow. All right?"

"Yeah," Pops said sullenly.

"Don't let me down. It's important."

"A'ight," he conceded. "Tomorrow. When will I know you've done something."

"You'll know."

Chapter Thirty-Five

MILTON TOOK the underground to Oxford Circus and emerged, blinking, into the hard bright light of another stifling summer's day. The temperature had continued its inexorable uptick into the mid-thirties, but now it had become damply humid, a wetness that quickly gathered beneath Milton's armpits and seeped down the middle of his back. The atmosphere lay heavy over the city, a woozy stupor that could only be alleviated with the inevitable thunderstorm that the forecast was predicting for later.

The Sig Sauer in its chamois holster was a heavy, warm lump beneath Milton's shoulder. The air in the tube had been cloying and dense, and Milton was pleased to have left it behind him. The confluence of Regent Street and Oxford Street was a busy scrum of sluggish tourists and frustrated office workers on their lunch breaks. Traffic jammed at the lights, taxi drivers leaning on their horns to chivvy along the busses that tarried to embark passengers. Tempers were stretched as tight as piano wire, arguments flaring and confrontations held just beneath the surface.

Milton's phone vibrated in his pocket.

"Hello?" he said.

"Is that John?"

"Who's this?"

"Rutherford. Is everything all right?"

"I'm a little busy."

"It's Saturday afternoon, I've been expecting your boy to come for training, but there ain't no sign of him. What's happening?"

"There's been a setback," Milton said as he crossed the road at the lights. "I'm taking care of it. I have to go."

Milton ended the call. He turned in the direction of the tall, crenulated finger of Centre Point. HMV was fifty yards along the road, the sound of heavy bass throbbing from the wide-open doorway into the cavernous space beyond. Milton surveyed the interior: racks of music and films; T-shirts; magazines; and, on a stage that had been erected in the middle of the shop, a table and a tall stack of CDs. A long queue of youngsters—mostly young boys, but also a handful of girls—snaked back from the table around the aisles and back almost to the entrance. Behind the table sat six members of BRAPPPP! The collection comprised the better known members of the collective: MC Mafia, Merlin, Icarus, Bredren. The female singer, Loletta, sat in the middle, haughty with her strikingly good looks, a highlight for the hormonal teenage boys who waited to be presented to her.

Milton recognised Bizness from the pictures on his Facebook and Twitter profiles. He was wearing a Chicago Bulls singlet, the top revealing an angular torso: long, skinny arms with the sharp points of his elbows and shoulders. His skin was extensively tattooed, and gold teeth glittered on the rare occasion when he disturbed the studied blankness of his expression to smile. He sat at the head of the table, the last member of the collective to receive the fans, like a king or a mafia don accepting the fealty of his subjects. They came to him, wide-eyed and open-mouthed, their CDs passed along the table with him finally adding his mark and sending them on their way. He spoke with some, bumped fists with others, but all left elated by their encounter with their hero. Milton could see, quite clearly, the power that the man—and the lifestyle he typified—had on them. He was an aspirational figure, living proof that the success he rapped about was possible to have. Milton did not respect him for this, but he recognised it and its influence, and filed it away for future reference.

A large display had been erected at the front of the shop, loaded with the collective's new album and an assortment of other merchandise. Milton took a copy of the record and a T-shirt and joined the end of the queue. It was moving slowly, and Milton guessed it would take half an hour to get to the front. He did not have the patience to wait for that, and taking advantage of the fact that it would have been difficult to imagine anyone less likely to jump the queue, he made his way to the front. "One minute," he said to the two young boys who were about to go forwards. "I just need a quick word with him. Won't hold you up long."

The table was fenced in by crowd control barriers, and two large bouncers stood guard at the entrance to the enclosure. They glared at him as he passed between them. Milton passed along the table, ignoring the others and making his way directly to Bizness.

He stopped in front of him. "Good afternoon."

Bizness bared his teeth in a feral grin, the golden caps sparkling. "Look at this." He laughed, jutting his chin towards Milton. The others laughed, too. "You in the wrong section, man. Old folks' music is over there."

"No, it's you I want to see."

Bizness threw up his hands and chuckled again. "Fine, bruv, where's your record, then? Give it here. What you want me to say?"

"I'm not here about your music."

"Come on, man, enough of this bullshit. If you ain't got nothing to sign, get the fuck out the way. Lot of brothers and sisters here been queuing hours to see us, you gonna end up causing a motherfucking riot you don't stop slowing the queue down."

"I need to talk to you. And you're going to listen to what I have to say."

"The fuck—?"

Milton ignored him. He stared at Bizness, his eyes icy and unblinking, with no life or empathy in them, until the confusion on the younger man's face faded and a cloud of anger replaced it. "I'm going to ask you nicely for two things," Milton said. "First, a woman named Laura has been associating with you. You are going to stop seeing her. If she comes to visit you, you are going to send her away."

"That's your first thing? A'ight, go on, you're an entertaining fucker. What's the second thing?"

"I know what you're planning for a young lad I know. Elijah Warriner. You call him JaJa. That is not going to happen. You are to stop seeing him, too. If I hear that you've been seen with him, there is going to be trouble. If just one hair on his head is hurt, we're going to have another conversation. But it won't be as civil as this one."

"You hear this motherfucker?" Bizness hooted at the others. They were all watching the exchange. "You asking me nicely, right? You better tell me, old man, just so I know, what you gonna do if I tell you to take your requests and shove them right up your arse? Tell me not-so-nicely? Raise your voice? Get out of here before you make me lose my temper. I ain't got time for this."

The bouncers took a step towards Milton, but Bizness stayed them with an impatient wave of his hand.

Milton did not look at them. He did not move away from the table. "You won't take me seriously now, but I'm going to give you a demonstration tonight of what will happen if you ignore my instructions. Something is going to happen to your interests, and I want you to think of me and what I've told you when you hear about it. Do you understand?"

Bizness surged up from his chair so quickly that it clattered behind him. "Do *I* understand?" Any vestige of his previous joviality was banished now, his eyes blazing with anger. "You come in here, with my bredderz around me, and you start making threats? Shit, man, you the dumbest motherfucker I ever met. I'm going to tell you one more time—get the fuck out of this shop before I throw you out my goddamn self. Do *you* understand?"

Bizness stepped around the table and took a step towards Milton. He did not flinch and, instead, fixed his pitiless stare on Bizness's face. "I've said what I needed to say. I hope you understand. I hope you remember. Do what I've told you, or the next time won't be so pleasant."

Bizness drew his fist back. Milton caught it around his ear before he could throw a punch and dug his thumb and index finger into the pressure point. Bizness yelped at the abrupt stab of white-hot pain and stumbled backwards, bouncing against the trestle table. The pile of posters tipped over, a glossy tide of paper that fanned out across the floor.

"Tonight," Milton said, smiling down at Bizness, a cold smile that was completely without humour. "Pay attention tonight. I want you to think of me."

He made his way to the front of the shop.

PART FOUR

Risky Bizness

Chapter Thirty-Six

MILTON PULLED OVER, extinguished the lights of the car, and switched off the engine. He left the radio on so that he could finish listening to the news. The bulletin reported that a protest outside a police station in Tottenham had deteriorated into a riot. Relatives of a man who had been shot by police two days earlier had gathered to protest his killing. Others had joined in, and the crowd had started to pelt the police with bottles and bricks. There were reports that cars and a double-decker bus had been set alight. Milton drew down on the cigarette he was smoking and blew the smoke out of the window. It was a hot night, close and humid. There was something in the air, a droning buzz of aggression. It wouldn't take much to ignite it.

He switched off the radio, opened the glove compartment, took out his holstered knife, and pulled up the sleeve of his right trouser leg. He wrapped the holster around his calf and fastened the Velcro straps. He checked in his mirrors that the pavement outside was empty, and satisfied that he would not be observed, he took his Sig Sauer from its holster and checked the magazine. It was full. He pumped a bullet into the chamber so that the gun was ready to fire. He slid it back beneath his armpit.

He looked around again. This part of Dalston Lane comprised a Georgian terrace of tall, two-storey houses with Victorian shop fronts that had been built over their front gardens when the railways arrived a hundred years earlier. The houses behind the shops had recently been used for social housing, but as time passed and their tenants were moved into the high-rise blocks that dominated the nearby skyline, they had been allowed to begin their long slide into decrepitude. Those that were

197

left vacant were boarded up. Damaged roofs were left unrepaired. Windows were shattered and left open to the rain. Four houses had been gutted by fire, the exposed bricks crusted black with soot and ash and the timbers exposed like cracked and broken bones. Those buildings had been condemned and demolished, tearing holes in the terrace like the teeth yanked from a cancerous mouth. Boards had been erected around the blackened remnants of the extension, and these had been scarified by graffiti and posters for illegal raves.

The Victorian extensions were occupied by local businesses. The entire house and extension at the corner of the road was a doctor's surgery, with bars on the door and the windows plastered with posters about sexually transmitted diseases and nutrition. Next to that was an Indian restaurant, then a shop selling musical instruments, a Laundromat, a business selling second-hand kitchen equipment, then a newsagent. Adjacent to that a façade announced the Star Bakery, but the shutters had been in place for so long that the rust had fastened the padlocks to their tethers. The property alongside had seen its extension occupied by a squatter. It had been a bicycle shop years before, the block typography of its original frontage still visible despite the etiolation of the weather and the fumes from the busy road. The wide picture windows were obscured by sheets of newspaper and a printed notice that had been glued to the door declared that the squatters enjoyed rights of occupation and could not be evicted without a court order.

Milton scanned it all quickly. The terrace behind the squat was one of Bizness's most profitable crack houses. Pops had told him everything. Heroin and crack were sold around the clock, rain or shine. Most of the customers were poor locals, drawn in from the surrounding Estates, but a significant minority of the customers were white, very often professional and middle class.

Milton got out of the car. He went around to the back,

opened the boot, and took out a jerrycan that he had filled with petrol from the garage on Mare Street. There was no sense in making his entry through the front door. It looked as if it was locked, just enough of a delay to allow for escape should the police arrive for a clean-up. Milton had another idea. The terrace was listed, and the plans were available online. He had visited the library and downloaded them, reviewing them before he came out. He knew that there was another way in. He followed the road to the junction, taking a right turn and then, before he reached a tawdry pub, another sharp right. A narrow cul-de-sac led around the back of the terrace. Overflowing dustbins were stacked up against the wall, and detritus had been allowed to gather in the gutter. Each house had a rear entrance, and the one that served the crack house was wide open. Silly boys.

Milton took out his Sig and went inside. The first room used to be a kitchen. Old appliances had been left to rot, with anything that could be easily removed long since sold for scrap. The walls were partially stripped and scabbed with lead paint, and the remnants of a twee wallpaper that depicted an Alpine scene had been left to peel away like patches of dead, flaking skin. Empty cardboard boxes and fast-food wrappers were scattered on the floor. A single man, strung out and emaciated, was slumped against the wall. He was unconscious, and Milton would not have been able to say whether he was dead or alive. He heard low conversation from the front of the house and set off towards it. The junkie's arm swept around sharply and his eyes swam with drunken stupor, but he paid Milton no heed as he passed through the room.

He moved through a hallway with a flight of stairs leading up to the first floor. Patterned linoleum was scattered with drug paraphernalia. A mattress rested upright against the wall. Another junkie was asleep on the floor. Milton tightened the grip on the butt of his pistol as he stepped carefully around him.

The noises were coming from the front extension. Milton paused in the shadows at the doorway to assess his surroundings. The only furniture was a sofa and a huge, monolithic television. It was a big unit with a cathode ray tube, and it had been left on, badly tuned, scenes from a soap occasionally resolving out of the distortion of static. The front door was ahead of him, barricaded with an old sideboard that had been propped against it. Vivid wallpaper with a woodland design had been hung on the wall, the paper stained yellow by months of smoke. There was no ventilation, and the atmosphere was thick and heavy, woozy, a sickly miasma.

There were a dozen people inside the room. Men and women, mostly supine, their heads lolling insensately, unfocussed eyes lazily flicking across the television screen. They were all black, dressed cheaply, feeble and thin. Plastic bottles were arranged in neat rows, each of them full of urine. A collection of shoes, random and unpaired, was pushed into one corner. Empty vials of crack had been ground underfoot, crunching like fresh snow as the addicts shuffled across the room to the two men who were sat on the sofa. They were clear-eyed and moved with crisp purpose as they exchanged vials of crack for their customers' crumpled banknotes. They were younger than their patrons; Milton guessed in their late teens, not long out of school. They were dressed in low-slung jeans, the crotch hanging down between the knees, there were diamond ear studs and golden chains, and both wore the colourful purple bandana of the LFB around their necks. These were the dealers, one step up from the shotters, Bizness's representatives on the street. They sold the drugs and then protected the house so that their customers had somewhere to get high and then buy from them again.

Milton shuddered in revulsion.

He assessed the situation. The junkies were too far gone to pose any kind of problem, and he discounted them. The two dealers looked fit and strong, and there was a kitchen knife resting on the arm of the sofa. That would be a problem if they could get to it before he had disabled them. He could not discount the possibility that they were armed, either.

Milton suddenly decided.

He sprang across the room and lashed out with the barrel of his pistol. He struck the bigger of the two men across the temple, a stunning blow that dropped him to his knees. The second man stretched across the sofa, but Milton had anticipated his move, firing out a kick that struck him in the side of the chest and brought a whistle of pain from him. The man's hand fell short, the knife dislodged from its perch by the attempt. Milton's hands grabbed the man in two places—bunching into his singlet and by waist of his trousers—and he heaved him off the sofa and onto the floor. The sharp edges of crushed vials and syringes bit into his face and throat as he tried to find his feet. Milton followed him to the floor, pinning the point of his knee between his shoulder blades and pressing down. He took the Sig and pressed the barrel into the cornrows on the top of the man's head.

"Pay attention," he said. "I want you to deliver a message to Bizness. Tell him that this is what I said would happen. If he doesn't do what I told him to do, tell him that this will keep happening. One crack house at a time. Do you understand? Nod if you do."

The man jerked his head awkwardly against the floor.

"All right. You're going to get up now, and you are going to clear these people out. Then you grab your friend over there and get him out, too. If you do anything foolish, I'll shoot you. Understand?"

Milton got up and backed away. He took the jerrycan and poured the petrol across the floor, on the sofa, sloshing it across the thick curtains. If the boy needed motivation, Milton's self-evident plan was it. He did as he was told, ushering the crackheads out the back and then returning to collect his friend, propping him up and helping him away.

The room quickly stank of petrol. Milton took out his lighter and thumbed it to flame. He played the lighter over a rag, and blue-white flame consumed it hungrily. Milton dropped it onto the sofa, and with a quiet exhalation, the fabric caught fire. The flame spread quickly over the upholstery, stretching higher and higher until it started to scorch the ceiling. It raced across the floor to the walls, a quiet crackling that quickly became a hungry roar, with black smoke billowing up to the roof and then spewing back down again.

Milton went out into the alley gun-first, only holstering the Sig Sauer when he saw that both boys had fled. He walked briskly, making his way back onto the main road and to his car. He unlocked the door and slipped inside.

Across the street, the squat was burning fiercely.

Chapter Thirty-Seven

CHRISTOPHER CALLAN paused outside Flat 609, and then, satisfied that it was the correct address, he knocked firmly, three times, on the door. He heard sounds of activity inside: the chink of pieces of crockery being knocked together, a door opening on a rusty hinge, and then footsteps approaching. A woman opened the door. Callan guessed that she was in her early thirties. Dark black hair, smooth skin, wide eyes, a slender build. She was wearing the uniform of a fast-food chain.

"Yes?"

Callan smiled. "Excuse me. Sorry for disturbing you. Are you Sharon Warriner?

Her eyes narrowed. "Who's asking?"

"I'm Detective Constable Travis."

Her face fell. "It's Elijah, isn't it?"

"Elijah?"

"My boy—what's he done?"

"No, Mrs Warriner, it's not that. Nothing to do with Elijah. Would it be all right if I came inside for a minute?"

"What's it about?"

She had the usual suspicion of the police, Callan saw. It was to be expected in a place like this. He reached into his jacket pocket and took out the file picture of Milton. "Do you know this man?"

She became confused as she studied the picture. "That's John."

"John Milton?"

"Yes. I don't understand. What's he done?"

"Can I come in, please? Just five minutes."

She reluctantly stood aside and let him through. They passed through the small hallway and into the lounge. It was a large room, the décor a little tatty and tired, an old sofa, a table with four chairs, a flat-screen television, PlayStation games scattered across the floor. Sharon stood stiffly; her suspicion had not been assuaged, Callan could see that, and he was not going to be invited to sit. Fair enough. He wouldn't be long. In some ways, he had already seen enough.

"How do you know Mr Milton?"

"He's a friend."

"How did you meet him?"

She paused, her face washed by a moment of worried memory. "I just did," she said. "What's this about, please?"

"What's he doing here?"

"I told you, he's a friend. He's helping me with my son."

"How?"

"I'm sorry, Detective, but I don't understand how any of that is relevant. What has he done wrong?"

"I'm afraid I can't tell you that. Please—how is he helping you?"

She waved her hand agitatedly. "My boy, Elijah, he can be a bit of a handful. Headstrong, like they all are at his age. Mr Milton is"—she paused, searching for the right word, and then repeated the same one again—"helping me with him, like I said. I don't understand why you're asking me—has he done something wrong? Should I be worried?"

Should she be concerned? Callan suppressed the smirk. She had no idea. None at all. "No," he said, "there's no reason to be concerned. I'm sorry I can't say any more than that."

She made for the door. "Then I'm sorry, Detective, if you can't tell me what Mr Milton has done, then I'm not sure what else I can do to help." She opened the door. "Do you mind? I have to get ready for bed. I start work early in the mornings."

"Of course," Callan said. "Thank you for your help.

Sorry again for disturbing you."

He looked around again as he allowed her to shepherd him to the door. Unpaid bills on the floor. Paint peeling from the walls. Bars across the windows. What was Number One doing in a place like this, with a woman like this? He supposed that she was pretty, after a fashion, but that wasn't a good enough reason to explain anything. The only thing that made any sense at all was Control's contention that something had broken inside Number One's head, and that, if it was true, would not be good for him at all. He politely bid the woman good night and walked over to the balcony as she shut the door behind him. He rested his elbows on the balustrade and looked out over the East End. It was a hot night, the air torpid and sluggish. Sirens wailed in the streets nearby, and a group of youngsters had gathered in the open space below, their raucous laughter reaching up to him. Callan did not understand any of it. His task was to gather evidence, not to draw conclusions, yet he could not help but wonder: what on earth had happened to Number One?

Chapter Thirty-Eight

STOKE NEWINGTON POLICE STATION was a modern three-story building with wide windows on the ground floor. They were all lit up, lights burning behind them. Pops walked towards the entrance but did not go in. They had one of those old-fashioned blue lanterns hanging from the wall, and he carried on beneath it and further along the road before he stopped, crossed over, and headed back in the same direction again. He had repeated the pattern for the last half an hour, passing up and down the tree-lined road, thinking about choices and consequences. What he was about to do would change everything for him. There was no point in pretending that it wouldn't, and the gravity of what he was contemplating frightened him. If he did as he had been asked to do, there would be no turning back for him. His life would be yanked off course and sent in a different direction.

There was a Turkish barber shop opposite the station. He sat down, resting his back against the window, and took the half-finished joint from behind his ear. He held it in the flame of his lighter and toked on it until it caught, drawing in a big breath of smoke. He held it in his lungs for a long moment and then blew it away. He needed to settle down, to relax. He drew his legs up to his chest and leant forwards, resting his forehead against his knees. He was hopelessly on edge.

Choices. He stared across the slow-moving traffic to the lit windows of the station. He knew that speaking to the police was a fundamental thing. It would make him a grass. He was at a junction; consequences one way, but consequences the other way, too. He had thought about it for long enough, before he met Elijah, before Bizness turned his back on him, before Laura, before Milton.

There were always choices, even when you thought there were none. It had been his choice to join the LFB, to start mugging and steaming, to start selling drugs. There had been different choices at every point, but the problem was that those alternatives were harder or less lucrative or less cool than the life he could have on the street. He had told the youngers that came up that the easy way was the best way, but he had always known that the stories he told them were lies. He had always known. He lied to them and to himself. He had persuaded himself that he was right, but now, well, now there was nothing else for it but to face the truth.

Because the truth of it was that there was always a choice.

The shopkeeper had a small television above the counter, and Pops could hear it through the open door. There was nonsense in Tottenham tonight, brothers getting together and wrecking the place. He could hear the reporter speaking from the scene, the sound of yelling in the background, things getting smashed up. Pops listened absently to it for a moment, not really paying attention, toking on the joint and letting the smoke slowly seep out from his nostrils. He finished it, sucking the flame down to his fingertips, and dropped it to the ground, grinding the roach underfoot.

He crossed the street, pushed open the door, and went inside.

A female officer was on duty.

"How can we help you?" she said.

"I want to talk someone about Israel Brown."

The woman looked at him askance. "Who's that, then?"

"You probably know him as Bizness. The rapper. He beat a boy half to death in Chimes last week. I was there. I saw it all."

Chapter Thirty-Nine

BIZNESS STARED out of the tinted window of the BMW at the burnt-out house. A fire engine was still at the scene, a fireman playing water over the smoking wreckage. The ceiling of the extension had collapsed, and the window had buckled and shattered from the heat, revealing the blackened mess beyond. He didn't own the house, and it wasn't worth shit, anyway, but that was not the point. It was Bizness's property. It served a purpose, and it made him a lot of paper. Now he was going to have to find somewhere else, spread the word, get things going again. It would cost him time and lose him money.

"Mother*fucker*," he said, slamming his fist against the steering wheel.

Mouse was in the passenger seat. "We got a problem, Bizness."

"You think? Shut the fuck up, Mouse. You don't know shit."

Levelz and Tookie, the two boys who had been working the squat, had told him what had happened. The man had attacked the place just after midnight, taking them by surprise. He had beaten them both, passed on his message, cleared the junkies out, and fired the place.

There would be a price to pay for that.

The door behind them opened, and a man slid into the seat. Bizness glanced up in the rear-view mirror. Detective Inspector Wilson glared back into his eyes.

"What's going on, lads? Who did this?"

"Someone who's gonna wish they never got involved with me. You don't need to worry about it."

"Are you sure about that? Because I'm pretty sure that when the fire service confirm that this is arson, there's going to be an investigation."

"Take it easy, a'ight? I know who did it. And I'm gonna sort it."

"You better make sure that you do. You've got to keep a lid on things. Having one of your places go up like it's bonfire night isn't good for my blood pressure. You want to operate around here without any trouble from me, you keep things quiet."

"Nah, man, me operating around here depends on you getting your cut every Friday."

Wilson ignored him and stabbed a finger against the window. "Things like that don't give me much confidence, son. I turn a blind eye to you because I don't have time to start worrying about lads from outside the postcode causing trouble. There are plenty of others who can keep a lid on things if you can't."

"That you making a threat?"

"No, that's me telling you that it's going to cost you ten from now on if you want to stay in business."

"Fuck, man, don't gimme that shit. You're doubling the fee?"

"There a problem with that?"

Bizness gripped the steering wheel hard. "Nah," he said. "Ten's fine."

"There are other benefits to working with me," Wilson said.

"Yeah? Like what?"

"Advanced warnings. You've got more trouble coming your way. Your boy Pops?"

"What about him?"

"He came into the nick last night. Says he's willing to give evidence against you."

"Against me?"

"So he says."

"For what?"

"Beating up that kid in Chimes."

"Man, that was nothing."

"Tell that to the kid's parents. He's still in hospital."

"Pops don't got shit."

"He's saying he was there."

"And he's gonna talk?"

"That's what I heard."

Bizness glowered through the tinted windscreen, watching as the passing cars slowed so that their drivers could gawp at the smoking wreck of the crack house. The problem with the man who did that and now this? Timing was bad. Timing was awful. Bizness nodded grimly. Fair enough, he thought. Timing was awful, but sometimes that's the way it was, the hand you got dealt. They were two small problems, and they could both be sorted. He started to work out angles, tactics.

"You've got to keep on top of things, son," Wilson said. "Do I have a reason to be concerned?"

"No," he said, gritting his teeth. "No reason. It'll all get sorted."

Chapter Forty

PINKY REACHED the door to Bizness's studio and pressed the intercom.

"Yeah?"

"I'm here to see Bizness."

"He ain't in. Go away."

"Don't talk chat, bruv. I saw him come in."

"Piss off, younger."

"Nah, it's about what happened at HMV yesterday. I got some information."

"You can tell me."

"Don't think so," he said. "I'll tell him myself, or I won't bother."

There was a click as the intercom was switched off. Pinky paused, holding his breath. The intercom crackled into life again. "Alright. Come up."

The lock buzzed, and the door clicked open.

Pinky climbed the stairs, the framed BRAPPPP! pictures on the walls on either side of him. He was nervous. Bizness had a reputation, a bad one, everyone knew that, and part of that reputation was that he could be unpredictable. All the stories Pinky had heard about him were at the front of his mind. He wasn't stupid, he knew plenty of them were made up for the sake of his image, but there were others he knew were true, and it was those that he was thinking about now.

He stepped through into the large room at the top of the stairs. Bizness was on the sofa, his feet propped up against the edge of the coffee table. A flat-screen television was fixed to the wall and tuned in to Sky News. Pinky had heard all about the riots that had started in Tottenham last night. He had been excited by it, at the idea of looting all those shops. Now it seemed like the trouble had spread to Enfield and Brixton. Footage from a helicopter showed a police car on fire.

"What's your name, boy?"

"Pinky."

"Alright, Pinky, you better have a good reason for coming up here. I'm a busy man, lot on my plate. I ain't got no time for signing no autographs."

"I'm not here for that," he said.

"Then you better tell me what you are here for."

"I got some information," he said. "That old man who got into it with you at the record signing—I saw it on YouTube."

"What?"

Pinky took out his phone. He had already cued up the video, and now he hit play. The video rolled; someone in the shop had filmed the conversation between Bizness and the old man. The camera was close enough to see the expressions on their faces, the implacability of the man and Bizness's growing anger. Their argument reached its crescendo, and Bizness lost his balance, stumbling backwards and tripping. The sound of laughter came as he sprawled amid the spilled posters and CDs.

"Who the fuck uploaded that?" he spat, grabbing the phone from out of Pinky's hand. There were several pages of comments, most of them jokes at Bizness's expense, and Pinky hoped that he would not read them. He did not; he played the video again and then tossed the phone back, his eyes flaring with anger.

"It's about the man," Pinky said.

Bizness's eyes narrowed, and the animation washed from his face. Pinky realised he would have to tread carefully. "Go on, then—don't just sit there, tell me what you know."

"There's a boy on the Estate, you've been asking him to do stuff for you—JaJa?"

"Yeah. What about him?"

"I was outside his mum's flat the day before yesterday.

It was in the morning. Early—we'd been up late, selling shit to the cats, we was just about to call it a night. Anyway, right, I saw Elijah coming out, looking all upset and shit, and then, right after him, out comes that man. It was definitely him, no doubt. He was half-undressed, had his shirt off."

"What you saying? It's Elijah's dad?"

"Nah, his dad's in prison."

"So who is it?"

"Dunno. His mum's a skanky ho—some bloke she picked up, I reckon."

Bizness zoned out as he tried to remember what the man had said to him. "He told me to stay away from the boy," he recalled.

"Him and Popa's bitch," Mouse offered.

"You know anything else?" Bizness asked.

"Nah, that's it. I thought it could be useful so I came over."

"It is useful, younger. I appreciate that, you making the effort. You done good."

"There was another reason for coming," he said. It had gone as well as he could have expected, and now here it was, the opportunity he had been hoping for.

"Go on," Bizness said sceptically.

"I been thinking," Pinky said. "I know you asked JaJa to do some things for you." He left the "things" vague, but he knew all about the incident at the launch party. "Between you and me, boy ain't up to much. He's just a little kid, gets scared about things."

"You ain't that much older yourself, younger."

"Nah, true enough, but me and him ain't got nothing in common. There ain't nothing you could ask me to do for you that I wouldn't get done. You know what I'm saying? You want to ask around, people will tell you. I'm reliable. I don't mess no one about. When I say I'm going to do something, I do it. You don't need to worry about it, it gets sorted, you know what I'm saying?"

"That so?"

"Yeah," he said. "Thing is, I'm looking for a change. I'm ambitious, man, and I'm getting bored hanging around in the same old crew. I want to do mad shit, but Pops don't have his heart in it no more. We just hang around these ends doing the same tired old shit day after day. The way I see it, I could do that kind of stuff with you."

Bizness looked over at Mouse and grinned. "The balls on this one, eh? Reminds me of what I used to be like."

"All you need to do is give me a chance—I promise I won't let you down."

"You don't take no for an answer, do you?"

Pinky shook his head.

"A'ight, I'll tell you what, younger, there is something you could do for me."

"Yeah?"

"Yeah." He reached into his pocket and pulled out a crumpled ten-pound note. "First of all, though, I'm hungry—go down to Maccy D's and get me a Ready Meal, a'ight? Here." He handed him the note as the other boys started to laugh.

Pinky felt the colour running into his cheeks. He pretended he wasn't bothered. "Alright."

"Big Mac and a Coke. And be quick. I ain't eaten all day."

Chapter Forty-One

POPS CAME out of the takeaway with a bucket of fried chicken. The boys were waiting outside, arranged around a bench opposite the parade of shops. Little Mark was cleaning his new Nikes with a piece of tissue; Kidz, Chips and Pinky were hooting at a couple of pretty girls outside the launderette; and JaJa was sitting facing half away from them, a scowl on his face. They were drinking a six-pack of beer that Little Mark had stuffed down the front of his jacket in the mini-market when they went in for chocolate earlier. Pops put the bucket down on the seat and took off the lid. He helped himself to a breast and bit into it. It was crisp, with just the right amount of grease to it. The others helped themselves.

"I'm hungry," Little Mark said.

"You're fat," Chips retorted.

"Piss off," he said, but his eyes shone. Little Mark didn't care if they teased him about his weight. He knew he was fat; he couldn't deny it, and he didn't care. He liked being the centre of attention.

"I'm bored," Chips said.

Kidz looked up. "What we gonna do, then?"

"Dunno."

"Go see a film?"

"Nah. Nothing on. All shit."

"What then?"

Chips raised his voice. "See if those fine girls fancy hanging out?"

The girls heard him, snorted with derision, and disappeared into the launderette.

"Something else, then."

"Dunno."

Pops looked at Elijah. He glared back at him sullenly.

His eyes were piercing, and for a moment, he wondered if there could have been any way that he could have found out about his visit to the station. No, he thought after a moment of worried consideration. No, there couldn't be. He had been careful. They would all know eventually, but not yet.

Little Mark spoke through a mouthful of chicken. "We could go and look at that crack house—you seen that shit?"

"That place Bizness had?"

"So they say," Chips said.

"In Dalston?" Kidz asked.

Chips nodded.

"What happened?"

"Burned to the ground," Little Mark replied, fragments of fried chicken spilling out of the corner of his mouth. "Some guy turns up, beats the shit out of the two boys who were there to look after the place, pours petrol around the place, and sets it off." He spread his fingers wide. "Whoosh."

"Who was it?"

"Fuck knows. Some cat, probably, didn't have any money for his fix and went mental or something."

"Whoever that cat is, man, I would not want to be him when Bizness gets hold of him."

"That shit's going to be epic."

"*Medieval.*"

"He should film it, stick it on YouTube. That's viral, innit."

"Stop it happening again."

"Nah," Little Mark decided. "Can't be bothered. Dalston's too far, and I'm still hungry."

"You always hungry, fatman."

"It wasn't no cat who did it," Chips said. "You hear what happened at the BRAPPPP! signing? Some old guy, like in his forties or some shit like that, he turns up in the queue and basically calls Bizness out."

"You see it?"

"Someone put it on YouTube. The old man goes toe-to-toe with him, stone cold, they have words, and he does this ninja death grip on his hand. Bizness ends up on his arse in front of everyone. What I heard, they reckon the guy who did that is the same guy who burned down the crack house."

"He's a dead man," Kidz said.

"You ain't wrong."

Elijah gave out an exasperated sigh.

"You hear about it, JaJa?" Chips said.

"Yeah."

"What you reckon?"

"I reckon none of you know what you're talking about."

Pops watched the five of them, the easy banter that passed between them. Only JaJa was quiet, the rest joshing and ribbing each other without affectation or agenda. They were what they were: young boys caught in the awkward hinterland between being children and men. He felt a moment of mawkishness. He had grown up with them. They were his boys, yet his days as one of them were limited now. When they learned that he was going to give evidence against Bizness, they would shun him as surely as if he had thumbed his nose at them personally. He would be a grass, and there would be beef between them, serious hype, and things could never be the same after that.

"Pops, man," Kidz said as he started on his second breast, grease smeared around his mouth. "What we gonna do?"

His train of thought depressed him. "I don't know," he said, his voice blank. "Do what you want."

"We could steam a bus?"

"Up to you, innit."

"What are you doing?"

"Stuff."

Little Mark looked at his BlackBerry. "Get this," he said. "Just got a message from my boy in Hackney. You know all that rioting and shit in Tottenham?"

"And Brixton."

"Yeah, now it's spreading all over. There's a big crowd getting together on the High Street. Hundred kids already and no sign of boi-dem anywhere. It's kicking off."

"Fuck we waiting here for?" Chips said. "That's what we doing tonight, right? Let's breeze."

They all rose.

"You coming, Pops?" Little Mark asked.

"Nah, bruv. I got things to do."

Pinky stopped and looked at him quizzically. "Where you heading?"

"Homerton."

"Going through the park?"

Pops said he was.

"I'll come with you."

"You're not going with the others?"

"Nah, bruv. I'm not into rioting and shit. Waste of time."

Pops shrugged. He would have preferred to walk to college on his own, but he wasn't ashamed of it any more. Who cared if they knew? And Pinky, more than the rest of them, needed to see that there were other alternatives to the street. Perhaps it would help give him a nudge to do something else. And if it didn't, if he thought worse of him, well, Pops didn't care about that any longer.

"A'ight," he said to the others. "Laters."

They bumped fists, and Pops had another moment of sentimental affection for them all. He quickly recalled some of the things they had done together. Long, hot summer nights, smoking weed in the park, watching the world go by. He smiled at the memories. Another world. It was all finished and gone now.

With Pinky loping along beside him, he set off towards the park.

Chapter Forty-Two

IT WAS SEVEN O'CLOCK and still bright and warm.

"Where you going, then?" Pinky asked him.

"Like I said, I got an appointment."

"Yeah?"

"That's right."

"Who with?"

Pops sighed. "No one, Pinky. I'm going to college."

"Course you are," Pinky replied, managing a wide grin.

"I'm serious."

"Bollocks, man."

"Twice a week. Night classes."

"Serious?"

Pinky was about to laugh again, but he saw that Pops was staring at him darkly and stifled it.

College, he thought. What was the point of that? Studying, books, teachers—he had no interest in any of it. Pinky had always been a little slow in school. It wasn't as if he had never tried. He had given it a go when he was younger, but it didn't seem to matter what he did; the others were always better at reading and numbers and shit, and coming bottom of the class again and again got to him eventually. In the end, he had just stopped bothering. Stopped going. The school did nothing about it, his mums didn't care either way, and no one seemed to miss him. Might as well just be philosophical about it. You couldn't be good at everything. He'd concentrate on the stuff he knew he was good at: robbing, tiefing, shotting, frightening people. Those were his skills. He'd work on them, get better at it. That was where the money was. That was where the power and respect were, too.

"Why's it so funny?" Pops asked him.

"Dunno. It's just—well, it's just not something I can

219

imagine any of the others being interested in, that's all."

Pops snapped, "Because they're not interested means it's a bad idea?"

"Dunno," he said, surprised at the heat in Pops's voice.

"So what's your plan? You must have one. Or you planning on being on the street all your life?"

"Hadn't really thought about it," he said. "It's not so bad, though, is it? I get to hang out with my mates, and I still make more money in a week than my mums does in a month."

Pinky could see that Pops was about to say something else, but he sighed and shook his head instead. "Never mind." He sighed. "You're right. School isn't for everyone."

They walked along the Old Ford Road and crossed at the shops. A police car, its lights flashing and siren wailing, rushed by at high speed. They walked up to the roundabout and crossed there, too, passing through the park gates and heading north. There were fewer people in the park than on the street. Pinky looked around. It was quiet. He felt his fingers start to tremble.

"You can disagree if you want, but if you want to get on in life, you need to have the grades."

"That's what you're doing? Exams and shit?"

"Yes."

"For what?"

"For a job. Work."

Pinky gestured around at the park and the streets beyond. "You don't want to do this no more?"

"Everything comes to an end."

Pinky had looked up to Pops when he started to make his way on the street. He had been a powerful figure, successful and feared, not afraid to get stuck in so that he could get what he wanted. He was what Pinky would have considered a role model. He couldn't believe how wrong he'd been about that. Bizness had shown him. Pops was nothing to look up to. He wanted out. He couldn't hold on to his woman. He was a fassy. A sell-out, a fraud who didn't deserve anyone's respect. Choosing to go back to school was just another example. And if what Bizness had said was true: going to the police? He felt sick when he thought about the way he had aspired to be like him. How could he have got it so wrong? He was nothing to look up to. He was nothing at all.

"Yeah," he said. "I guess."

"What are you going to do with your life?"

"Smoke a lot of weed." He laughed. "Work on my rep, make sure everyone knows who I am."

"Can't do this forever, man."

"Why not?"

"You just can't."

"Nah," Pinky said, suddenly overcome with the urge to put Pops in his place. "You're talking shit, man. Just because you ain't got the stomach for it no more don't mean the rest of us have to feel the same way."

He had never spoken to Pops like that before. A week ago, he would not have had the nerve, but he knew more now. There was no reason to fear him. And he didn't need to listen to his sanctimonious nonsense.

Pops gave a gentle shake of his head but did not rise to it.

They walked on.

Pinky's bag bounced against his hip as he walked. He held it in place with his right hand; it was heavy, and it felt solid.

"Where you going, anyway?" Pops said. "Following me around like a bad smell."

"Just fancied a walk," he said. "Nice night, innit?"

He stopped, letting Pops take several steps forward until he was next to a park bench.

He opened the bag and reached inside. He took out the gun that Bizness had given him. It was a Russian gun, an old Makarov. He had practiced with it in the quieter part of the park, getting used to the weight of it, how it felt in his hand.

"Oi," he said. "Pops."

Pops stopped and turned. "What is it?"

Pinky pulled the gun up and levelled his arm, bracing his shoulder for the recoil.

"This is from Bizness," he said, just as he had been told.

Pops started to say something, but he didn't, his voice just tailing off. Perhaps he was going to explain, to apologize, to beg for his life, but what he must have seen in Pinky's dead eyes made it all useless. Maybe he just accepted it. The gun cracked viciously again and again—four times—and then fell silent. Pops fell back against the bench and sat for a moment, looking up at the darkening sky. His fingers opened in a spasm as he clutched at his chest. Then his head fell sideways and then the right shoulder and finally the whole upper part of his body lurched over the arm of the bench as if he were going to be sick. But there was only a short scrape of his heels on the ground and then no other movement.

Pinky looked around. There was no one near them. He started to giggle, nervous at first and then faster and faster, unable to control it. He tugged his hood down low over his face and set off, crossing the wide-open space at a jog and then cutting through a straggled hedge and into a patch of scrub beyond. He paused there, taking a moment to catch his breath.

His heart was racing. He had done it. He had lost his cherry, killed a man.

Breathing deep and even, but trembling with adrenaline, he clambered over a wall and dropped down onto the pavement beyond. As he set off back towards the Estate, he heard the sound of police sirens in the distance.

Chapter Forty-Three

MILTON SAT in the front room with the pieces of his Sig Sauer arranged on the table before him. He often stripped and cleaned the gun whenever he needed to think; there was something meditative about the process. He removed the magazine and racked the slide, ejecting the chambered round. He disassembled the gun, removing the slide, barrel, recoil spring and receiver, wiping away the dust from the barrel with a bore brush before squeezing tiny drops of oil onto the moving parts. The routine had been driven into him over the course of long years. He had seen men who had been shot after their weapons jammed; two of his own victims had been damned by their bad habits when they might otherwise have held an advantage over him.

He had piggy-backed next door's Wi-Fi and was streaming the radio through his phone. The riots had spread to Hackney now, too, and there were reports of disturbances in Birmingham and Manchester. Milton thought of Elijah and hoped that he was sensible enough to stay out of the way. Aaron had left him a message earlier in the day: he had not noticed any real change in the boy; he was still hanging out with the other boys although he was, Aaron thought, quieter than usual. He said that he seemed to be angry about something but that he had not spoken with him to confirm it. As far as he knew, there had been no new contact with Bizness.

Milton tapped out one of his Russian cigarettes and lit up. He considered Bizness. Last night's message would have been received, and if he had any sense, it would have been listened to. Perhaps he had taken Milton's advice and was going to stay away from Elijah. Perhaps. Milton wet an ear bud with cleaning solvent and inserted it into the breech end of the barrel, working it back and forth and swabbing out the chamber and bore. Perhaps not. No, Bizness was not the kind of man who would back down. He had made his point, but he had anticipated that it would be necessary to underline it. Another demonstration would need to be made. Milton looked over at the scrap of paper on the arm of the sofa. Aaron had provided the address for a second crack house. He planned to take it down tonight.

He heard the boom of heavy bass from a car stereo, gradually increasing as it neared the house. The thudding rattled the windows in their frames. He pulled aside the net curtains to look at where it was coming from. A car with blacked-out windows was moving slowly along the side of the road, and as he watched, the passenger-side window rolled down. The car drew up alongside the house. A figure leant out of the window, bringing up a long assault rifle. With something approaching a mixture of professional curiosity and alarm, Milton recognised the distinctive shape of an AK-47. The car passed into the golden cone of light from a streetlamp, and Milton could see Bizness' face, his features contorted with a grin of excitement that looked feral.

Milton threw himself to the floor as the AK fired. The glass in the window was thrown out by the first few rounds, splashing down around his head and shoulders and shattering against the floorboards. Bullets studded against the thin partition walls, dusty puffs of plaster exhaling from each impact. The mirror above the fireplace was struck, cracking down the middle with each half falling down separately against the mantelpiece. A jagged track was pecked across the ceiling, more plaster shaken out to drift down like the thinnest of snow. The thin door was struck, the cheap MDF torn up and spat out.

Outside, someone screamed. Milton crawled behind the sofa, pressing himself into cover. The table with the pieces of his Sig was out of reach; he dared not make an attempt to retrieve it, and even if he had been able to get it and assemble it, he would have been badly outgunned. The AK had been fitted with a drum, and he knew that it would have around seventy-five rounds if it was full to capacity. At a standard rate of fire the gun would chew through that in fifteen seconds.

As he was considering this, the shooting stopped.

He stayed where he was, waiting. Residual bits of glass fell from the wrecked frame, tinkling as they shattered against the floorboards. Milton's breath was quick. He did not move.

He heard a loud whoop of exultation, a car door opening, and then—panic spilling into his gut—he saw a small metallic object sail through the smashed window, bounce against the wall and fall back, landing on the sofa with a soft thump. A second followed. Milton knew what they were and scrambled up, desperately trying to find purchase for his feet as he threw himself out of the door and into the hall. The first grenade detonated with an ear-splitting bang, ripping the door from its hinges and sending a thousand razor-sharp fragments of shrapnel around the room. The second exploded seconds later. Shards sliced through the partition wall and into the hall, spiking into the masonry like tiny daggers. Milton shielded his head with his hands, pieces of debris bouncing off him.

He heard a car door slam shut, an engine rev loudly, and then the shriek of rubber as tyres bit into the road. He opened the bullet-shredded front door and stepped out onto the street. The BMW was speeding towards Bethnal Green, turning the corner and disappearing from view. Pedestrians on the other side of the road were staring in open-mouthed stupefaction at the scene before them. Residents of the block opposite were hanging out of their windows. The house had been sprayed with bullets. Most had passed through the window, but others had lodged in the brickwork. Dozens of spent cartridges glittered on the road and the pavement, a host of red-hot slugs, many still rolling down towards the gutter.

Milton was not interested in discussing what had happened with the police, and there was no reason for him to stay. He quickly piled his clothes into his bag, collected the pieces of the gun, shut the door, got into his Volvo and set off.

Chapter Forty-Four

MOUSE WAS DRIVING the new whip, the BMW. Bizness was in the passenger seat, and Pinky was in the back. Traffic was crawling along Kingsland Road. There were youngers everywhere, hundreds of them, kids from the gangs with their faces covered and white kids you'd never normally see this deep in the heart of Hackney. As he watched, he saw different kinds of people in the crowd: professionals in suits, older people, plenty of girls, not so much watching the boys as involved up to their necks themselves. Ahead, they saw two boys in tracksuits with hoods pulled up over their caps dragging an industrial bin into the middle of the road. Another boy poured something into the bin and then dropped a flame into it. The fire caught quickly, and in seconds, a powerful blaze was reaching up to the roofs of the three-storey buildings on either side of the road. Opposite them, a single hooded boy stood in the middle of a trashed Foot Locker, empty boxes and single, unpaired trainers strewn all about him. An old man, must have been seventy, grabbed a hat and bolted. A kid came out from the warehouse, balancing eight boxes of shoes. Ahead of them, a people carrier with a disabled badge in the window pulled over, and the grown man waiting for it quickly filled it with protein shakes from Holland & Barrett. Two girls pushed a wheelie bin full of the clothes they had taken from one of the local boutiques. Bizness had been following events on Twitter all afternoon: kids were rioting in Tottenham, Brixton, Enfield, Edmonton, Wood Green, all over London. And the feds were nowhere.

The car came to a halt. "Fucking *look* at this," Mouse exclaimed. "Shit is mental."

Bizness couldn't keep his eyes off the scene before

him: a group of boys had gathered along the same side of a Ford Mondeo, heaving it in unison until they had it on two wheels and then, with a final effort, tipped it onto its side. They hooted in satisfaction before moving on to the Vauxhall parked ahead of it. Bizness grinned at it all. "Boi-dem shoot a brother like they did, what they expect? This was always gonna happen. People got no money, got nothing to do. It's been a riot waiting for an excuse for months round here."

He craned his neck around so that he could look into the back at Pinky.

"You done good tonight, younger. Did exactly what I told you. Ain't no way no one's going to be able to tie that back to us, and anyway, it's all gonna get lost in all this nonsense."

"Yeah," Pinky said proudly. "Thanks."

"First time you done that, right?"

"Yeah."

"How was it?"

"Cool," Pinky said. "You should've seen his face when I pulled the gun on him." He giggled. "Looked like he was going to shit his pants. Then"—he made the shape of a gun with his forefingers—"blam, blam, blam, blam."

Bizness looked at him. There was a smile on his face, but there was no emotion in his eyes. They were blank and empty. Boy was a stone-cold killer. It was a little unsettling. He could see he wasn't the smartest kid, and he knew he'd end up getting merked himself eventually, but until that happened, he'd keep him close. People like him, with no empathy, they were hard to find. They were useful, too. There were plenty of people he could do with having out of the way. Wiley T, for a start. Finish the job that JaJa never even started.

"That's sorted out your problem, then?"

The boy craved his approval, like they all did. He laughed derisively. "There ain't no case without Pops. That's finished."

"Won't hurt with the stuff on YouTube, either," Mouse offered.

Bizness felt his mood curdle just a little. He remembered that someone had recorded the old man standing up to him at the record signing, posting the clip online. There had been traffic on his Facebook page, too, and he had been called out for it. Mouse was right: when word got around that he had put out the hit on Pops and that had shot up the old man's house, things would soon be back the way they were supposed to be again. No one would be stupid enough to stand up to him now. Bizness wasn't the things they were saying. He wasn't a hoodrat. He wasn't a kid you could just scare off. He was a serious player. A gangster with a reputation to defend. An authentic, one hundred percent OG.

"Yeah," he agreed. "That shit's gonna be good for business."

That brought his thinking around. Business. It had been easy to find a replacement for the Dalston Lane crack house that the old man had torched. It wasn't as if Hackney was short of empty properties, and Levelz and Tookie had found a new place ten minutes away. They were already setting up again and putting out the word. Bizness hated crack heads, and he hated crack houses, but they brought in plenty of Ps, and he knew how to make the business work. It was like any business; you just needed to advertise, create a little demand, that was all. In this case you let it be known that there was cheap crack to be had, and then you waited for your punters to come. Easy. It was like spreading shit and waiting for the fungus to grow.

"No way through here," Mouse said. "We gonna have to detour." He edged the Beamer further along the road until they could take a side street. He buried the pedal, and they lurched forwards, wheels squealing as the rubber gripped. Bizness stared out of the window as they passed the rows of terraced houses and then the ugly boxes of the

Estate.

Youngers were gathered on the street corners, their eyes following the car. Bizness wondered whether they knew who it belonged to. Some of them did, you could tell from their faces; he loved it when they nudged their friends and told them that it was him, loved the open mouths and their surprise. It made him feel good. He had been one of them, once, stood around on the streets and doing nothing, shotting a little if he could get his hands on any merchandise, getting into beefs with other boys, looking for hype with lads from outside the postcode. He liked to remind himself how far he had come, how far he had left them behind. He was a player now; there was no question about it. He was a Face, and everyone knew it. Some had started calling him the God of Hackney. He liked that. Maybe he'd change his name, release a solo record under that next. The God of Hackney. Had a ring to it, for sure. BRAPPPP! couldn't go on forever, and after all, as far as most people were concerned, he was BRAPPPP!, anyway.

"We picking up JaJa now?" Pinky said.

"Yeah. You know what to say to him?"

"Just what I saw, innit," he said. "Ain't no problem."

The boy was the last loose end he had to snip. He was waiting for them next to the entrance to the lido in London Fields. Mouse had BBMed him earlier and told him to wait for them. He slowed the car to a stop. The boy got in next to Pinky, shut the door, and Mouse accelerated away again.

"A'ight, younger. How you doing?"

"Alright," Elijah said hesitantly.

Bizness was pleased to see that the boy was still nervous around him. That was good.

"What's he doing here?" Elijah said, nodding at Pinky.

"He's in the crew now," Bizness said. "You heard about Pops?"

He looked down at his new trainers pressed close

together in the footwell of the car. "Yeah."

"What you hear?"

"He got shot."

"Other people know, too?"

"People are talking about it."

Bizness folded his arms. "He had it coming to him, younger. Mandem was up to no good. First rule—you don't ever, *never*, grass to the feds. You do that, you're worse than a dog. I know you know that, but it pays to keep it at the front of your mind. Pops forgot, see? And so he got what was coming to him. Ain't no reason to feel bad about it."

"You did it?"

"Nah. I made it happen."

"Who, then?"

"You sitting right next to him."

Elijah gaped at Pinky. "Him?"

"Yeah. Boy did good, just what I told him to do. Put four bullets into him. Ice cold. You want to pay attention. You got a lot to learn."

"What do you mean?"

"I ain't forgotten what happened with Wiley T, little man. You still got to make up for that."

Elijah kept his eyes fixed on the floor. Yeah, Bizness thought, boy was real scared, of him and now of Pinky, too. That was just how he wanted it. You could get someone who was scared to do just about whatever you wanted them to do.

He changed the subject. "Reason you're here, I want to talk to you about something. This man, the old fassy who burnt down my property—you know what we did to him today?"

He shook his head.

"There's an AK-47 in the boot. We shot his house up."

"You killed him?"

"Nah—we saw him come out, but he probably got shot, though, either that or the grenades we tossed in through his window would've done him. Messed his place up good. He won't be bothering us no more." He grinned at the thought of it. "It's the same thing as Pops, see? Can't have people questioning me, disrespecting me. You have to make an example out of people like that. You get me?"

Elijah nodded. It was a small, timid gesture.

"So," Bizness went on, "the thing is, I heard something that's troubling me. I heard you know who he is."

"I—"

"Don't mess me around on this, younger. It's important. Pinky?"

"I was outside your mum's flat last week, wasn't I? I saw him coming out. The HMV thing, too, I recognised him from there. I got an eye for faces, know what I mean? It was the same old man, I'm sure of it."

"Come on, then, younger, what's his name."

"Milton."

"You know what he does?"

"He never told me," he replied quietly. "Said he ain't police, though."

Bizness sucked his teeth. Police didn't typically burn down crack houses, so he was happy that the old man wasn't lying about that. "If he ain't police, you know why he's putting his nose in our business?"

"Dunno—honest."

"He's been staying with your mums, though. Right?"

Fear washed over the boy's face. "Not staying. One night."

"Like a boyfriend or something?"

"Dunno."

"Is it to do with her some way or another?"

"Dunno—"

"Come on, younger. There's no need to worry. Nothing's gonna happen to you or your mums, I just need to know what's going on so I can make sure he don't do no more damage than he's already done. Is he helping her?"

"I think maybe she asked him to keep an eye on me. I ain't told him nothing, though, I swear. I don't want nothing to do with him."

"A'ight, younger. That's all I needed to know. That'll do for now. Stop the car, Mouse—we'll let him out here."

They were near Bethnal Green now, nowhere near where they had picked him up. Another big group of hooded kids had gathered, heading along Mare Street towards Hackney's High Street. They passed the blacked-out windows of the Beamer, some of them staring, fire in their eyes. The busses weren't running; JaJa was going to have to walk home. Dizness didn't care about that. He picked up his phone and shuffled through his contacts for the number he wanted. He watched Elijah shuffling away with his head down as the call connected.

"You there?" he said.

"Yeah, man," Tookie said.

"Do it."

Chapter Forty-Five

MILTON STOPPED to fill up with petrol and then drove across to Blissett House. The traffic was heavy, and it had taken him longer than usual. A large crowd of teenagers, their faces covered by bandanas and hoods, suddenly swept across the street, bringing the traffic to a halt. Milton clenched his jaw as he sat waiting for them to clear out of the way. An Audi was three cars behind him; Milton watched in the rear-view mirror as bricks started to bounce off the roof and bonnet. The windscreen caved in, a missile landing square in the middle of it. A police Matrix van was behind the Audi, the officers inside it powerless to do anything. A kid, his face wrapped in the purple bandana of the LFB, ran up to it and swung the golf club he was carrying into the side of the van, swinging it again and again and again until the wing was crumpled and bent.

He banged his fist against the dash. The stakes had been raised, and he was suddenly very afraid. He had not expected Bizness to back down, but neither had he expected him to do what he had done. He operated without compunction, with no regard for restraint. Milton was concerned that he would do something else, something worse.

He took his mobile and called Aaron. The phone rang five times, then six before the call connected.

"Hello?"

Milton did not recognise the voice. "Can I speak to Aaron, please?"

"Who is this?"

He hesitated. "I'm a friend of Aaron's. Who are you?"

"Detective Constable Wilson, Stoke Newington CID. Who is this, please?"

"Where is Aaron?"

"I'm afraid Aaron has been shot, sir."

"Is he all right?"

"I'm sorry. No, he's not—he's dead, sir. Please—"

Milton cut off the call and bounced his mobile across the passenger seat. The lights were still red. He felt a tightening in his gut, a cold knot of fear and dread. He slammed his palms on the steering wheel.

Come on, come on, come on!

The lights changed, and he stamped on the accelerator, the rubber shrieking as he took a hard right turn. The traffic thinned out a little, and he was able to make better progress, pulling out and bullying his way along the opposite lane whenever it slowed.

He knew something was wrong as soon as he reached the Estate. A thick plume of smoke was rising into the darkening sky. As he got closer, he saw that it was wreathed around the side of the block, lit by the spotlights on the corners of the building as it crawled up and pitched into the sky as a dirty, clotting cloud. He swerved the car onto the forecourt. A crowd had gathered around the foot of the building, their eyes fixed on the sixth floor. Thick smoke was gushing from one of the flats. A window shattered and more spilled out. Milton stared into the source of the smoke and saw the orange-red of the fire.

Sharon's flat.

He sprinted across the forecourt to the stairwell, shouldered the door aside, and took the stairs three at a time. He reached the sixth floor, slammed through the door and onto the walkway. He recognised Sharon's neighbours among the group that had gathered at the end of the walkway. He grabbed one, the old lady who lived next door, and tugged her to one side. "Is she still in there?" he asked.

"I haven't seen her come out. Her boy, neither."

Milton released her arm and ran down the corridor. The heat climbed until it started to singe his eyebrows, a solid wall that washed over him and made it hard to breathe. He took off his coat and wrapped it around his hand, reaching out to the red-hot door handle and twisting it open. The room beyond was an inferno: the carpets, the furniture, even the walls and the ceiling seemed to be on fire. The flames lapped across the ceiling like waves. The smoke was dense and choking, and the sound of the hungry fire was threatening.

Milton heard a single scream for help, quickly choked back.

He draped his coat over his head and shoulders and stepped inside.

Chapter Forty-Six

RUTHERFORD LEFT THE HOUSE, locking the door behind him. It was another sultry, sticky night. The sound of sirens was audible in the distance, an up-and-down ululation that seemed almost constant and seemed to be coming from several directions at once. He paused at the door of his car, took off his jacket and tossed it onto the passenger seat. There was something else in the atmosphere tonight, an almost tangible edge. He could not define it, but it made him uneasy. This part of Hackney often had the hint of menace to it, especially at night, but this was different. Something was wrong.

Milton had called him five minutes earlier. He had sounded anxious. Rutherford hardly knew him, but he was not the sort of man that he would have associated with worry. He had explained that there had been an accident, and that Elijah's mother was in Homerton hospital. Rutherford asked what had happened, but Milton had ignored the question, asking him to find the boy and bring him to the hospital as quickly as he could. Rutherford had been eating a takeaway curry in front of a film, but he had put the plate aside at once and put on his shoes.

Rutherford opened the door and settled in the driver's seat. He had asked Milton where he could find Elijah. Milton said that he wasn't at home, but save that, he had no idea. That wasn't helpful, but Rutherford said that he would do his best.

He started the car, put it into gear, and drove west.

There were more kids on the streets than usual, gathered in small groups on the corners and outside shops. They wore their hoods up, and some had scarves and bandanas around their faces.

He reached for the radio and switched it on. Capital

FM would normally have been playing chart music at this hour, but instead, there was a news bulletin. There were serious disturbances across London, and Hackney was said to be especially bad. Rutherford had read the reports in the newspaper about the gang banger who had been shot and killed, and it seemed that the protests in Tottenham and Enfield had spread, metastasizing into something much bigger and more dangerous.

As he turned off the main road, a bus hurried towards him from the opposite direction, driving quickly and erratically. As it rushed by, Rutherford saw that it had no passengers. All of its windows had been shattered. He drove on until he reached Mare Street; he had to slow to a crawl as the crowd on the pavement started to drift out into the road. Ahead of him, the crowd was a solid mass. He stared in stupefaction as a group of teenagers smashed the window of a parked police car. One of them reached in with a black bin bag and spread it across the passenger seat. He lit the bag, the flames taking at once, the upholstery going up and flames quickly curling back down again from the ceiling. The crowd cheered jubilantly. The windows that had been left intact blackened and then started to crack. Someone marshalled the crowd to stand back and then, on cue, the petrol tank exploded. A hundred mobile phones were held aloft, videoing the scene.

Rutherford had seen shit like this before in Baghdad, but this was London.

He found a side road and reversed the car into an open parking space. He set off, walking briskly. He didn't know where Elijah was, but he did know what youngers would be like with something like this happening on their doorstep. They would be drawn to it like cats to free crack. His best chance was just to follow the mayhem.

Shop owners were closing their businesses early, yanking down the metal shutters to cover the doors and windows. People looked up and down the street anxiously.

Rutherford stopped at the stall where he liked to get his coffee in the morning. "You know what's going on?" he asked the owner.

"Trouble," he said. "It's already crazy, and they say it's going to get worse. I'm closing up."

Rutherford and the man turned and watched as a young boy, no older than twelve, sprinted down the pavement towards them. He was struggling with a large box pressed against his chest. The youngster ran past, screaming, "I got an Xbox, bruv, believe it! There's bare free stuff down there."

Rutherford made his way further up the road. The shops were all shut now.

A large crowd had gathered in the high street. Forty or fifty of them, their faces covered with bandanas or hoods, were attacking the shuttered windows of the shops. Another two or three hundred were watching, laughing and pointing at what they were seeing, on the cusp of getting involved themselves. A large industrial bin had been wheeled into the centre of the street, next to the bus stop, and set alight. Thick black smoke gushed out of it as the rubbish inside caught fire. The crowd whooped and hollered as young men took it in turns to launch kicks into the window of a Dixons. The glass was tough and resistant, but kick after kick thudded into it, and it gradually started to weaken. A spider web of cracks appeared and spread, the glass slowly buckling inwards. "Out of the way!" yelled one of the crowd, a fire extinguisher held above his head. He ran at the window and threw the extinguisher into the middle of it. The glass crunched as it finally cracked open, the fire extinguisher tumbling into the space beyond. The crowd set on the wrecked display like jackals, kicking at it and clearing away the shards with hands wrapped in the sleeves of their coats. The televisions inside were ferried out, some of them put into the back of waiting cars, others wheeled away in shopping trolleys. The looters climbed into the window and disappeared into the shop beyond. Others moved on to the next one along.

Rutherford's attention was drawn to a scuffle at the mouth of an alley fifty yards ahead of him. Four larger boys were surrounding a fifth person; his face was obscured by the T-shirt that had been put over it like a hood, and he was identifiable as a police officer only by his uniform. The boys were dragging him into the alley, occasionally pausing to kick or punch him. Another one was tearing a fence down for the planks of wood it would yield; Rutherford knew what they would be used for. He changed course to head in their direction, shouldering people out of the way as he picked up speed.

"Oi!" he shouted to them. "That's enough. Let him go."

One of the boys turned, an insolent retort on his lips, but his expression changed as he saw what he was facing. Rutherford was big, and there was fire in his eyes. He called out to the others, and they all faded back into the crowd.

Rutherford pulled the T-shirt from the officer's head. He could only have been in his early twenties: a new recruit tossed into the middle of the worst disturbances London had seen for years. His nose was streaming with blood, and Rutherford used the shirt to mop away the worst of it. "You all right, son?"

The man wore an expression of terror. "There's nothing we can do," he said, his voice taut with hysteria. "They're like animals."

Rutherford took him by the shoulders and looked right into his face. "You don't want to be here," he said, loosening the straps that secured his stab vest. "Ditch your gear and get back. It's not going to take much more for it to get worse. Lynching, you know what I mean? Go on— breeze, man."

People buffeted Rutherford as he was swept further up the street. He had never seen anything like it. There were no police anywhere, and the crowd continued to grow and swell. The atmosphere was manic, and the riot seemed to be gathering momentum, a life all of its own. Glass smashed and shattered, shards tumbling into the street to be trodden underfoot. Alarms clamoured helplessly, the sirens swallowed by the deafening noise of the mob. At the far end of the High Street someone had set fire to another bin, and plumes of dark smoke billowed upwards into the dusk. A police helicopter swooped overhead, hovering impotently, its spotlight reaching down like a finger to stroke over the mob.

He was tall enough to look out over the top of the crowd, but there was no sign of him. A teenage girl slammed into him and turned him to the left, and there he was: with a group of boys, each of them taking turns to shoulder-barge the door to a newsagent's.

"Elijah!"

He turned. His face was full of exhilaration, but it softened with shame as he recognised him. "What you want, man?" he said, the false bravado for the benefit of his friends.

"I need to talk to you."

"Nah. Don't think so."

Rutherford reached out and snagged the edge of his jacket. "You need to come with me."

"Get off me!" He saw Rutherford's face, and the sudden anger paled. "What is it?"

"It's your mum."

"What about her?"

"Better come with me, younger."

Elijah's face blanched. Rutherford made his way back through the angry crowd, holding the edge of Elijah's jacket in a tight grip. The boy did not resist.

Chapter Forty-Seven

RUTHERFORD PARKED his car in the car park and led the way to the entrance of the hospital. Elijah had asked what the matter was as they made their way to the car. Rutherford had explained that he didn't know, that he had received a message from Milton and that was it. The boy had been quiet during the ride, and he remained silent now. Rutherford reached down and folded one large hand around the boy's arm, just above the bicep, his fingers gripping it loosely. Elijah did not resist.

Rutherford stopped at the reception and asked, quietly, for directions to the Burns Unit. The hospital was sprawling and badly organised, and it took them ten minutes to trace a route through the warren of corridors until they found the correct department. A long passageway gave access onto a dozen separate rooms. A nurse was sat behind a counter at the start of the corridor.

"Sharon Warriner?"

"Are you related to her?"

"This is her boy."

The nurse looked at Elijah, a small smile of sympathy breaking across her face. "Room eight."

They walked quickly and in silence, the soles of their shoes squeaking against the linoleum floor. The door was closed, with a sign indicating that visitors should use the intercom to announce themselves.

Rutherford paused. "Are you all right?" he asked Elijah.

The boy's throat bulged as he swallowed. "Yeah," he said, his voice wobbling.

"It might not look good now, but your mum is going to be all right. You hear me? She'll be fine."

"Yeah."

"And I'm here if you need me."

Rutherford buzzed the intercom and opened the door. He stepped inside, leaving his hand on Elijah's shoulder as they made their way into the ward. A series of private rooms were accessed from a central corridor. Milton was standing outside a room at the end. They walked up to him, and he stepped aside.

It was a small space, barely enough room for a bed and the cheap and flimsy furniture arranged around it. A window looked out onto a patch of garden, the ornamental tree in the centre of the space overgrown with weeds and bits of litter that had snared in its lifeless branches. A woman was lying in the bed, most of her body wrapped in bandages. The skin on her face was puckered across one side, angry blisters and weals started at her scalp and disfigured her all the way down to her throat. Her head had been shaved to a stubbled furze, and the eyebrow to the right had been singed away. An oxygen masked was fitted to her mouth, and her breathing in and out was shallow, a delicate and pathetic sound. Her eyes were closed.

Rutherford felt a catch in his throat. He squeezed Elijah's shoulder.

The boy's hard face seemed to break apart in slow motion. The hostility melted and the premature years fell away until he looked like what he really was: a fifteen-year-old child, confused, helpless and desperate for his mother. Rutherford's hand fell away as the boy ran across the room to the bed.

Rutherford stepped back from the bed to give the boy some space. He turned. Milton was standing at the back of the room, his arms folded across his chest. His face relayed a mixture of emotions: concern for the woman, sympathy for the boy, and beneath everything else, the unmistakeable fire of black anger. Rutherford knew all about that, it had landed him in trouble as a young man, and he had learnt to douse it down whenever it started to flicker and flame. He could see it smouldering behind Milton's eyes now. His fists clenched and unclenched, and his jaw was set into an iron-hard line. He was struggling to keep it under control. It didn't look as if he wanted to. As he looked at the darkness that flickered in those flinty, emotionless eyes, he was afraid.

"What happened?"

"Arson."

"Do you know—"

"I know."

Rutherford lowered his voice even lower and flicked his eyes towards Elijah. "You said he was in trouble—is it because of something he was mixed up in?"

Milton nodded.

"Have you told the police?"

His voice was flat. "It's gone beyond that."

"So?"

Milton put his hand on Rutherford's arm. "You need to do me a favour. Look after the boy. Keep an eye on him, keep on at him to train, he needs something like that in his life, and we both know he's got talent."

"What about you?"

Milton ignored the question. "He needs a strong figure in his life. Someone to look up to. It's not me—it was never going to be me. I'm the last sort of example that he needs."

"What you talking about, man?"

"It doesn't matter. Just say you'll look out for him."

"Of course I will."

"Thank you."

Rutherford pressed. "What about you?"

The feeling was suddenly bleached from Milton's expression again. It became cold and impassive and frightening. "There's something I have to do."

"Let me help."

"Not for this."

"Come on, man. I don't know what you're thinking

about, but whatever it is, it'll go better if you've got someone to watch your back."

"Look after the boy."

"You're going after them, aren't you?"

"Look after the boy. That's more than enough."

Chapter Forty-Eight

JOHN MILTON set off for Dalston. The radio said that the rioting was getting worse, and the evidence bore that out: the streets were choked with people, groups of youngsters making their way into the centre of Hackney. A girl was standing on a corner wearing her shorts and bra, her T-shirt wrapped around her face, both middle fingers extended towards a police car as it sped by. Shop windows were smashed: broken TVs were left on the street, unwanted T-shirts were scattered about, empty trainer and mobile phone boxes and security tags lying where they had been thrown. Milton watched as a young boy cradling a PlayStation box was punched by two older boys and the box stolen, in turn, from him. The occasional police van went past, lights flashing, but not as many as Milton would have expected.

He passed a police station. It was surrounded by a large crowd, and as he watched, he saw the thick line of looters bulge and surge and then pour inside through a smashed door. Lights were turned on, and within moments, thick smoke started to pour through the windows. Rioters emerged again, some of them wearing police stab vests and helmets. They launched the helmets at the police and turned over the cars parked in the yard. Surely the authorities had not been caught out? he thought as he carefully skirted the crowd. Milton didn't mind. This would serve as a valuable distraction for what he was intending to do.

The main road was eventually blocked by the sheer number of people in the street, so he picked a way to Bizness's studio around the back streets, driving slowly and taking a wide path around clutches of rioters, their faces obscured by scarves and hoods, hauling away the

246

goods they had looted from wrecked shops. He was stared down by huddled groups of people on the corner. They had boxes at their feet: consoles, stereos, flat-screen TVs.

He parked the car two hundred yards away and went around to the back. The light inside the boot cast a sickly light on the interior, a travel blanket lay across a collection of items that revealed themselves as bumps through the fabric. He looked around cautiously. There was no one close enough to see what he was doing.

He took a pair of latex gloves from a cardboard dispenser and fitted them carefully onto his hands. He checked the street again and, satisfied, pulled the blanket aside. A sawn off shotgun was laid across the floor of the boot and, next to it, his Sig 9mm automatic. He took a rag and wiped both guns carefully. He checked the Sig was fully loaded and holstered it under his shirt, inside the waistband of his jeans, the metal pressed into the small of his back. There was a box of shells next to the shotgun, and he stuffed a handful into his pocket. He wiped the gun with the rag, carefully removing any prints, and wrapped it in the travel blanket. It was eighteen inches from tip to stock, and he slipped the bundle underneath his jacket, barrel pointing downwards. He had a dozen shells for the shotgun and seventeen rounds in the Sig. Twenty-nine in total. He hoped it would be enough. He dropped a pair of flashbangs into his pocket and closed the boot.

The sound of alarms filled the air, loud and declamatory, and beneath their sharp screech came the occasional noise of windows shattering and the hubbub of shouts and shrieks from the rioters on the street. Police riot vans raced down the street towards Hackney Central, and at the same time tens of kids with scarves over their faces came running in the other direction, laughing and screaming.

Milton made his way towards the main road.

Chapter Forty-Nine

"SHIT'S GOING ON OUT THERE," Mouse whooped. "You see that brother? He just put a dustbin through the window of the Poundland."

"Brother needs his head examined, looting a motherfucking Poundland."

Pinky was speaking on the phone. "It's going down at the shopping centre, too," he reported. "They've bust in through the front doors, and there ain't no security or police nowhere doing anything about it. There's a Foot Locker in there. What we doing here, anyway? It can wait. I want me some new Jordans, man. Come on, bruv. Let's get involved. We can be there in five minutes."

Bizness looked at Pinky. The boy was immature. He was enthusiastic and full of energy, but he was going to get on his nerves if he didn't take it easy.

"It's hot in here, man. Don't you ever open no windows?"

"Have a beer. Smoke something. Just stop fucking getting in my face, a'ight?"

They had been in the room for two hours, and it smelled of dope, sweat and cigarettes. Mouse had been out to find out the news and had returned to report that Pops's body had been found in the park and that Elijah's mother's flat had been razed to the ground. Bizness was not worried. He had been careful, and there was nothing to connect him to either crime. The best policy, in a situation like this, was to sit tight for a few hours until the initial fuss had blown over. If the police wanted to talk to him, they knew where he was. They would say that they had been in the studio all day.

He had told himself he wouldn't do any of the blow, but it had been a long wait. They had a lot of it, and there wasn't anything else to do. He felt twitchy, and a vein in his temple jumped now and again, a nervous tic that was beginning to irritate him.

Mouse took out his phone. "I'm gonna go call my woman."

"Do it in here," Bizness said.

"Place smells rank, man," Mouse countered. "If I don't get some fresh air, I swear I'm gonna faint. I'll speak to her for a bit, have a look on the street, see what's happening, then get back inside. Won't be long."

Chapter Fifty

MILTON WALKED briskly to the entrance to the studio. Bass was thumping through the walls of the building, rattling the door in its frame. He scouted it quickly. If there had been time, he would have prepared a careful plan for getting inside and taking Bizness out. He would have found a distraction, perhaps disabled the electricity to put them on the back foot. Or he could have broken into the building opposite and sniped them from the second floor. The road was only twenty metres wide, and he could have managed that in his sleep. He dismissed both ideas. There wasn't time for either of them, and anyway, he wasn't inclined to be subtle.

He tried the handle: it was locked. Milton took a step back and was preparing to kick it in when the lock clicked, the handle turned, and the door was pulled open. A man was standing there, shock on his face, an unlit cigarette dangling from his lip. Milton released his grip so that the blanket fell away from the sawn-off and shoved the stock into the man's face. His nose crumpled, and blood burst across his face. He lost his legs and began to fall. Milton followed him as he staggered back inside, swiping the stock like a club, the end catching the man on the chin as he went down. He was unconscious before he fell back and bounced off the stairs.

The light over the stairs was on. Milton flicked it off.

"Mouse?" came a voice from upstairs. "You alright?"

Milton turned the sawn-off in his hands, holding it loosely and aiming it diagonally upwards. He stepped over Mouse and started up the stairs, slowly, one at a time.

"Mouse?"

Milton climbed.

"You hear something?" came an angry voice from

upstairs.

"Nah."

"Go and check."

"He's outside on the phone. It's nothing, Bizness."

"Then there's nothing to worry about going and making sure, is there?"

"Fuck it, man, all I want is a smoke and a relax."

"Get down there."

Milton kept climbing the stairs.

He thought of Aaron: shot dead in the park like an animal.

He thought of Sharon: breathing through a tube in a hospital bed, bandages wrapped around her face.

He thought of Elijah and his brutally short future if he let Bizness live.

No, he could not go back. Too much blood had been spilt. Milton had offered Bizness a way out, but he had decided not to take it. That was his choice. Ignoring his offer came with consequences, and those had been explained to him, too. There was nothing else to do; he had to finish it, tonight.

A second man appeared at the top of the stairs. Milton recognised him from the crack house. He squeezed the trigger and shot him in the chest, the impact peppering him from his navel to his throat. He staggered, his hand pointlessly reaching for the knife in his pocket. Milton fired a second spread. Spit and blood foamed at the man's lips as he pirouetted back into the room above, dropping to the floor.

The music suddenly cut out.

Milton paused, crouching low.

"A'ight," Bizness called down to him. "That you, Milton?"

He gripped the barrel in his left hand, the index finger of his right hand tight against the trigger.

"I know it's you. I don't know what your beef is with me, but I ain't armed. Come up. Let's sort this out."

Milton took another step, then another.

"We can settle this thing. It's about JaJa, right? That's what you said. You want the younger, man, you can have him. Little shit ain't worth all this aggravation. Come up. We'll shake like men."

Milton was at the top of the stairs.

He took a quick step and flung himself into the room.

Two Mac-10s spat out.

Tck-tck-tck-tck-tck.

The bullets thudded into the sofa, spraying out fragments of leather and gouts of yellowed upholstery. Milton landed next to the table and scrambled into the studio beyond, more spray from the automatics studding into the floor and wall as he swung his legs inside and out of the line of fire.

Tck-tck-tck-tck-tck.

Chunks of wood sprayed out as bullets bit into the frame. The wide glass panel spider-webbed and then fell inwards in a hundred razored fragments as bullets cracked into it. Milton crabbed backwards so that the solidity of the mixing desk was between him and Bizness's dual autos.

He had dropped the shotgun. He fumbled for the Sig, pulled out the magazine and checked it, slapping the seventeen-shot load back into the butt. He cranked a bullet into the chamber and held the weapon in front of his face.

"What—you thought you could embarrass me in front of my friends and my fans with no consequences? You could burn down my place and that would be that, no hard feelings, let bygones be fucking bygones? You must be out of your mind, man, coming here. You're a dead man."

There was a moment of peace. It was not silence—bits of debris still spattered down and the crowd was loud outside the window—but the firing had ceased.

"You dropped your shotgun," he called. "Got anything

else?"

Milton gritted his teeth.

"You ain't got nothing like what I got here."

"I gave you a choice," Milton called out. "You just needed to leave Elijah alone."

"See—there it is again, *arrogance*. What makes you think you can tell me what to do? You don't tell me nothing, bruv."

Tck-tck-tck-tck-tck.

The Mac-10s fired again, and the room flashed, bullets spraying into the recording booth opposite Milton. He glanced up and saw the twin muzzle-flash reflected in the jagged remains of the booth window before bullets stitched across it and sent the shards crashing down on top of him. Bizness was behind the sofa. The bullets thudded softly into the upholstered sound insulation, and the studio was filled with a fine shower of powder and dust.

"Come on. Come out, and let's get it over with. You know there's no way out for you. What you got—a nine? You just pissing in the wind, bruv. I got two Mac-10s and enough ammo for a month. Stop hiding like a bitch. I ain't gonna lie, you ain't getting out of here alive. Come on. But you come out now, I promise I'll do you quick."

Milton straightened his back against the mixing desk and reached inside his jacket. His fingers touched a smooth, rounded cylinder. The flashbang fitted snugly into his palm.

"Funny thing is, even this won't stick on me. You and my two boys had a gunfight, and you all got done. There won't be no sign of me. I've got a woman in Camden, she'll alibi me up for now and earlier. All this—you gonna get dooked for nothing, bruv."

Milton pulled the pin, reached up, and tossed the grenade through the broken window and into the room beyond.

There was a fizz and a burst of the brightest white light

as the phosphorous ignited.

Milton rolled out of the door, bringing the Sig up, and fired. The first shot missed, but there was enough light from the flashbang for Milton to see Bizness just as he popped up from behind the sofa to return fire. He brought the Sig around and aimed quickly, squeezing the trigger twice. Bizness staggered backwards through a sudden pink mist, the Mac-10s firing wildly into the ceiling. The boy toppled into the sofa. It tipped over so that he lay across it on his back, his legs splayed out over the now vertical seats. He was pressing his hand against his chest. A bullet had hit him there, and blood was pulsing out between his fingers.

Milton had seen plenty of gutshots before. The boy was finished. No treatment could save him now.

He advanced on him, the Sig aimed at his head.

"You think you're better than me, don't you?" Bizness gasped out, the words forming between bloody gurgles. Milton kicked away the machine guns. He crouched down at Bizness's side. The boy took a ragged, wheezing breath. "You know what you are?" he said. "You people? You're a bunch of fuckin' hypocrites."

A ringing sound danced in Milton's ears, and his eyes stung with sweat. The smell of cordite was acrid, and he gagged a little. A trickle of blood, specked with bubbles of breath, dribbled from Bizness's mouth.

"You sit in your cosy homes… with your soft, comfy lives… nothing bad ever happens…" He coughed, a tearing cough that brought blood to his lips. "You look at us and… you shake your head. You *need* people like me so you can shake your fuckin' heads and say, 'See that guy, he's bad,' just so you can feel better about yourselves."

Milton reached down and collected one of the cushions that had scattered away from the sofa.

"And you know why you… people are scared of a proud black man? I'm a threat to the way you see the world to be. The black kid in school… his mums can't put food on the table. The black kid who's got no future... no prospects 'cept slaving for some fucked-up... system that sees him as a second-class citizen." He gasped. "You should be scared, bruv... Those kids running around outside tonight... I give them a purpose. I'm proof, man, living proof... that there ain't no need to bow down to fuckers like you and those fuckers you represent. You want something, it's a'ight, you go on and take it. JaJa, you can tell him what you want... but see how he feels this time next year when you've fucked off and he's doing twelve-hour shifts in Maccy D's because that's the only place that'll give him a job." He gasped again; the words were harder and harder to form. "He'll think about me... the taste I gave him of the life... and he'll ask himself, 'Why not me? Why can't I have me some of that good stuff?' You know I'm right. You've seen it in his eyes... same as I have."

"You don't know that. Maybe he will. Maybe he won't. But he'll see he's got choices. You can take the short cut or do things properly. You chose the short cut. The easy choice. It hasn't worked out so well for you."

"Fuck you, bruv. You don't know shit."

"I know he wouldn't think your life looked so appealing now."

Bizness tried to retort, but he coughed on a mouthful of blood.

Milton took the pillow and placed it over his head, one hand on each side, pressing down. The boy struggled, but Milton had his knees pressed down so that his arms were pinned to his side. His legs thrashed impotently, the kicks becoming less frequent until they subsided to spasms.

The spasms stopped.

Milton gently released the pressure, and the cushion, covered in blood, fell aside. Milton had it smeared across his trousers and on the latex gloves, too. He looked up and was suddenly aware that there was another person in the room. He stared into the eyes of a teenage boy, the same age as Elijah. He was tall and skinny, his chin pressed down hard into his chest, just his eyes showing. It took a moment, but then he recognised him: it was the boy from the park, the one who had threatened him on his first night in Hackney. He was in the corner of the room, pressed tight against the wall. He had a Makarov revolver in a trembling hand. The gun hung loosely from his fingers, pointed down at the floor. The boy looked young and frightened.

For a moment, Milton was back in France again, on the road in the mountains.

He stood and walked across the room, reaching down for the Makarov. The boy released it without speaking. He located the spent cartridges from the shotgun and pocketed them. He collected the sawn-off and put it, the Sig and the revolver into a Nike holdall he found in a cupboard. The boy's eyes followed him about the room, wide and timid, but he stayed where he was against the wall. He checked the room one final time to make sure that he had not left anything behind, and satisfied that he had not, he closed the door behind him and descended to the chaotic street below.

PART FIVE

Group Fifteen

Chapter Fifty-One

NUMBER TWELVE SAT IN HIS CAR. He was parked on the opposite side of the road to the church hall. The street was eerily quiet. A battered old minibus was parked directly in front of him, the stencilled sign on its dirty flanks advertising a Camden gym. He had watched the dozen youngsters pile out of the bus and file into the hall, different sizes and ages, all of them carrying sports bags. The local kids had arrived within the space of half an hour, all similarly equipped. Milton's car was parked fifty yards away; Callan had followed the tracking beacon from across London. He had not seen him and assumed that he was inside.

His mobile chirped.

"I have orders for you."

Callan recognised Control's voice. "Yes, sir."

"Do you know where Number One is?"

"He's in the East End. I have him under surveillance now. What do you want me to do?"

"The Committee has reviewed your report. It's been decided that he is a risk we cannot take. His behaviour, his likely mental condition—national security is at risk. We have decided that he needs to be retired."

Callan kept his voice calm and implacable. "Yes, sir. When?"

"Quickly."

"Tonight should be possible."

"Very good, Twelve. Let me know when it is done."

The line went dead.

Callan put the phone back into his pocket. He would have preferred a little longer to plan an operation like this, against a target of Number One's pedigree, but he didn't think it an impediment that need detain him. Number One had no idea that he had been marked for death. Callan had the benefit of the element of surprise, and that would be the only advantage that he would need.

He opened the door, went around to the boot of the car, and popped it open. He pulled up the false floor and ran his gaze across the row of neatly arranged weapons. He reached down and stroked his fingers across the cold metal stock of a combat shotgun. He pulled a bandolier over his shoulder and filled the pouches with shells. He didn't think he'd need more than the two that were already loaded, but it didn't hurt to be prepared. He shut the boot and locked it and got back into the car again. All he needed to do was wait for the right moment.

Chapter Fifty-Two

MILTON STOOD with Rutherford next to the ring, both of them watching the action. Elijah was fighting one of the boys from the Tottenham club. The two of them were well matched: the Tottenham boy was a year older and a little bigger, but Elijah was faster and his punches were crisper, with a natural technique that couldn't be taught.

"Boy's doing good," Rutherford said, his eyes fixed on the action. "Landing everything he throws. If he don't knock him out, he'll take him on points, easy."

Milton thought that was probably right, but it didn't mean that he wasn't nervous. His own fists jerked a little with each punch, and he caught himself holding his breath as the other boy moved in tight and clinched, snagging Elijah around the shoulders and hugging him. Elijah tried to struggle free, but the Tottenham boy was strong. The referee called for the break, but before he could step in, the boy released his right hand and punched, twice, into Elijah's groin.

The bell sounded.

Elijah spat out his mouthguard. "You hit me low!" he yelled at him.

"Yeah?" the boy called back across the ring at him. "What you gonna do about it, Hackney?"

Rutherford stepped between the ropes. "Elijah!"

"I'm gonna fuckin' dook you!"

Rutherford reached out a long arm, snagged the collar of Elijah's singlet, and dragged him back to the corner. "Deep breath, younger."

"He hit me in the nuts!"

Rutherford put one big hand on each shoulder and turned him away. "Yeah, he did, and you lose your temper like you're fixing to do, chances are this boy ain't got what it takes to hold you off, and you'll probably knock him out. But losing your temper like that gets to be a bad habit, and eventually, you'll come up against someone who's good enough to get you all fired up and take advantage of it. You're good enough to go a long way, younger, maybe even make a nice career out of it. You don't want to get into bad habits that'll get you in trouble in a fight that really means something—like for your future. You hear what I'm saying?"

Elijah scowled down at the canvas. "Yeah."

"Now then—you know why he hit you low?"

"'Cos I'm better than him."

"That's right, younger. Better than him. Much better than he'll ever get to be, too. There's one more round coming, a'ight? I'm going to let you go, and you're going to get back out there, touch his gloves in the middle of the ring like you respect him even though we know you don't, and then you're going to box him. You keep your cool, follow the plan we talked about, and wait for the opening. When he gives it to you, *then* you punish him for hitting you low—you got it?"

"Yeah."

"All right then." Rutherford pushed the mouthguard back into Elijah's mouth and let go of his shoulder. "Touch his gloves and away you go."

The bell was rung to signal the start of the third round, and the two boys met in the centre of the ring again. They tapped gloves and then sprang apart. Elijah did exactly as Rutherford had instructed: he kept his opponent at arm's length, stinging him with his jab whenever he tried to get in too close. The older boy tried to rush him, but Elijah skipped out of the way, banging in straight rights and lefts into the side of the boy's face as he sailed harmlessly past. As the seconds wound down, he stepped back and lowered his guard, indicating his chin with a clumsy touch of his glove. He's showboating, Milton thought, a grin breaking out across his face. The other boy swore at the goading, his words muffled by his guard, and rushed in again. Elijah took a step to the side, pivoted on his right foot, and swung a strong right hook into the boy's guts. His momentum was stopped at once, and his guard dropping to shield his stinging ribs, Elijah powered a left hook that knocked him backwards, and after a comical stumble, he landed on his behind.

The bell sounded, and the fight came to an end.

That's my boy, Milton thought, before he caught himself. Elijah ducked his head to the referee and bumped his right fist against Rutherford's. He turned to look at Milton but looked away again quickly. Milton nodded at that. Fair enough, he thought. He didn't know anything about what had happened, and as far as he was concerned, he had caught Milton in bed with his mother. All things considered, he deserved his mistrust.

A week had passed since the riots. Milton had spent most of the time with Elijah in the hospital. Sharon's condition had stabilised to the extent that the doctors were happy to plan the skin grafts that would fix some of the damage that had been done to her face and the rest of her body. Elijah had refused to leave her side, so Milton had arranged for him to have a spare bed in a suite that was held back for relatives. He made sure that the boy ate and did whatever he could to reassure him that his mother would make a recovery, although he kept some of the information to himself. The doctors were confident that they would be able to help, but she had been very badly burnt, they said, and she was always going to be badly scarred. On the sixth day, Sharon was moved from the Burns Unit to a general ward, and Milton started to feel more confident that things would start to improve.

He had returned to the hospital after disposing of Bizness. He said nothing about it to Rutherford, but he didn't need to. The story was on the news that night, buried beneath the clamour of the riots, but once the streets had calmed down again, it rose to the top of the

263

bulletins. Bizness, referred to by his given name of Israel Brown, had been murdered by a person or persons unknown. Two of his associates had also been shot and killed. It was quickly dismissed as a gangland argument that had escalated into something more. Bizness was revealed to be a man of many enemies and, when it all came down to it, not many friends. It was difficult to find anyone who was prepared to say that he would be missed.

Milton had been ready to find a hotel, but Rutherford told him there was no need for that: he could stay with him. Eventually, Milton had agreed. There was a long list of things that needed to be done to make the hall more suitable for the club's business and staying nearby enabled him to start earlier and finish later. Rutherford had a small house with two bedrooms, the second used as the office from where he ran the club. There was a sofa bed, and once the desk was pushed to the wall, there was enough space for Milton and the handful of things he had rescued from the rented house. They had spoken about Elijah, and once he was ready to leave the hospital, Rutherford had promised that he would be able to stay, too. Milton doubted that there would be space for all three of them, but he knew that that was moot: he didn't plan to stay for much longer.

Milton had quickly settled into a routine: he would rise early, at half-five, and go for his run. He would work until eight, and then, after showering at the club, he would drive across to the hospital to see Elijah and Sharon. After an hour with them, he would return to Hackney and work through until five, stopping only to buy his lunch from the arcade of takeaways at the end of the road. He stayed at the hospital for a second time until visiting closed for the night, worked until nine or ten and then, finally, returned to the house for something to eat. Rutherford would usually be watching the television, and he would join him for half an hour before calling it a day.

It was a hard schedule, but it had allowed him to get a

lot done. He had fixed the roof properly, replacing the tiles that had been dislodged. He had given the equipment a thorough cleanse, scrubbing the canvasses in both rings until the stains that had been trodden in over years of use had been mostly scoured away. He had whitewashed the walls and mended the damaged fixtures in the toilets.

Rutherford approached him. "You coming?"

"In a couple of hours? I want to finish wiring the plugs." The biggest task left to do was to renew the wiring, but he had made a start and was keen to press on.

"You work too hard."

"It'll get done sooner this way."

"I'm still not sure why you're being so good about this."

"It's nice to be able to help," he said. "I'll see you later."

"A'ight," he said, clapping Milton on the back.

Rutherford went to collect his coat. Milton was about to fetch his tools from the office when Elijah stepped in front of him.

"Hey," he said, a little awkwardly.

"All right, Elijah?"

"Thanks for coming."

"Are you kidding? I loved it. I said you'd be cut out for this, didn't I?"

He paused awkwardly. "I never said thanks."

Milton smiled at him. "There's no need."

"It was—you know…"

"You don't have to say anything. I didn't handle things as well as I could have done, either. That's how things get to be, sometimes."

Elijah was struggling for the words. "It's just—I don't want you to think I'm ungrateful, that's all."

"You've done well. That fight, tonight, the way you handled him—I'm telling you, Elijah, that was something. I know a little bit about boxing, and when Rutherford says you've got potential, I reckon he's about right. You keep working hard and stay away from the street, I'd say there's a very good chance you're going to end up doing something pretty useful with these." He tapped the back of the boy's hands. "That left hook of yours"—he exhaled theatrically—"it's something, Elijah, it really is. I wouldn't want to get on the other side of it. Your mother will be proud of you when she sees what you've been doing."

The mention of Sharon quietened him for a moment.

"You know she'll be all right," Milton said.

He looked up at him. "Why did you help us? You never said." His eyes were wet.

Milton didn't know how to answer that.

"JaJa!" Rutherford called. The three of them were the last people in the hall. "I want a curry. You coming?"

Elijah hadn't taken his eyes off Milton's face.

It was his turn to feel discomfited. "Doesn't have to be a reason, does there?"

Elijah paused for a moment and then reached out his hand. Milton took it and held it for a moment. "See you later, Milton," the boy said. He self-consciously scrubbed the back of his hand across his damp eyes. "We're getting take-out curries. What do you want?"

"You choose. I'm not fussed."

"You like it hot?"

"Not really."

Elijah grinned. "Pussy."

Milton watched the boy make his way back to Rutherford. They made their way out, shutting the door behind them. Milton headed to the back and the small office. There was a desk, a filing cabinet and a battered leather sofa. He collected his bag of tools and went over to the plug that he was fitting. A curry with them sounded good. He was planning on leaving tomorrow, and it would be nice to have had an evening with them before he did.

Chapter Fifty-Three

RUTHERFORD AND ELIJAH walked along the perimeter of the park. All the boy wanted to do was recount the fight from earlier, constantly asking Rutherford for his opinion and his suggestions for how he could eliminate his faults. It made him smile to see the boy so animated. The evening had been an escape for him, Rutherford could see that, a distraction that meant that he did not have to think about his mother or the ordeal of the last few days. He was a lively, engaged boy, and in his enthusiasm Rutherford could see the premature aging endowed by the street quickly peeled back. He saw him for what he was: a sweet fifteen-year-old boy full of the usual insecurities, the usual need for encouragement and acceptance. He was a little full of himself at times, but what young boy wasn't? Rutherford remembered that he had been much worse.

"Damn it," Rutherford said.

"What's the matter?"

"I put the alarm on. Milton will set it off if he opens the door."

"Want me to run back and tell him?"

"I better do it." He handed over a set of keys and pointed. "No need for you to come too—we're nearly there. You know my house? Last one on the left. Let yourself in, make yourself at home. I'll get the takeaway on the way back—what do you want?"

"Curry," he said. "Milton, too. Chicken korma for him. Beef madras for me."

"Two chicken kormas and a beef madras, then. There are DVDs in the living room—put one on if you want. Go on, get inside. Don't hang around outside, you hear? It still ain't right around here."

Rutherford waited until Elijah had crossed the road and was at the door to the maisonette. The door opened and closed, the boy disappearing inside. Satisfied, Rutherford turned on his heel and retraced his steps back to the church hall.

Chapter Fifty-Four

MILTON PUT down his screwdriver and concentrated on the aches and pains that registered around his body. His joints throbbed with a dull ague, his muscles felt stiff, and there was a deep-seated fatigue all the way in the marrow of his bones. There was no point in pretending; he was getting old. Old and stiff.

He recognised, dimly, that he needed sleep more than anything else.

He was screwing the cover onto the new socket when he heard a knock on the door from outside. He waited, wondering whether he had misheard, but the knock was repeated. Three times, quite hard, urgent. He stood. His eye fell on his Sig Sauer hanging in the shoulder holster against the back of the nearby chair. There was no need. It was Rutherford or, in the worst case, kids who were mucking about. He tossed it behind the ring, out of sight.

He crossed the wide space to the front door, unlocked it, and pulled it back.

Milton did not recognise the man outside.

The man brought up a gun and pointed it directly at his chest.

"Back inside," he said.

The gun was a Sig Sauer 9mm, like his own. He knew what that meant.

"About time," he said.

"Inside."

"Control sent you?"

The man didn't answer.

"I don't think I've seen you before. Who are you? Eleven? Twelve?"

"Twelve," he said. The muzzle was aimed at his heart, unwavering in a steady hand, and the man's face was blank and inscrutable. There would be no sense in appealing to his better nature. He would have no better nature. Twelve followed him into the hall and pushed the door closed with his foot. Milton assessed him. He looked like an athlete with wide shoulders and a tapered trunk. The eyes stared out coldly from beneath pale lashes.

"What's this about?"

"Are you armed?" Twelve said. His voice was flat, the sentence trailing away on a dead note.

"No."

"Pull up your shirt."

Milton did as he was told.

"Turn around."

He did.

"Where is it?"

"In the car."

"Anyone else here?"

"No. Just me. Why don't you tell me what this is all about?"

Again, there was no response. Milton assessed. Was there any way of putting Twelve off his stride? Upsetting his balance? He knew with grim certainty that there was not. Twelve and all the other young agents in Group Fifteen were brutally professional. Milton knew how well he had been trained—he would have gone through the same programme as he had, after all—and he was able to anticipate all of the variables that he would be considering. First, he would assess the threat that Milton posed: significant, but limited as it stood. Second, he would confirm that the surroundings were suitable for an elimination: perfect. Once those quick assessments had been made to his satisfaction, he would carry out his orders. It would be quick and efficient. Milton guessed that he had a handful of seconds. A minute if he was lucky and could muddy the waters.

He would not go down without a fight. If there was a chance, a half-chance, he would take it. He assessed the situation himself. Six feet separated him from Twelve. Another indication that the agent was good; not enough to compromise his aim but enough to make sure that Milton could not attack before he could fire. Milton explored his own body, his posture, tensing his muscles and assessing how quickly he might be able to move. The position of his feet. The angle of his hips, of his shoulders. He would need to be decisive, but even then, he knew that his chances were slim. He would certainly be shot before he could reach him, and even if he was not, he did not fancy his chances in unarmed combat with Twelve. He was younger, his muscles more pliant and less damaged and scarred than Milton's.

"Control sent you?" he asked again, probing for a weakness, some conversational gambit he could spin out into hesitation, then work the hesitation into doubt.

Nothing. He took a step into the hall. The gun did not waver.

"He doesn't trust me?"

Nothing.

"Come on, Twelve. I'm owed a reason."

Finally, he answered the question. "Your mental health is in question."

"Don't be ridiculous."

Twelve's eyes darted left and right, taking in his surroundings, scanning for threats. "Look at this place! What are you now, a handyman?"

Milton ignored that. "It might have been in question before, but it isn't now. Ten years doing what we do, it's enough to make you hate the world. I'm not doing it anymore. I'm finished—I've never been more certain of anything in my life."

Twelve turned his gaze back onto Milton. "I used to look up to you," he said, a cruel smile briefly creasing his alabaster-white skin. "You were a legend. But that was then, wasn't it? Before whatever it is that's happened to you."

"Is that what Control thinks? That I've gone mad?"

"I've been following you. Moving into that dump of a place down the road. That woman you've been seeing. And going to those meetings. You're saying you're an alcoholic now, with all the intelligence you're privy to? Fuck, after what happened in France, what did you think he'd think? How could he possibly let that stand? You've been classified as a security risk. 'Most Urgent, Marked for Death.' What else did you expect? He can't have you running around like that, can he? You're a liability."

He tried to think of something that might deflect Twelve from his mission, but there was nothing. "There's no need for this," he said hopelessly.

"Comes to us all in the end. And I can't lie—this will be the making of me. I'm the one who gets to retire the famous Number One."

Behind them, the door handle pressed down. Milton saw it first, an advantage of a second or two that his body spent readying itself for sudden action. Twelve heard it too, and the gun continuing to cover Milton, he took a sideways step and then a quarter turn, allowing him to see both Milton and the doorway at the same time. The door opened inwards.

Rutherford stood there.

Oh no.

A warning caught in Milton's throat, stifled by the steady gun.

"Forgot to tell you about the alarm—" Rutherford said, the sentence trailing away as he noticed the tension in Milton's posture. His face creased with confusion as he looked to the right, at Twelve, and then that became anxiety as he saw the gun.

"Come inside, and shut the door," Twelve instructed him in the same cold, flat voice.

Milton knew Rutherford had seconds to live. He was a witness, and there could be no witnesses. He had to act, right now, but the gun remained where it was, as if held by a statue, pointed implacably at his heart. Rutherford did as he was told, stepping inside and pushing the door behind him. The mechanism closed with a solid click.

"You don't need to shoot him," Milton said, desperately trying to distract Twelve from the course he would already have determined the moment Rutherford set his hand on the door. "He doesn't know who you are. He doesn't know who I am. Let him go. We can settle this between us."

"We're going to settle it," Twelve said.

He swung the gun away from Milton and aimed it at Rutherford.

Chapter Fifty-Five

IN ONE VIOLENT corkscrew of motion, Milton threw himself across the room.

The gun spat out once and then swung back towards Milton again.

Twelve's reflexes were unbelievably quick, and a second—unaimed—shot rang out.

The bullet caught Milton in the shoulder, razor shards of pain lancing down his arm. Milton disregarded it, shut it down, and threw himself into the younger man. He tackled him around the waist, his momentum sending them both stumbling backwards until they clattered against the wall. Twelve tried to bludgeon him with the butt of the gun, but he blocked the clumsy swipe, their wrists clashing and the gun falling to the floor. They collapsed downwards, Milton ending up on top, and he drove the point of his elbow into Twelve's face. He felt the bones of his nose crumple and snap as they crunched together, blood immediately running over the pale white skin. Milton rolled away and scrambled for the gun. His fingers closed around it as Twelve sprang up to his feet, his face twisted with fury.

"Don't," Milton said. The pain from his shoulder washed over him in nauseous waves, but he managed to aim the pistol.

Twelve stopped. He was six feet away. Blood ran freely from his broken nose. His eyes shone with anger.

Milton slowly got to his feet. His left shoulder felt as though it had been mangled, the arm hanging uselessly down by his side. He was woozy from the pain. He knew, from experience, that it would get worse. It was the adrenaline that was holding him together, but the pain would overwhelm him eventually. He held the advantage, but he would not have it for long.

"Put the gun down," Twelve said.

Milton looked across the room. Rutherford's body was sprawled across the floor. Twelve's shot had struck him in the forehead. He had landed in an untidy sprawl, his arms outflung. His body was still. There was no hope for him.

Milton tightened his grip on the pistol. He felt the old, familiar flick of his anger. His finger tightened around the trigger.

"Put it down," Twelve said calmly.

He tried to tune out the pain. Twelve had sunk down a little, spreading his weight between both legs. He could see that Milton was injured. He would have noticed the way that his aim was slowly dropping, his gun arm gradually falling towards the floor. He would be making the same calculations that Milton had made moments earlier. The distance between them. How quickly he could close it. The odds of a shot stopping him before he could reach his target. Milton knew his weakness was obvious; Twelve would be able to smell it like a shark smells blood.

Milton fought the anger and the pain. "I'm not going to kill you," he said, his voice quiet. "I'm finished with that, not unless there's no other choice, and if you're sensible, you won't back me into a corner."

"All right," Twelve said, showing him his open palms, placating him. "I won't. Take it easy."

"I'm not going to kill you, but you know I can't have you following me."

Milton stiffened his arm, switched to a lower aim, and pulled the trigger.

The bullet struck Twelve in the right knee. His face distorted with agony, and he fell back.

Milton closed in and swept his good leg. Twelve dropped to the floor. Milton backed away, covering him with the gun until he reached the door. "Tell Control not to come after me."

"He'll come after you," he gasped through the pain.

"Tell him I'm out."

Twelve grunted; Milton realised that he was laughing. "We're never out."

"I am. Tell him if he sends anyone after me, I'll send them back in boxes. And then I'll bring him down."

He looked again at Rutherford's unmoving body, then at Twelve, staring up at him through a mask of pain. He reached around and pushed the gun into the waistband of his jeans and pulled out the tails of his shirt to cover it. The pain was reaching a crescendo.

He had to move now.

Right now.

He opened the door and hurried across the road towards the unlit stretch of park. He passed through the open gate and kept going until the darkness swallowed him.

Chapter Fifty-Six

THE HOUSE WAS EMPTY. Milton had forced his way in through a door to the garden; he'd put his fist through the glass and unlocked the door from the inside. It was on one of the most expensive streets in the neighbourhood, a long curved cul-de-sac that faced onto the peaceful expanse of a common adjacent to the main area of the park. Expensive SUVs and four-by-fours competed for space on the road. The houses were large, set behind railed front gardens with wide bay windows and broad front doors.

Milton had started to feel faint as he crossed the common. The pain had started to dull and fade; a sensation he knew was dangerous. He kept his hand clamped to his shoulder, but the blood kept coming. He knew enough about battlefield medicine to know that a lodged bullet could sometimes be a blessing, plugging up the entry wound until it could be carefully removed and the blood staunched. Milton had not been so fortunate. This bullet had nicked a vein, and the blood continued to seep out around it, squeezing through his fingers and soaking into the fabric of his shirt.

He found a packet of ibuprofen in a first aid box in the bathroom cabinet. He tapped out three and swallowed them dry and then laid out his tools on the kitchen table. He placed an adjustable mirror before the chair and stood an anglepoise lamp next to it, the shade turned so that the bright cone of light was cast back onto the chair. He opened the first aid box again and took out a tube of antiseptic gel, a gauze dressing and a roll of bandages. He crossed the room to the gas hob and removed the small kitchen knife from where he had rested it, the blade suspended in the blue flame. He raised the knife before his

277

cheek; the metal glowed red and radiated heat. That was good. He lodged the blade of a larger, broader metal spatula in the flame instead.

He went back to the table and took off his shirt, using it to mop the blood from around the wound. He sat in the wooden chair, adjusting the lamp so that its light fell on the wound, and then turned the mirror so that he could stare right into it. A neat hole had been burrowed out, blackened around the edges and scabbed in parts with partly congealed blood. He grimaced with pain as he reached his left hand back up to his left shoulder and then gasped as he used his forefinger and thumb to spread the edges of the wound, opening it so that he could look a little way inside.

He took the knife and, biting down hard on a dish cloth, prodded the hot and sharp tip into the wound, digging deeper until he saw the silver sparkle of the bullet, lodged like a spiteful tumour an inch deep in his flesh.

He took a deep breath and pushed the knife further into his flesh, the sharp point sliding through the skin and into the muscle beneath. The pain yanked him back to wakefulness and then kept climbing; every millimetre of progress, every nudge and tap, was rewarded with a lance of agony that seared into his brain.

He thought about Elijah and Sharon.

He thought about Rutherford.

He felt the tip of the blade touch against the bullet, and with the pain and his weakness shimmering like heat haze before his face, he pressed down harder and then prised the blade back, levering the slug from its burrow and pressing it out until it dropped from out of the wound and onto the table.

The pain flared once, a crescendo that Milton met by slamming his fist against the table, and then slackened off.

Halfway there.

He swallowed another two ibuprofen and reached over to the hob for the spatula. Closing his eyes and pressing his teeth together, he took the blade and pressed it against the wound, the skin sizzling as the red-hot metal cauterised it. Milton gasped at another vicious wave of pain, clenching the edge of the table until it, too, passed. He inspected the seared, puckered flesh in the mirror. A huge, purple bruise had already bloomed around the wound, but the bleeding had stopped. He had done a decent job.

There was no time to pause.

Milton went upstairs and stripped off, taking Twelve's Sig Sauer into the bathroom with him, and showered in the en suite bathroom. He dried himself, daubing antiseptic gel onto the clean wound and then dressing it with the gauze pad, fixing it in place with the roll of bandage. He went into the bedroom and tore through the wardrobe, finding a T-shirt and jeans that fitted him and putting them on.

He had noticed a key fob on the radiator cover in the hall. The fob was attached to a leather swatch decorated with a BMW badge. He left the house through the front door, his pistol hidden beneath a leather jacket he had taken from where it had been slung over the end of the banister. He aimed the fob at the line of parked cars and pressed. There came the familiar double blip and the illumination of the courtesy lights of a large black BMW X5 that had been parked a little way down the road.

Milton opened the door and slid inside. He put Twelve's pistol on the passenger seat and pressed the engine start. The display reported a full tank of diesel. He let the handbrake out, put the car into gear, and pulled slowly into the quiet road.

EPILOGUE

Chapter Fifty-Seven

PINKY TOOK A SEAT on the see-saw and looked around. They were in the playground next to Blissett House. He looked up at the sixth floor. The fire had been contained there, but Elijah's old flat and the ones on each side had been gutted. Black ash and soot were everywhere, the windows and doors had been boarded up, the damage sticking out like an ugly bruise on the concrete face of the block. Pinky didn't have strong feelings about what had happened. Elijah and his mums had brought it on themselves. What else was Bizness supposed to have done, the two of them sending that man after him like that? Pinky had no sympathy for them.

He had sent messages to the other boys, and they had been waiting for him when he had arrived five minutes earlier. They were all there: Little Mark, Chips, Kidz and a couple of the primary school kids from the Estate who had been hanging around with him for the last week. Time they got promoted, Pinky thought, time they had something useful to do. The boys were spread out; Chips and Kidz sat on the swings, Little Mark leant against the chain-link fence, the youngsters kept together, eyeing the older boys with a mixture of bravado and nervousness. The older boys were smoking from the joint that Pinky had rolled and passed around.

It had been a crazy few days, and Pinky had not slept much. It didn't matter, though; he still felt good. There was no point in pretending that he hadn't been frightened, but nothing had happened to him, and now he was in the clear. He had searched the studio after Milton had left; he figured he had a little time before the feds came, and he knew that there was bound to be stuff worth taking. He had been right about that: he had found more than ten grand in a holdall and dozens of little bags filled with cocaine, ready to be distributed to Bizness's dealers, the network of shotters that he had on the street. Pinky had put the Mac-10s and the drugs into another bag he found and left the studio by the fire escape at the back.

It had been hairy getting back. London had been a war zone that night, police cars and vans speeding through the back streets under blue lights, but he had not been stopped. He had stored the guns and money under his bed at home, hiding it beneath his empty trainer boxes and dirty clothes. His mums had given up trying to get him to keep the room tidy long ago, and she had stopped going inside. He knew they would be safe there for a day or two until he could think of somewhere better.

Pinky cast his gaze around the group. They all knew Pops was gone, but no one had said anything about it. Pinky guessed that they had heard that he was responsible, and while he wasn't stupid enough to admit that it had been him, he was happy for them to speculate. He wouldn't own up to it, but he wouldn't deny it, either. A little bit of fear was a good thing, especially with what he had planned. It helped to build respect. That had been a long time coming, and he was going to make sure that he took advantage of it.

Pinky reckoned that he had been given an opportunity. After always being second best, now he had a chance to really do something with his life. Make a name for himself, make some money; he wasn't going to fuck it up, no way.

He got up from the see-saw. "A'ight," he said. "First things first. I'm in charge now. Anyone have a problem with that?"

No one spoke.

"Didn't think so." He grinned. He lifted the holdall onto the roundabout and pulled back the zip. Dozens of little bags full of white powder were snuggled together inside. "Pay attention," he said, making sure that they had all seen the stash. "Things are going to change around here. We're going to make some mad cash. I'm going into business, boys—if you got the balls to be a part of it, listen up. This is what we're gonna do."

Chapter Fifty-Eight

GROUP FIFTEEN had its own private medical facilities attached to a well-known London teaching hospital. State-of-the-art facilities, the best doctors in the country, absolute discretion. Control watched through the window as the surgeon bent low to examine the damage that had been done to Twelve's knee. The man—and his three colleagues—were wearing green smocks, their faces covered by surgical masks and latex gloves over their hands. Twelve had been anaesthetised and was laid out on the operating table, covered by a sheet with a long vertical slit that allowed easy access to his right leg. The surgeon had already sliced open his knee, a neat incision that began just below the quadriceps and curved around the line of his leg. The opening was held open by medical clips, and a miniature camera on an articulated arm had been positioned overhead, its feed visible on the large screen that was fixed to the wall in the observation suite.

Milton's bullet had ruined the knee, smashing through the anterior and posterior ligaments and shattering the patella. They had examined the damage with an arthroscope first and determined that repairs were not possible; a full arthroplasty was necessary. The surgeon had removed what was left of the patella and had shaved the ends of the femur and tibia so that he could fix the replacement joint. One of his colleagues was preparing the bone cement while the other was checking that the prosthesis was ready to be implanted.

Control watched the screen, his eyes a little glazed. He was not bothered by the blood and the gore; Heaven knows, he had seen enough of it over the years, and much worse than this. He was not really concentrating on Twelve at all. His mind was on Milton.

His liquidation should have been straightforward. Twelve had had the benefit of surprise, and Milton was not as young as he had once been. And, yet, here they were, with a badly injured agent and Milton a ghost.

He had been working on damage control ever since Twelve had limped out of the church hall and called for emergency pickup. He had taken the response team himself to ensure that there was no trace of Twelve ever having been there. The blood from his leg had been scrubbed away and footage from local CCTV cameras had been deleted. The dead man—Rutherford—was left where he was. Twelve had explained what had happened. The surprise of Rutherford's appearance had saved Milton's life, so now, in death, he would have to pay back the damage that he had caused. His body would prove to be useful. It was easy to fabricate the story. CCTV footage placed Milton at the scene and showed Rutherford arriving moments before he was shot.

A camera at the entrance to the park had footage of Milton heading north. He was wounded, too, a bullet to the shoulder. They had immediately checked local hospitals for admissions, but it was perfunctory; Milton was much too savvy to do something as foolish as that. An hour later they had intercepted a call to local police of a break-in. A couple had returned to their house on the edge of the nearby park to find that someone had forced the door to the garden. Their car and a few clothes had been stolen. That, in itself, would have been enough for Control to have investigated, but they had also reported that their first aid cabinet had been ransacked, that a lamp had been moved onto the kitchen table, and that kitchen utensils had been found covered in blood.

Control took command of the investigation himself and visited the house. He went through into the kitchen and sat at the table, glancing at his reflection. He knew that Milton had been sitting in the same chair a couple of hours earlier. He had operated on himself, cleaned the wound, and made it safe until he found someone that he could trust to do the job properly. He had showered, changed clothes, taken their car and fled. The police were looking for the vehicle, but they had not located it yet. It wouldn't matter. They would find it eventually, abandoned at the side of the road when Milton switched vehicles. It would be too late then. He would stay ahead of them unless he made a mistake or he chose to be found.

Control focussed on the screen again as the prosthesis was carefully placed into Twelve's wrecked joint.

John Milton was a chameleon. He had twenty years' experience of blending into the background, surfacing only to do the bloody work of his trade before sinking out of sight again. Control felt an icy knot in the pit of his stomach. Milton was the most dangerous man he had ever met, and now he knew that the State wanted him dead. He had no idea what he would do next, and that was the kind of thought that would keep a man up at night.

Chapter Fifty-Nine

THE MOTORWAY stretched away into the distance, the slow-moving row of tail lights painting a lazy swipe across the valley. There had been a crash outside Wolverhampton, and the traffic had backed up, filtering slowly through two lanes while the grim wreckage was craned away. Milton cursed the accident. He knew that it would only be a matter of time before the details of the stolen BMW were added to the national registry. The motorway was equipped with the CCTV masts that serviced the police's number-plate recognition system, and the longer he stayed on the road, the greater the chance that the car would be noticed. He felt vulnerable, and even though he knew it would make no difference, he tugged down the brim of the baseball cap he had found in the glove compartment so that his face was partially obscured.

He was tired, and his shoulder throbbed. He had been driving for three hours. His instinct was not to stop until he reached Manchester, but as he passed the sign advertising the services at Stafford South, he decided it was worth the risk for a strong cup of coffee.

Milton moved carefully into the crawler lane and pulled off the motorway.

The car park was quiet, a wide-open space lit by a series of tall overhead lights. Milton parked in a shadowed area and walked across to the complex of buildings. There were very few drivers around, a handful of red-eyed travellers drinking coffee in the small Starbucks concession. Milton bought a packet of Nurofen from WH Smith and then ordered a double espresso and a bottle of water from the bored-looking barista.

Milton looked up at the screen fixed to the wall. The BBC's rolling news channel was showing. He sipped from the Styrofoam cup as the anchor recapped the day's news. The riots were the main focus. The worst of the disturbances had abated, but the police were short-handed, and there was talk of calling in the army. Milton was stunned by their severity. Large parts of Croydon had been set alight, and a furniture store that he recognised had been razed to the ground by a ferocious blaze. There was footage from Hackney and Tottenham, crowds of rioters with scarves obscuring their faces, packs of looters that descended on retail parks and local businesses alike, taking whatever they could lay their hands upon. A police superintendent was interviewed, and promised that the culprits would be caught and punished. Milton thought of Elijah. Had they got to him in time?

"And in other news, police have launched a murder hunt after a man was found dead in the boxing club he ran in London's East End. Dennis Rutherford was found this evening by one of his students. He had been shot."

A picture of Rutherford was displayed. He was with a group of youngsters, holding a trophy and smiling into the camera. The picture switched to an outside broadcast. A reporter was standing in front of the boxing club, a policeman standing guard at the entrance.

The reporter spoke into the camera. "The Metropolitan police and London ambulance service were called here at 10.20pm, where the victim, from Hackney, was subsequently pronounced dead. A post-mortem is due to take place tomorrow, but it is understood that he died from a single gunshot wound. Police sources say that they want to speak to John Milton, last seen in the London area. He is described as a middle-aged white male, six foot tall, well built and with short dark hair. They recommend that he is not approached and that members of the public with information on his whereabouts should contact officers as soon as possible."

A head-and-shoulders picture of Milton flashed onto the screen. He recognised it: the picture had been taken from his Group file. Control was behaving exactly as he knew that he would. He would organise a manhunt, co-opting all the other agencies: the intelligence service, the police, everyone. His picture remained on the screen as the report continued. Milton looked around at the other customers anxiously. No one was paying the television much attention, but he replaced the cap on his head regardless.

He took his coffee with him and went back out into the hot night. The steady hum of the motorway was loud, the stand of trees that had been planted at the edge of the car park doing little to dampen the noise. Milton ignored the BMW. It had served him well, but he knew that it would have been reported by now. He found a spot that was poorly served by CCTV and approached a Ford Mondeo. He forced the door, slid inside, and hot-wired the engine.

The digital clock on the dashboard showed a little after three in the morning as he rejoined the motorway heading north. He passed through the gears, making sure to stay below the speed limit. In an hour and a half, the lights of Liverpool sparkled in the distance. Milton turned off the motorway and drove into town.

SAINT DEATH

is out now!

ADOLFO GONZÁLEZ lowered his AK, and the others did the same. They were stood in a semicircle, all around the three stalled trucks. There was no noise beyond the soporific buzz of the earth baking and cracking under the heat of the sun. Dust and heat shimmered everywhere. He looked out at their handiwork. The vehicles were smoking, bullet holes studded all the way across the sheet metal. They were all shot up to high heaven. The windscreens had been stove in by the .416 calibre rounds that the snipers had fired. Some of the holes that ran across the cars were spaced and regular from the AKs, others were scattered with uneven clumps from number four buckshot. The Italians had come to the meet in their big, expensive four-wheel-drive Range Rovers. Tinted windows, leather interiors and xenon headlamps. Trying to make a big impression. Showing off. Hadn't done them much good. One of them had tried to drive away, but he hadn't got far. The tyres of the car were flat, still wheezing air. The glass was all shot out. Steam poured from the perforated bonnets.

Adolfo looked up at the hills. He knew Samalayuca like the back of his hand. His family had been using this spot for years. Perfect for dumping bodies. Perfect for ambushes. He'd put three of his best snipers up on the lava ridge. Half a mile away. They had prepared covered trenches and hid in them overnight. He could see them coming down the ridge now. The sun shone against the dark metal of their long-barrelled Barretts and reflected in glaring flickers from the glass in the sights.

He approached the nearest Range Rover, his automatic cradled at his waist. Things happened. Miracles. It paid to be careful. He opened the door. One of the Italians, slumped dead over the wheel, swung over to the side. Adolfo hauled his body out and dumped it in the dust. Bad luck, *pendejo*. There were two more bodies in the back.

Adolfo walked around the end of the truck. There was another body behind it, face up, mouth open. Vivid red blood soaked into the dirt. A cloud of hungry flies hovered over it.

He went to the second truck and looked through the window at the driver. This one had tried to get away. He was shot through the head. Blood everywhere: the dash, the seats, across what was left of the window.

He walked on to the third vehicle. Two men inside, both dead.

He walked back to the first truck to where the body lay.

He nudged the man's ribs with his toe.

The man moved his lips.

"What?"

The man wheezed something at him.

Adolfo knelt down. "I can't hear you."

"*Basta*," the man wheezed. "*Ferma.*"

"Too late to stop, *cabrón*," Adolfo said. "You shoulda thought of that before."

He put the automatic down and gestured to Pablo. He had the video camera and was taking the footage that they would upload to YouTube later. Leave a message. Something to focus the mind. Pablo brought the camera over, still filming. Another man brought over a short-bladed machete. He gave it to him.

The dying man followed Adolfo with his eyes.

Adolfo signalled, and his men hauled the dying man to his knees. They dragged him across to a tree. There was blood on his face, and it slicked out from the bottom of his jacket. They looped a rope over a branch and tied one end around the man's ankles. They yanked on the other end so that he fell to his knees, and then they yanked again, and then again, until he was suspended upside down.

Adolfo took the machete with his right hand and, with his left, took a handful of the man's thick black hair and yanked back to expose his throat.

Adolfo stared into the camera.

He went to work.

GET A FREE BEST-SELLER, TWO NOVELLAS AND EXCLUSIVE JOHN MILTON MATERIAL

Building a relationship with my readers is the very best thing about writing. I occasionally send newsletters with details on new releases, special offers and other bits of news relating to the John Milton, Beatrix Rose and Soho Noir series.

And if you sign up to the mailing list I'll send you all this free stuff:

1. A copy of the John Milton introductory novella, 1000 Yards.

2. A copy of the introductory Soho Noir novella, Gaslight.

3. A free copy of my best-seller, The Black Mile (averages 4.4 out of 5 stars and RRP of $ 5.99).

4. A copy of the highly classified background check on John Milton before he was admitted to Group 15. Exclusive to my mailing list – you can't get this anywhere else.

5. A copy of Tarantula, an exciting John Milton short story.

You can get the novel, the novellas, the background check and the short story, **for free**, by signing up at http://eepurl.com/Cai5X

Enjoy this book?
You can make a big difference

Reviews are the most powerful tools in my arsenal when it comes getting attention for my books. Much as I'd like to, I don't have the financial muscle of a New York publisher. I can't take out full page ads in the newspaper or put posters on the subway.

(Not yet, anyway).

But I do have something much more powerful and effective than that, and it's something that those publishers would kill to get their hands on.

A committed and loyal bunch of readers.

Honest reviews of my books help bring them to the attention of other readers.

If you've enjoyed this book I would be very grateful if you could spend just five minutes leaving a review (it can be as short as you like).

Thank you very much.

ABOUT THE AUTHOR

Mark Dawson is the author of the breakout John Milton, Beatrix Rose and Soho Noir series. He makes his online home at www.markjdawson.com. You can connect with Mark on Twitter at @pbackwriter, on Facebook at www.facebook.com/markdawsonauthor and you should send him an email at mark@markjdawson.com if the mood strikes you.

ALSO BY MARK DAWSON

Have you read them all?

In the Soho Noir Series

Gaslight

When Harry and his brother Frank are blackmailed into paying off a local hood they decide to take care of the problem themselves. But when all of London's underworld is in thrall to the man's boss, was their plan audacious or the most foolish thing that they could possibly have done?

The Black Mile

London, 1940: the Luftwaffe blitzes London every night for fifty-seven nights. Houses, shops and entire streets are wiped from the map. The underworld is in flux: the Italian criminals who dominated the West End have been interned and now their rivals are fighting to replace them. Meanwhile, hidden in the shadows, the Black-Out Ripper sharpens his knife and sets to his grisly work.

The Imposter

War hero Edward Fabian finds himself drawn into a criminal family's web of vice and soon he is an accomplice to their scheming. But he's not the man they think he is - he's far more dangerous than they could possibly imagine.

In the John Milton Series

One Thousand Yards

In this dip into his case files, John Milton is sent into North Korea. With nothing but a sniper rifle, bad intentions and a very particular target, will Milton be able to take on the secret police of the most dangerous failed state on the planet?

Tarantula

In this further dip into his files, Milton is sent to Italy. A colleague who was investigating a particularly violent Mafiosi has disappeared. Will Milton be able to get to the bottom of the mystery, or will he be the next to fall victim to Tarantula?

The Cleaner

Sharon Warriner is a single mother in the East End of London, fearful that she's lost her young son to a life in the gangs. After John Milton saves her life, he promises to help. But the gang, and the charismatic rapper who leads it, is not about to cooperate with him.

Saint Death

John Milton has been off the grid for six months. He surfaces in Ciudad Juárez, Mexico, and immediately finds himself drawn into a vicious battle with the narco-gangs that control the borderlands.

The Driver

When a girl he drives to a party goes missing, John Milton is worried. Especially when two dead bodies are discovered and the police start treating him as their prime suspect.

Ghosts

John Milton is blackmailed into finding his predecessor as Number One. But she's a ghost, too, and just as dangerous as him. He finds himself in de ep trouble, playing the Russians against the British in a desperate attempt to save the life of his oldest friend.

The Sword of God

On the run from his own demons, John Milton treks through the Michigan wilderness into the town of Truth. He's not looking for trouble, but trouble's looking for him. He finds himself up against a small-town cop who has no idea with whom he is dealing, and no idea how dangerous he is.

Salvation Row

John Milton finds himself in New Orleans with a debt to repay. The family who sheltered him during Hurricane Katrina need his special kind of help. But a man emerges from Milton's past and it might be that he has been given more than he can handle.

In the Beatrix Rose Series

In Cold Blood

Beatrix Rose was the most dangerous assassin in an off the-books government kill squad until her former boss betrayed her. A decade later, she emerges from the Hong Kong underworld with payback on her mind. They gunned down her husband and kidnapped her daughter, and now the debt needs to be repaid. It's a blood feud she didn't start but she is going to finish.

Blood Moon Rising

There were six names on Beatrix's Death List and now there are four. She's going to account for the others, one by one, even if it kills her. She has returned from Somalia with another target in her sights. Bryan Duffy is in Iraq, surrounded by mercenaries, with no easy way to get to him and no easy way to get out. And Beatrix has other issues that need to be addressed. Will Duffy prove to be one kill too far?

Blood and Roses

Beatrix Rose has worked her way through her Kill List. Four are dead, just two are left. But now her foes know she has them in her sights and the hunter has become the hunted.

Standalone Novels

The Art of Falling Apart

A story of greed, duplicity and death in the flamboyant, super-ego world of rock and roll. Dystopia have rocketed up the charts in Europe, so now it's time to crack America. The opening concert in Las Vegas is a sell-out success, but secret envy and open animosity have begun to tear the group apart.

Subpoena Colada

Daniel Tate looks like he has it all. A lucrative job as a lawyer and a host of famous names who want him to work for them. But his girlfriend has deserted him for an American film star and his main client has just been implicated in a sensational murder. Can he hold it all together?

Made in the USA
San Bernardino, CA
19 August 2018